'I think that I love you, Mr Ritchie—so what do I do now?'

'Nothing,' he replied, inwardly cursing his disguise. Oh, to be Richard Chancellor again and be able to approach her honourably.

Pandora said, her face mournful, 'And that is all? Nothing?'

'As we are now,' Ritchie told her, and he was prevaricating, he knew, 'there is nothing that we can do.'

She was intelligent enough to catch the possible underlying meaning in what he had just said. 'Do you mean that there could come a time when matters between us might stand differently?'

'My dear, we live in the here and now, where you are mistress and I am servant, and we must both do nothing which might dishonour us—however much we might desire to act otherwise.'

Pray God that this mission might soon be over, but what then might Pandora think of a man who had so consistently lied to and tricked all those about him

Dear Reader

I thought that it might interest myself and my readers if I wrote two novels about twin brothers who were not at all alike either in looks or in character: the elder, Russell, being carefree, gallant and fair, and the younger, Ritchie, being quiet, serious and dark. I decided that Russell would be the heir to an Earldom, while Ritchie, who had wanted to be a scholar, was ordered into the Army by his father.

As a result of reading about the huge industry which smuggling became during the Napoleonic Wars, it was Ritchie's story I wrote first. He discovers his duty to his country and his own honour are in conflict when, in the course of carrying out the mission on which the Home Office has sent him, he meets the pretty, lively and wilful Pandora... As for Russell, his story is quite different: disliking the idle life on which his father has insisted, he tries to change it and, while doing so, meets again the quiet and clever beauty, Mary Wardour, whom he once loved and lost...

I hope you enjoy Ritchie's story in *Major Chancellor's Mission*. Russell's will follow in early 2002.

Paula Marshall

MAJOR CHANCELLOR'S MISSION

Paula Marshall

MILLS & BOON and MILLS & BOON with the Rose Device are registered trademarks of the publisher.

First published in Great Britain 2001
Harlequin Mills & Boon Limited,
Eton House, 18-24 Paradise Road, Richmond, Surrey TW9 1SR

© Paula Marshall 2001

ISBN 0 263 82753 4

Set in Times Roman 10½ on 12 pt.
04-1101-85233

Printed and bound in Spain
by Litografia Rosés S.A., Barcelona

Prologue

Early spring, 1813

'Who in the world was responsible for giving me such a ridiculous name?' demanded Pandora Compton of her aunt Em. She had burst through the drawing-room door without so much as 'So there you are, Aunt', or 'Pray do forgive me for disturbing you at your canvas work, but I have a question to ask of you.'

Used to Pandora's downright ways, her aunt replied placidly, 'I can't quite remember, my love. Oh, yes, now I come to think of it, it was your poor dear mama. When she was expecting she had been reading a very pretty book about a young woman called Pandora. Such a nice name, she told me, so much more romantic than Charlotte or Amelia: boring names only fit to be given to the offspring of German kings and princes…'

'Aunt,' said Pandora, setting her teeth at life as usual, 'I wish I *had* been given a really boring name. Before they meet me everyone expects to see a sweetly pretty version of Lady Caroline Lamb, not an Amazon out of a Greek legend, as tall as most men. And then I get to be nicknamed Dora—which is, I suppose, better than Pan, which Jack always calls me—but only just…'

'Oh, but Dora is a sweetly pretty name, too,' said her aunt placidly, adding a stitch to a large cabbage rose.

'That's not the point!' exclaimed Pandora vigorously. 'This afternoon at Lady Larkin's, I met yet another young man who looked quite downcast when we were finally introduced. He had apparently been told that he must meet me—presumably because I'm due to inherit the money from my maternal grandfather Julian's estates, but that's not until I'm twenty-seven so that William can't touch it. The Trust Julian set up gives me a small but useful income—but even that couldn't sweeten the fact that I am about six inches taller than this particular young man.'

'But would having a boring name change matters?' returned Aunt Em reasonably.

'Well, my name had obviously raised *his* expectations because I overheard him telling Roger Waters that he thought he was going to be introduced to a dear little creature called Pandora, not a beanpole who made a fellow feel smaller than he was. Worse than that, he'd also been told that I was running Grandfather's estates for him, my half-brother being only interested in pleasure. It seems that most men want decorative, rather than useful, wives. At this rate I shall never get married—not that the prospect pleases me, you understand, nor can I afford to do so at the moment—but there is a certain quality of failure about a woman who remains a spinster at the advanced age of twenty-three, I suppose.'

Her aunt Em, the widow of a man whom she had loved dearly, said quietly, 'Yes, I quite understand that, but you could have married your cousin Charles Temple. He has, after all, offered for you three times.'

'True, but the thought of spending the rest of my life

with him doesn't attract, and I know that he was only after my money: his sister told me so.'

'Not very nice of her.'

'But truthful, you must admit. Oh, dear, I do wish that life wasn't so complicated. And now we have to find a new tutor for Jack since the old one was such a failure. For a tutor to get one servant in the family way was bad enough, but to get two was not only careless but the outside of enough! Besides being such a bad example for Jack.'

'Really, Pandora,' sighed her aunt, 'you shouldn't know about such things, let alone talk about them so familiarly.'

'Since I was left to clear up the mess he left behind when he eloped with a *third* servant, I could scarcely pretend that I didn't know what he was about! Grandfather Compton is a forgetful invalid who needs quiet and you are unable to be unkind to anyone, let alone organise anything more than a small tea-party. My half-brother William is never here; when he is, he spends his time roistering with half the county. My brother Jack is only thirteen years old, so who but myself is there left to see that Compton Place runs properly?'

'Well, you do have the land agent to assist you.'

'Rice...you mean Rice? He is a complete incompetent, and a clothhead to boot. You know perfectly well that because he has managed the Compton Estates ever since the Domesday book was written Grandfather refuses to pension him off. So that leaves me. I do wish that my poor father had never married again after William's mother went to her last rest, which would have meant that Jack and I would never have been born, and I should not be left to pick up the pieces of a bankrupt estate, and Jack would not be running wild.'

Her aunt stared at her, aghast. 'How can you say such

things, Pandora! If you talk like this in company, no wonder you never receive any offers. Most unladylike of you.'

Pandora rose and began to pace the room. 'Would you
prefer to starve, Aunt, and Jack and Grandfather, too?
Grandfather's illness and the mismanagement of my father
and then that of William mean that had I not taken over
when I reached twenty-one we should all be in Queer
Street, begging for a crust on its pavements!'

'Don't exaggerate, dear.'

'Now that is what I complain of,' exclaimed Pandora.
'A refusal to face the true facts of our condition. At the
moment we have our heads just above water. The bank
has ceased to speak of foreclosing, and if we can hold on
until I reach twenty-seven then some of my grandfather
Julian's legacy may be used to ensure that we are A-one
at Lloyds again.'

'You even talk like a man,' complained her aunt. 'Such
slang! Whatever would your poor mother think if she had
lived to hear you?'

'That is neither here nor there since she didn't. Besides,
the task of hiring a new tutor for Jack—and finding the
money to pay his wages—means I have another worry.
From where is William getting the money to live as high
as he does? Not from the estate, that is sure. He comes
in and out of this house every few months or so and each
time that he does he has a wardrobe of new clothes. To
cap everything, he has somehow acquired an expensive
and luxurious curricle and a pair of prime chestnuts for
it. The good Lord alone knows what that must have cost.

'If he *is* in thrall to London money-lenders, then a day
of reckoning is sure to come. They will probably try to
distrain on what passes for his inheritance—and at the
moment he hasn't got one, so he'll be doomed to spend
the rest of his life in the Marshalsea.'

She sat down, saying, 'Simply to think of all this exhausts me.'

Her aunt put down her canvas work. She could not deny that every word Pandora had spoken was other than the truth—but, oh, how she wished that it wasn't. Her one fear now was that Pandora would never marry, particularly since she thought that her quixotic niece might be foolish enough to waste her entire inheritance on restoring the Compton family's fortunes—and who would want a woman past her last prayers then?

The worst of it was that if she took care of her appearance she could be a striking beauty with her abundant wavy chestnut hair, her striking green eyes and a porcelain complexion which, of course, she was trying to ruin by running around in the mid-day sun and becoming as brown as a milkmaid! Her height was a drawback, one had to admit, but her looks and her inheritance would more than make up for that.

'You need a holiday,' she said abruptly before thinking, Oh, dear, what a stupid thing to say! She knew that Pandora's sense of duty would outweigh the need for a holiday.

'And a London Season, too,' said Pandora sarcastically, leaning back in her armchair, her eyes closed. 'I now know why men in my parlous state get drunk. Alas, being a lady, even that is denied to me!'

Aunt Em ruefully acknowledged that she ought to be trying to help her niece rather than simply be carping at her; after all, she was doing the work of several men, so it was not remarkable that she was so exceedingly strong-minded, and loud with it.

She thought for a moment before saying, 'I will write to my cousin, Lady Leominster, about a reliable tutor for Jack and beg her to ask her circle of friends in London for the name of one—so that is something which you need not worry about.'

'Well,' said Pandora, rising and stretching herself in a most unladylike way, 'I can only hope that, if you do, she will send word soon. Jack is likely to run even more wild, and to think of him following in William and Papa's footsteps is another thing likely to make me feel ill. He needs a man about the place with a strong sense of duty, as well as a sound knowledge of Latin hexameters and classic Greek. Best of all would be if Lady Leominster could find someone who has a good grasp of numbering as well; I could do with some help with the estates' books!

'In the meantime, I must persuade Grandfather to sign a few documents which will enable us to pay for some necessary improvements to the Home Farm. Like old Rice, he is addicted to what served in the past, but times change and Compton Place must change with them.'

She was out of the room in as big a haste as her entrance had been. Her aunt sank back, desolate, leaving her canvas work neglected on the side-table where she had placed it.

She's such a good girl, and if she were fashionably dressed and could be persuaded to behave as a young lady ought, she would be as attractive as my poor late sister; nay, more so, for she has a presence my sister never had. What's more, she would make some man a splendid wife. Alas, whoever is going to want to marry her as she is now, a strong-minded virago who walks and talks like a man?

That's it, perhaps a man as strong-minded as she is might be able to tame her—and, oh, what a pair they would make!

But this is to dream of cloud cuckoo land, not the here and now.

Chapter One

'Miss it, do you?' drawled Russell Chancellor in the direction of his younger twin brother, Richard, who was busy reading the *Morning Post*. 'Being a soldier boy, I mean.'

Major Richard Chancellor of the Fourteenth Light Cavalry, always known as Ritchie to his friends and family, looked up. Russell was lying lazily in a large armchair, both booted legs on a foot stool, a glass of something or other at his elbow. He was dressed to kill, the most celebrated dandy in London. With his stunning good looks, his bright golden curls, windswept in the latest fashion. and his athletic physique, he had broken the heart of nearly every young woman in London, and was, in consequence, the envy of every young man.

The twins, both in their late twenties, were not identical ones, so Ritchie resembled his brother not at all. He was as severe and dark as his brother was bright and fair, and the flamboyance which came naturally to Russell was missing in him. His dress was moderate as was his manner. His eyes were grey, and a little piercing; he was as athletic as his brother and a better rider and, until he was injured, had been campaigning in Spain as a staff officer in Wellington's army there.

His injuries had been severe enough to result in his being seconded to the War Department in London to act as what Russell rudely referred to as a senior clerk.

Ritchie, always a silent creature, had never talked about how he had acquired his injuries. Perhaps, his twin had decided, he would be happier in his temporary Government appointment than he had been as a serving officer. After all, his original wish had been to take up a scholarly career, except that their father, the Earl of Bretford, had forbidden it and demanded that he be a soldier.

'It has been the habit of the Chancellor family for the last two hundred years to send their younger sons to defend the realm in which we live,' he had roared. 'I have no mind to be the first to break that rule, seeing that I am not likely to have any more sons to give to my country.'

So Ritchie had done his duty, and had pursued his bent for scholarship as privately and quietly as he did everything.

He said now, 'Yes, I do, but we cannot always have what we wish—which was a lesson I learned early. The only problem at the moment is that, after being a soldier, a quiet life in a bureau or office is somewhat boring.'

'I never thought that you would enjoy being a soldier,' said Russell frankly. 'On the other hand, I do know that whatever you do, you do well. So I suppose you will succeed in Whitehall in the end.'

Ritchie, putting his newspaper carefully down on a boulle table, smiled suddenly. His brother wished that he would do so more often. It quite transformed his overserious face.

'Well, there's a compliment from you I didn't expect, and I have no time to enjoy it. I've an appointment at the

Home Office, God knows why, only that Lord Sidmouth wishes to see me urgently. I suspect, knowing Sidmouth, that he wishes to see everyone urgently. It's his habit, I'm told, which should make him a good Home Secretary.'

'True,' agreed Russell. 'But it won't make him popular, that's for sure. May I persuade you to attend Lady Leominster's reception this evening? Or do you intend to find a grotto and remain a hermit forever?'

'No, and no, to each part of your question,' returned Ritchie. 'I've no desire either to take part in the Season or to live in a grotto—it seems a damned uncomfortable place to me—always cold and wet whatever the weather outside. I'll see you tomorrow at breakfast.'

'I doubt it,' drawled his brother. 'A party of us are going on to the Coal Hole after Lady Leominster's, and the good God alone knows what time I shall be home again. I suppose that it's no use asking you to join us there later on?'

Halfway to the door Ritchie shook his head at his brother. Much though he loved him, there were times when he wished that Russell was not so determined to live a life of total pleasure. Would the day ever come when he decided to settle down?

Their father had once bellowed at his late wife, 'I wish that Russell had some of Ritchie's steadiness and Ritchie a little of Russell's wildness—that would, I suppose, make two perfect human beings of them, which is, I know, an impossibility!'

Well, it was their father's worry, not his, and meantime he must hurry along to find out what Sidmouth wanted of him. He had met him years ago when he had been a boy and Sidmouth had been simple Henry Addington, Pitt's rival: he wondered whether Sidmouth had remembered him, but doubted it.

* * *

Sidmouth's office was as large and beautiful as befitted a man who was in charge of England's security in the middle of a major war. M'lord came round his desk to greet Ritchie warmly.

'I don't suppose that you remember that we met some years ago when you were only a boy. You asked me a learned question about the role of elephants in Hannibal's war with Rome. I heard later that you had become a cavalry officer—making do with horses in lieu of elephants, eh?'

'Elephants were in short supply in Spain, sir, I do admit,' replied Ritchie, wondering what all this chit-chat was leading up to. He doubted that he had been summoned to Whitehall to talk about tactics in Carthage's war with Rome.

Nor had he, for after he had accepted a glass of port and a comfortable chair, Sidmouth rapidly came to the point.

'I have sent for you, Chancellor, to ask if you will undertake for your country at home the kind of service which I understand that you performed for Wellington in Spain and Portugal. Yes, I know that you were a cavalry officer who behaved gallantly on the field of battle, but I am also aware of something which is not generally known: that you were a member of Wellington's intelligence service and acted as a liaison officer with groups of Spanish guerillas when the occasion demanded. While doing so you were captured by the French, and your command of Spanish, as well as your bravery, was such that you succeeded in deceiving them as to your true nationality. Not, however, before you had been severely injured during repeated questioning, so that when you managed to escape with your information Wellington recommended that you be sent home on furlough in order to recover your health as a reward for the vital information which you had provided him.'

Ritchie's face was, for once, a picture. 'I shall not ask you,' he said at last, 'how you came to learn of this, m'lord, but I would like to know what bearing it has on my work here in London.'

'I know,' said Sidmouth, 'because I was told that if I should ever need a resourceful and courageous man to carry out a difficult task, then I ought to be aware that one existed in Horse Guards. It has recently come to my knowledge that the amount of smuggled goods entering this country illegally has become a veritable torrent. The loss to the Customs and Excise department is enormous: not only that, but we have reason to believe that French agents are entering the country through ships secretly docking on the Sussex coast.

'Sadly, many otherwise good citizens find it amusing, as well as profitable, to betray their country not only by engaging in this trade, but also by keeping the names of the smugglers and their means of distributing the goods a secret. It is almost impossible for us to discover some genuine information about their activities. As you must know, smuggling is in breach of the Continental blockade which the Navy is attempting to enforce and which forbids trade with our enemy France and her allies—so those participating in the trade are, in effect, traitors.

'What we need is to have on the spot someone used to covert operations, who is unknown to the organisers—and also to the Revenue officers, some of whom, I fear, have been bribed to help the criminals, for that is what they are. Someone who can try to identify not only where the goods are coming in, but also who is behind the trade. Now you would fit the bill perfectly. You could go there in some innocent capacity and keep your ears and eyes open.'

Ritchie put down his wine glass, saying, 'I shall, of course, accept such a task, if that is what you and my superiors in the Horse Guards wish, my lord. Alas, however, I know no one in Sussex or its neighbouring counties. As you must be aware my father's estates are all in the North, and I have few friends in England—those I do have are still with Wellington.'

'No matter,' said Sidmouth. 'By pure chance I have an excellent disguise for you. I heard only the other night, through my sister, that Lady Leominster has asked her friends if they could recommend a reliable tutor for Sir John Compton's grandson, Jack, a boy aged thirteen. Sir John's estate is in Sussex and lies between Lewes and the sea. I understand that, added to your other accomplishments, you are also an excellent scholar. My suggestion is that I ask my sister to speak to Lady Leominster immediately and suggest that she recommends you to her friend. Apparently they are experiencing difficulty in finding someone reliable.

'Your presence there would thus not in any way be remarked on since no one would think that a tutor posed any threat to anyone—other, of course, than to his charge! Should you agree to undertake this mission, we must find you a name and an innocent address for you to write to should you wish to pass information on urgently. I fear that it is likely that there is no one in the neighbourhood you can trust, not even the local magistrates. What is your answer to my proposition, Major Chancellor?'

Ritchie smiled to himself and thought: I was saying to myself not long ago that my life had become somewhat boring. This offer seems certain to enliven it.

Aloud he said, 'That I am ready to undertake this enterprise, my lord. I cannot promise you success, but I shall do my best. May I suggest that I adopt as a surname my own nickname, which is Ritchie. I shall thus have no difficulty in answering to it. If you agree, I shall be Edward Ritchie, an unassuming and innocent pen-pusher. Edward is my second Christian name.'

'Excellent,' said Sidmouth warmly. 'We will set up an accommodation address for you immediately. I doubt that you will be in any real danger, but it might be as well for you to go warily.'

Ritchie smiled again. 'Oh, that's my habit, m'lord. I am not one for derring-do, whatever you may have been told.'

If Sidmouth thought that the young man before him was being over-modest, he did not say so. Instead, he rose and offered Ritchie his hand, something rarely done. 'I shall inform you when the news arrives that Sir John will interview you. I take it that you still have your Latin and Greek?'

'Enough to convince anyone that I am what I claim to be.'

'Good luck go with you, then.'

It was over, and while leaving by the servants' entrance so as not to be seen at the Home Office, Ritchie thought that for better or worse he had undertaken something which might remind him of what he had lost when he had left the Army.

One thing he had already decided on: he would pose as a timid soul, and would arrange to buy some plain-glass spectacles—one would expect a tutor to be both short-sighted and retiring.

'Really, Aunt, I could well have done without having to entertain half the county this afternoon. Mr Ritchie, Jack's new tutor, is due to arrive this morning. Rice is asking me to check his books again, and William's arrangement this afternoon to host a grand get-together with a pack of people with whom I have nothing in common could not have come at a worse time. To say nothing of what the get-together will cost in money which we haven't got.'

'Now, Pandora, do not carry on so. A get-together will do you good. It is time that you wore a pretty *toilette* and had your hair dressed properly.'

'That does it, that is the outside of enough,' exclaimed Pandora. 'I have no time for such frippery, so I shall not attend at all. *You* may act as hostess, and you may offer what excuse best pleases you to account for my absence.'

'No such thing, Pandora,' began her aunt, cursing her own tactlessness. She wondered which had annoyed her niece the more: speaking of having her hair dressed or of her wearing a pretty *toilette* instead of stalking about in something which a servant would be ashamed to wear.

She was about to continue when the butler, old Galpin, wandered in, his head hanging as usual.

'There's a Mr Ritchie arrived to see you,' he mumbled. 'He says that he's come to be Master Jack's tutor. I've put him in the library.'

'The library!' exclaimed both women together of the room which Pandora's father, Simon, had looted of most of its treasures in order to raise a little more money to pay for his rowdy life.

'Oh, did I do wrong, Miss Pandora?' he muttered looking more downcast than ever.

'No, as well there as anywhere,' replied Pandora and, with a last fling at her aunt, called out when she passed her, 'You may be sure that I shall be absent this afternoon,' she left to interview the man whom Lady Leominster had found for them.

One more person for her to worry about. It was to be hoped that he would be experienced enough to be able to tame Jack, who was at present confined to the schoolroom for running off with the cook's boy to swim in the over-grown lake in the once-beautiful park, regardless of the fact that he had been told never to do any such thing.

Ritchie was examining his surroundings with some interest. He had just endured an uncomfortable journey to Nether Compton on top of an inexpensive coach that was little more than a farm cart, since a supposedly poor young tutor would not be able to afford either the Mail Coach or an inside seat on a cheap one.

All that he had seen when he had been driven in an ancient gig through Sir John Compton's park reeked of poverty. His home was no different. The room in which he had been left, farcically called the library, was typical of everything else from the entrance hall onwards in that it bore every sign of advanced neglect. Yes, there were books in it, but not many and most of the shelves were empty. The desk at the far end of it was the only thing which showed any sign of use. What, he thought, would his employer be like when he finally met him?

When he had ushered Ritchie into the entrance hall the elderly butler had grimaced at him and mumbled, 'Sir John, is it? Is it Sir John you want?' He had then argued with himself about whether to take the new arrival to the drawing room or upstairs. Finally he had said, 'The library, perhaps. Miss Pandora works there.'

Miss Pandora? Now who might she be? Sidmouth, just before he had left for Sussex, had told him of Sir John, and of his grandson, William. 'A bit of a wastrel, I understand.'

Ritchie had heard of William Compton. Russell had

mentioned him once or twice, but not in a fashion which suggested any great friendship or affinity with the man. 'A gamester,' he had said. 'Not too successful.' Did that account for the poverty? Partly, perhaps, but the land and the house both looked as though they had been neglected for years.

He was still pondering this, and preparing himself to look duly humble as befitted a mere tutor, when the large oak door at the other end of the room opened and a young woman came in. She skirted the desk, and walked towards him in a manner which could only be described as purposeful. She was taller than most women, being only a little shorter than his own six feet one inch. She was wearing an old-fashioned and elderly green cloth dress, so shabby that it looked as though it had been handed down through several generations like an odd heirloom.

Her hair was a red-gold flame, her eyes were green, but her shapely mouth, indeed her whole face, was set in such severe lines that any beauty she might have possessed was quite dimmed. Her hands, when he was able to see them properly, were callused as though she were used to working hard with them. Was this conceivably Miss Pandora, and if so, was she the housekeeper?—she could scarcely be a member of the family.

'Ma'am,' he said, and bowed. It seemed the safest thing to do.

'Mr Ritchie, I believe,' Pandora replied.

It might be fair to say that she was as surprised as Ritchie at what she was seeing. Whatever she had been expecting, it was not this tall young man with a thin, clever face. She had assumed, if she had assumed anything, that the new tutor, recommended because of his reliability, would be some plump, middle-aged, anxious-looking clerk. Well, to be fair, the young man did look a little anxious, particularly when he bent down and groped in a valise, which, with a battered-looking small trunk, was standing by his feet.

What on earth had possessed Galpin that he had not taken charge of the newcomer's luggage? Oh, dear, he must be becoming more forgetful than ever. He was another relic of Sir John's earlier rule who should have been put out to pasture long ago with a nice little pension. Except that her grandfather would not hear of it, not having to endure Galpin's vagaries overmuch himself.

I am wool-gathering—which is stupid of me, she told herself fiercely. I have met young men before, many of them, and all better looking than this shabby young fellow who cannot even look me in the eye. I really must say something sensible. It's not his fault that he is oversetting me in this odd way.

'I hope your journey here was not too trying,' she began. 'I must introduce myself; I am Miss Pandora Compton, Sir John's granddaughter. When I have checked your credentials, which I have been assured are impeccable, I shall take you to the schoolroom where you may be introduced to my brother Jack who is to be your new charge.'

She held out her hand—for the credentials, Ritchie presumed, wondering why he was not to be immediately introduced to his employer. No matter, he decided to be suitably humble, as well as a little backward socially—both unfortunate attributes which could be considered to be due to his low birth.

'Sir John,' he said, fumbling with his new, gold-rimmed spectacles and the papers which he had fetched from his valise, and looking unhappy while he did so. 'I understood that my employer was to be Sir John Compton—forgive me if I am wrong.'

Don't overdo it, he told himself as fiercely as Pandora had reproached herself, I am supposed to be a gifted scholar. On the other hand, gifted scholars are also supposed to be vague creatures uninstructed in the finer arts of living.

'Indeed,' replied Pandora, a little disturbed by Ritchie's apparent distress. 'But Sir John is an invalid. He never leaves his rooms, which are on the first floor. I shall take you to see him when you have met Jack, but all of your instructions while you are employed here will come through me. It is I with whom you must consult over Jack's tuition and welfare. In some sort I act as my grandfather's agent in all matters connected with the running of the house and the estate.'

And what is William Compton's position in this strange household—after all, he is the heir? Ritchie asked himself. And how the devil does he have so much money to throw about in London when it is plain that his inheritance is on its last legs? Of course, he couldn't ask Miss Compton a question which might solve this odd little puzzle since he wasn't supposed to know that William Compton existed. In any case, it would appear most forward of him were he to do any such thing.

So, 'Thank you, Miss Compton,' he said softly. 'Here are the papers for which you have asked and which will assure you that I am who I claim to be.'

Pandora took the letters of recommendation, all skilfully concocted by Sidmouth and Ritchie himself, from him. In the doing, though, their hands touched—with an immediate consequence for both of them. They had sufficient command not to allow their joint surprise at the shock which they each received; Ritchie, being the more expert dissembler, was the first to recover himself.

What was it about this bossy female which had caused

that? He could surely not be attracted to her—she was quite unlike any woman he had ever fancied before, and, despite his mild appearance and his brother's assumption of him as an innocent, he had fancied quite a few. But never one like this.

Pandora, who had never before reacted so strongly to a man's touch—indeed, had previously disliked any such contact with one of the wretched creatures—turned swiftly away from him lest he see how affected she had been, and sat down before the battered desk.

'I shall not detain you more than a moment, I hope. Pray take a seat, Mr Ritchie. I fear you must be tired.' And so must I be, to allow the simple business of hiring someone to tutor Jack to have such an odd effect on me.

A few moments crawled by.

Finally Pandora looked up. 'Most satisfactory,' she said approvingly. 'I confess that I am a little surprised that you have not attained a position more suited to your un-doubted talents.'

Ritchie bowed his head. 'There were family circum-stances that prevented me from doing so. Happily they now no longer exist and I may be able to re-order my life more to my liking. Until then I must find suitable em-ployment to allow me to live—if humbly.'

Well, at least the first sentence was true, even if the rest was a fairy story! But it had served to convince Miss Compton that here was a suitable person able and willing to tutor her brother.

'I hope, Mr Ritchie,' Pandora said, rising, 'that you will be more fortunate in future.'

He bowed, and followed her upstairs to the schoolroom on the top floor where Galpin had told Jack to wait for them. He was sitting on a high stool before a tall, old desk, his face a picture of apprehension.

'Well, Jack,' said Pandora brightly, 'here is your new tutor, Mr Ritchie. He is a very learned gentleman and I am sure that you will do your best to please him.'

Jack, who had slid down from his stool, bowed in Ritchie's direction and muttered something which might be construed as assent to this unlikely statement. He was tall for his age and that, together with his flaming hair and his green eyes, meant that he greatly resembled his sister.

Ritchie said, 'How do you do, young man. I trust that we shall deal well together.'

He looked around the schoolroom, which was by no means as shabby as the rest of the house. There were drawings—crude it was true, but with a certain vigour— stuck to the plastered walls. They were mostly of soldiers throughout the ages, with those of Ancient Rome in the majority.

'Yours, I presume?' he asked Jack, who flushed and nodded his head.

'It is customary,' Ritchie said, a little severely, 'to give a proper answer to a civil question. Nodding the head is neither a sufficient, nor a correct, way to reply.'

He was of the opinion that he might as well start as he meant to go on.

Pandora smiled appreciatively at this early display of authority.

Jack flushed again and said, more politely this time, 'Yes, I drew them. I admire soldiers—particularly the Roman ones because they conquered everywhere they went. Like us,' he added.

'Excellent,' said Ritchie. 'If you show the same talent and diligence when you work with me, we shall get on famously. Otherwise…' and he shrugged his shoulders.

'I don't like otherwises,' retorted Jack. 'Old Sutton was full of them when he was my tutor.'

'Mr Sutton to you, Jack.' Pandora was sharp. 'Respect is always due to one's elders.'

Ritchie watched Jack's face change on hearing this. 'Not to Mr Sutton it wasn't. Mr Ritchie ought to know what he got up to—if only to avoid it himself,' he added considerately.

'Jack!' Pandora's reprimanding voice was worth at least a dozen exclamation marks, thought an amused Ritchie, who was immediately determined to discover exactly what it was that 'old Sutton' *had* got up to.

Best to support his new employer, though. In his most quietly severe manner he came out with, 'The first rule of etiquette, Master Jack, is never to make personal remarks. You might care to write that out for me ten times in your best hand while your sister takes me to be interviewed by Sir John.'

'You're going to meet Grandfather! I thought that he never saw anyone these days, Pandora.'

'Now, Jack, you know as well as I do that I have to introduce all the new senior members of the household to him. He likes to know what is going on in his own home.'

Jack opened his mouth to say something unforgivable about his grandfather and his ways, but, catching the new tutor's stern eyes on him, he closed it again. There was something daunting about this new fellow that they had wished on him. He already had the notion that it might not be a good thing to get on his wrong side. Like his sister, he had already grasped—how?—that there was something about this new man which was a little troubling, and only the Good Lord—whom the cook's boy was fond of invoking—could know why. He looked meek enough, but best not to provoke him yet.

Clever, but spoiled, and his last tutor scarcely seemed to have been a good influence on him, was Ritchie's verdict on Jack when he followed Miss Compton to Sir John's suite of rooms. The cub needs to be licked into shape, which would be a challenging, if pleasant, task for a man who had been good at putting his subordinates through their paces.

Once they had reached the double doors to Sir John's suite, a footman flung them open and announced 'Miss Compton and Mr Ritchie to see you, sir.'

Ritchie found himself in the only room in the house which was in splendid condition. Sir John's chair was before a window and he sat in it, fully dressed, but with a blanket over his knees. A glass of port stood on a low table by his elbow. Through an open door could be seen a huge state bed, also in excellent condition.

Sir John waved a hand to Pandora to sit, leaving Ritchie standing a little way in front of him.

'Brought the new tutor to see me, have you?' he said abruptly to his granddaughter.

'Yes, Grandfather. He has already met Jack.'

'John, he has met John,' said the old man pettishly, turning his bleary eyes on Ritchie. 'What is your name, sir?'

'Ritchie, Sir John. Edward Ritchie.'

'Hmph. An Oxford man, Pandora told me…after that silly woman had recommended you to her. Prefer Cambridge myself, but never mind, you'll probably do.'

There seemed to be little to say in answer to that, so Ritchie said nothing.

The old man barked at him, 'Cat got your tongue, sir?'

Ritchie inclined his head and dared to say, as humbly as possible, 'Fortunately not, Sir John, or else I should not be able to assist your grandson.'

The old man looked away and through the window before mumbling inconsequentially, 'It's been raining, Pandora. Rotten summer this, we haven't seen the sun for days.'

He swung his head round to stare at Ritchie before barking at Pandora, 'What the devil is this fellow doing in my room, hey, Miss Compton? Do you have an explanation for his presence?'

Pandora sighed. Sir John was in one of his forgetful moods again. They were coming more often these days. 'He's Jack's new tutor, Mr Ritchie, Grandfather.'

'Don't gammon me, my girl,' he muttered at her. 'A soldier, that's what he is. Fellow's a soldier. I'd know one anywhere, in or out of uniform!'

Ritchie stiffened, and hoped that by some horrible mischance the old fellow had not smoked him out before he had even begun his mission. Particularly when Sir John repeated his last three sentences again on a rising note. He did the only thing he could think of to disabuse his supposed employer. He fished his spectacles out of his coat pocket where he had stowed them away after leaving the library and put them on again to peer owlishly in Sir John's direction.

Pandora sighed. It really was too bad of the old man. What in the world could have made him think that this humble clerk was, of all things, a soldier?

'Grandfather, Mr Ritchie is Jack's new tutor. I introduced him to you not five minutes ago.'

Sir John's sudden apparent acuteness had deserted him. He stared blearily first at Ritchie and then at Pandora before coming out with his usual litany after he had committed such a gross error as this.

'If you say so, my dear, if you say so.'

Except that the last thing Ritchie heard from him as they left the room was a muttered, 'All the same, I know damn well that he's a soldier. Sticks out a mile.'

Fortunately Pandora's hearing was not quite so good as Ritchie's so she did not catch his mutinous outburst, while Ritchie was left wondering what about him had caused the old man's shrewd and immediate understanding of his true character.

It was as well that everyone, particularly Pandora Compton, obviously thought Sir John senile or Ritchie's tenure of office as Jack's tutor might now be short, but not particularly sweet!

Chapter Two

'Do you know anything about soldiers, sir? Mr Sutton didn't. He knew about the Roman armies, but not about present-day ones.'

They were eating their nuncheon in the schoolroom. Ritchie looked up from his cold beef, wondering why everyone at Compton Park was so inconveniently interested in soldiers. What sort of answer could he give the lad to satisfy him, and still keep his own secret? He must be careful what he said.

'A little,' he finally replied. 'Why?'

'I want to be a soldier when I grow up. Younger sons often are and I'm a younger son. William's not interested in soldiers.'

'William?' Ritchie thought it advisable to appear ignorant.

'My half-brother, the heir. Not that he's here much to talk about them, or anything else for that matter. He's staying at the Waters's place at the moment, but he'll be present at the party he's giving here this afternoon. Starts at three—all the county will have been invited, but I haven't. Not that I mind that. Are we beginning lessons this afternoon, sir?'

'No,' said Ritchie. He was not going to be a mad ped-
agogue, determined to teach at all hours of the day. 'You
can take me for a tour of the house and grounds so that
I shan't get lost, and be found twenty years later, a heap
of whitened bones in some coppice halfway to London.'

Jack nearly choked with delight over his beef at this
splendid flight of fancy. 'Oh, capital, sir. Yes, I'll show
you round. I don't suppose Pandora could find the time.
She won't be present at William's party, too busy doing
the accounts with old Rice.'

It was becoming increasingly plain that Jack's world
consisted of two women and a lot of men who were so
old that the word had become part of their names. Which
was a pity, Ritchie thought, since he was a sturdy lad of
good physique and was clearly not a fool. Exactly how
clever he was it would be his duty to find out.

'Excellent,' he said, pushing his plate away. 'Do you
know anything about fossils? I gather that they're plentiful
in this part of the world.'

Ritchie was mildly interested in them and thought that
it would be a useful excuse or explanation for his proposed wanderings about this part of Sussex. Wanderings
which would be necessary if he were to uncover anything
in this unlikely mission he was undertaking for Sidmouth.

'A little. Old Sutton explained about them once. Why?'

'Well, I've a bit of a passion for them, and we could
go fossil hunting. You can often find traces of them in the
stones of old churches.'

'Oh, old churches!' Jack's interest in fossils promptly
diminished. 'When do you want us to go for a walk, sir?'

Ritchie pulled a battered watch from his pocket. It was
a relic of his own childhood, recently fished from a drawer
to replace his present excellent gold hunter—which was
not something a penniless tutor would own.

'Some time soon, when I've had time to unpack my luggage and find my compass. I always take one on walks.'

It looked as though the man was going to be an improvement on old Sutton, but only time would tell that. Something about him told Jack that he might be a tough nut when it came to lessons about which old Sutton had been casual.

Mid-afternoon found them walking along an overgrown path outside the grounds. Jack had already informed him that it led towards the sea.

'I'm not supposed to leave the park,' he confessed, 'but since you're with me I suppose that doesn't matter now.'

'True,' said Ritchie, who was busy making a map of his new surroundings in his head. Wouldn't do to get lost on future forays—or perhaps it might. One never knew in this line of work.

They broke through the scrub to arrive at a clearing— where neither the sea nor the house they had left behind them was visible—to find that someone was already there.

The someone was Pandora Compton, who was supposed to be doing the books with old Rice! She was sitting on the ground, reclining against a tree, her skirts spread about her, reading a book. She had lifted her head at the sound of their voices, and stared at them quite unembarrassed. She was amused to discover that Jack was already introducing the new tutor to his favourite walk—the one he had been forbidden to take.

'Thought you were with old Rice this afternoon, Pan,' Jack blurted at her.

'So I was, earlier,' she said untruthfully, closing her book with a sigh. 'Good afternoon, Mr Ritchie.'

'Good afternoon, Miss Compton,' he said, giving her

the small bow with which he favoured everyone. 'I am sorry that we have disturbed your siesta.'

'That's a Spanish word, isn't?' she asked, more for something to say than for any other reason. 'I thought that it meant an afternoon sleep.'

Ritchie, who was regretting using the word at all since it had overtones of the country where he had spent his time soldiering, said as pedantically as he could, 'I suppose that is its exact meaning, Miss Compton, but could it not be extended, perhaps, to mean simply taking a rest from one's duties?'

Dear, dear, what an earnest creature he was to be sure! He had leaned his head towards her while he offered her this pearl of wisdom, rather like a schoolmaster in a play. Perhaps schoolmasters in a play did that because they were imitating schoolmasters in real life. And what an odd thing to think.

'I suppose so,' she told him, before adding, 'I think that I have finished my rest, and if you would offer me your hand, Mr Ritchie, I might be able to stand up more easily than if you didn't. Would it interfere with your time with Jack if I suggested that we might walk back together, dodging William's party while we did so?'

'Certainly, ma'am,' and he bent to do as she asked, lifting her in one supple movement which kept her skirts decently around her, thank goodness.

'As for my time with Jack, we are having a little holiday this afternoon before our real work together begins. It is essential,' he continued, falling into a pedagogical mode again, 'that we get to know one another as soon as possible. That is one of the arts of instruction, I have found.'

What an odd mixture he was. Did he never forget that he was a tutor, and unbend a little? Mr Sutton had spent too much of his time unbending and doing other, even more relaxed, things, like seducing the servants. This fellow was apparently cut from a different cloth.

Pandora was not to know that, for once, Ritchie was not lying to her about himself. He had been thinking of his time as a young officer, convincing the men above and under him in rank that he was a worthy fellow to live—and die—with. Now, should he offer her his arm, or not? Ritchie was not sure. Better, perhaps, to do nothing rather than make a mistake.

Pandora briskly solved his problem for him by falling in on the other side of Jack so that they either walked in single file through the scrub or as a threesome.

'Is this your first visit to Sussex, Mr Ritchie?' she asked him.

Well, at least he could tell her the truth again by saying, 'Yes. The view from the coach revealed it to be even prettier than I had thought it, nearly as much so as Kent, the garden of England.'

'Oh, Jack and I would be sure to dispute that with you,' said Pandora with a smile. 'I believe that quite a number of counties lay claim to the title, but we like to think that it belongs to us.'

Well, this was all innocuous enough, thought Ritchie, and so long as they continued to discuss the beauties of English scenery he was not likely to give himself away. So he replied by admitting that he knew the North of England better than the South. 'I have lived and worked there for some few years,' he offered to her.

'So your credentials said,' was Pandora's reply to that.

Once they were back in the park where the distant sound of merriment told them that William's party was in full swing, they were given no more time to exchange banal pleasantries such as these since the noise of it stopped discussion for good.

Alas for Pandora—her hopes that they might be able to avoid William as well as his party were doomed. They were walking along yet another overgrown avenue lined with tall shrubs, which lay parallel with the lawn on which food, drink and a battered old archery set had been provided for the visitors' entertainment, when a flurry of laughter and running footsteps heralded the arrival of a pretty young girl.

She took one look at the three of them, put both hands in front of her mouth after blushing, and exclaimed, 'Oh, dear!' before crossing their path and disappearing rapidly into the shrubbery on their left.

Immediately afterwards a man in his early thirties arrived, running and laughing, only to stop abruptly and stare at them in an embarrassment which he attempted to conceal by saying roughly to Pandora, 'So there you are! I was told that you were working and here you are strolling round the grounds—and who the devil's he?' he finished unpleasantly, waving at Ritchie. 'More to the point, what are *you* doing with him?'

'More to the point, William,' said Pandora coldly, 'is what do you think that *you* were doing, chasing after Sarah Tracy? She's half your age and needs your care, not your carelessness. The gentleman with me is Jack's new tutor, Mr Ritchie. Jack was showing him around the grounds where they came upon me quite accidentally. We decided to walk home together.'

'Gentleman?' sneered William Compton, eyeing Ritchie up and down and grimacing at his shabby appearance. 'I hope that you will be paying him enough to allow him to buy some clothing which will appear halfway decent for a servant in our household. And if *you* value my friendship, you will climb out of that dowdy get-up and attend my party in something halfway decent yourself. Miss Compton of Compton Place should not be running round looking like a servant when she ought to be helping me to entertain the county. So tell your pen-pusher to take himself off, and his charge with him.'

Now isn't it fortunate for Mr William Compton, thought Ritchie furiously, that I am posing as a servant and am not present in my proper guise since, if I were, I would give myself the pleasure of thrashing such an unpleasant cur as he appears to be until he howls for mercy. As it is, I will have to do as he bids and take myself off.

Before he could do any such thing Jack roared furiously in his sister's defence. 'You are not to talk to Pandora like that! She is slaving herself stupid to keep this moth-eaten old place going and to provide you with some sort of income which you will only spend on pleasure. As for Mr Ritchie, he is a thoroughly decent sort, quite unlike old Sutton, and by his conversation knows a great deal more about everything than you will ever do.'

'Dear, dear,' said his half-brother unpleasantly. 'After that, my first order to this paragon whom Pandora appears to have dragged from the gutter is to tell him to take you away and give you a good thrashing for your impertinence. Pandora will come with me.'

'No, she won't,' said Pandora before Ritchie could do so much as bow himself out of William Compton's sight, dragging a mutinous Jack with him. 'I have no intention of coming to your wretched party until you have apologised to Mr Ritchie for speaking of and to him so vilely. You know nothing of him.'

'Nor do you,' put in William, which was, Ritchie thought sardonically, no more and no less than the truth. Neither of them knew anything of the true Ritchie. What the untrue one needed to do was to stop this ghastly family brouhaha in its tracks.

'Forgive me,' he said, so greasily humble that both Jack and Pandora stared at him, he was so unlike the cheerful man with whom they had been talking on the way home. 'I feel that it is incumbent upon me to remove myself to the house with Master Jack, and leave both Mr and Miss Compton to settle their differences in private. Come, Jack,' and he took the red-faced boy by the ear and began to lead him away.

Jack tried to wrestle himself out of Ritchie's grasp, opening his mouth to protest against leaving Pandora while he did so. Except that, looking up at his tutor, he encountered a glare of such cold severity that he quailed before it and meekly allowed himself to be walked towards the house.

The expression on the faces of the two remaining Comptons was oddly similar.

'Well,' exclaimed William at last. 'I never thought to see anyone make such short work of Jack. That tutor fellow took one look at him and that was enough to make him behave himself. Wherever did you find him?'

'I didn't,' said Pandora shortly. 'Lady Leominster recommended him to Aunt. I suppose that I ought to point out that he made short work of us, too.'

'So he did,' said William struck by this judgement and admitting its truth. He was beginning to grasp that, annoyed by being found romping in the shrubbery with the very young daughter of their immediate neighbour, he had subsequently behaved in a stupidly intemperate fashion. He was neither such a boor, nor even such a fool, as not to recognise that he had not distinguished himself greatly in his recent encounter with Jack's new tutor.

He decided to try honey to bend Pandora to his will
since gall had not proved successful.

'Look, sister,' he wheedled, 'do me the favour of joining me shortly as my hostess. I own that I should not have
spoken to you as I did.'

'Nor to Mr Ritchie, either,' replied Pandora, 'and if you
will admit that, I will join you.'

'Oh, I apologise to you for that as well,' said William,
who was reminding himself that he did not really wish to
be at outs with the half-sister who was saving him the
trouble of worrying about Compton Place and that old
fool, Sir John, who was refusing to do the decent thing
and die.

Pandora met Mr Ritchie on her way downstairs to join
William after he had obliged her by apologising for his
boorish behaviour.

They stared at one another.

Pandora's stare was because there was something about
Mr Edward Ritchie which she found most discomposing
and she could not tell what it was. William was right, his
clothes were deplorable. He was not extremely handsome,
nor was he any of the other things which women were
supposed to find attractive in men. True, he was tall and
reasonably good looking. Perhaps it was his eyes that she
was finding so compelling.

Yes, it was his eyes. They were grey—almost silver.
They were cold and hard and quite at odds with the rest
of his mild appearance. He had certainly seemed to use
them with good effect on Jack.

Ritchie's stare was because Pandora in clothes which
befitted her station was a sight to see. The delicate blue
of her high-waisted dress with its elegant lace frill around
her swan-like neck, the silver ribbon which bound her tiny

waist, her white kid shoes and her glorious hair now piled high and carefully dressed presented a picture quite at odds with that of the flyaway hoyden he had so far seen on this, his first day at Compton Place.

As a supreme act of defiance—against whom she did not know—Pandora had decided that for once she would do what her aunt had been imploring her to do for years: allow her maid to dress her to advantage in the kind of *toilette* which she despised and would rarely condescend to wear.

The consequence was that Ritchie could not stop himself from overstepping the mark which decreed that a humble tutor should only speak to his employer when spoken to.

He said, 'You decided to attend the party after all.'

This time his stare was so penetrating that Pandora half-quavered at him, 'Is there anything wrong, Mr Ritchie?'

Again he risked all by replying, 'No, not at all, Miss Compton. You look superb.'

She surprised him by faltering, 'Do I? Do I really?' She was not accustomed to masculine admiration, but Edward Ritchie's so far impassive face was now registering exactly that. So affected were both of them, each for their different reasons, that they stood looking at one another in silence.

Ritchie was the first to break it. This would never do! He said, 'Forgive me, Miss Compton. I should not have spoken to you so personally. It was presumptuous of me.'

'Not at all,' she said, repeating back to him his words to her. 'It was I who asked you to remark on me, not the other way round.'

Again they stood silent.

Ritchie said, at last, 'Jack asked me to discover whether he and I might share in some of the goodies provided for

Mr Compton's feast. I had better find out or he will think me lost.'

'Try the kitchen, Mr Ritchie. Tell Cook I sent you.'

For some reason that seemed to break the spell which was holding them in thrall.

He bowed.

She bowed back.

They parted.

Cook was kind and Jack and Ritchie feasted happily in the schoolroom—while Pandora, bored, talked with folk whom she scarcely knew, and wished that she were in the schoolroom with them.

And what an odd thing that was to wish!

'I never like it when William stays here,' said Jack resentfully to Ritchie a few days later. 'He's always so unkind to Pandora and me. I wish he'd stayed with the Waters as he usually does. I asked him why he didn't and he gave me a stiff roasting for being curious.'

'Quite right, too,' said Ritchie, looking up from the Latin exercise which he was busy correcting while Jack bent his mind to the finer part of mathematics, something for which he was beginning to show a talent. 'When next we have a shot at improving your penmanship, you can write out a series of maxims designed to instruct you in the finer points of etiquette.'

'I don't like it when you talk to me in that stiff fashion,' Jack mumbled into his untidy cravat. 'I much prefer it when we're having a bit of fun together.'

'Life,' said Ritchie, playing the severe tutor again, 'isn't meant to be all fun.'

'But don't you wish it were,' said Jack, mumbling again.

Ritchie forgave him his muttered mutiny if only because Jack was, unintentionally, giving him a great deal of information about life around Compton Place.

Two afternoons ago, while walking back to the house after playing at single-wicket cricket with Ritchie, who seemed to have a surprisingly good command of the game given that he was a bookish, semi-reverend gentleman, Jack had begun to talk about one of Sussex's favourite occupations: smuggling.

'The Gentlemen were always at it on this coast in my father's time,' he had told Ritchie. 'Nobody paid the proper price for anything. It all came in by sea. George told me about it once.'

Ritchie already knew that the men who brought illicit goods ashore by night were always called Gentlemen. Why, he had no idea, and since he didn't wish to appear over-interested, he didn't like to ask.

George was the head, and only, groom who with one stable boy looked after the three nondescript horses which the Comptons owned when William was away. When he was in residence William, as well as his valet, brought a groom, a tiger, a stable boy, his curricle and two splendid horses with him, as well as a fine but temperamental hunter named Nero.

'How did George know about it?' Ritchie had asked idly. 'And does it still go on?'

'Well, George says,' Jack had offered importantly, 'that the government brought in the Revenue Officers from the Board of Custom to try to check it, and so the trade died down. I suppose that he knew about it because everyone did.'

'Nothing comes in now, then?'

'Rumours, George told me once. There are rumours that it still does, but he doesn't know anything definite, or so he says,' Jack offered in a disappointed voice. He thought that he might have liked to run around the Downs at night, dodging the authorities. 'No one ever peached on them, George said.'

So they wouldn't betray what they might know now, Ritchie had thought. Thus far he had been so busy establishing his false identity that he hadn't had time to forage around. He had already decided that William Compton might bear inspecting so, unlike Jack and Pandora, he was pleased that the fellow had decided to settle for a time at Compton Place where he could keep an eye on him.

Jack now said, his maths finished, 'Cook says that the housekeeper has asked us to the kitchen for tea today. There's an honour for you. She wouldn't have Mr Sutton in the place—she didn't like him at all.'

The kitchen and the servants' hall, Ritchie already knew from his own boyhood, were the only places where the servants were in charge, and their rules of etiquette and behaviour were as strict, in their different fashion, as those of their masters. He guessed that Sutton was not welcome because he preyed on the young girls. He wondered why he was welcome.

Late afternoon found the pair of them in the kitchen among the staff seated around a long table, which stood before a tall dresser covered with elderly and battered copper pots and pans. The kitchen, too, bore all the signs of the poverty which afflicted Compton Place. The table had been designed for a staff twice the size of that which was busy eating and drinking and enjoying a short break from their duties.

Ritchie had been presented to the housekeeper, Mrs Rimmington, who sat at the top of the table, by Galpin, who sat on her right. George Davies, the groom, was on her left, with William Compton's groom, Brodribb, on his.

Jack was given the place of honour at the bottom with
Ritchie on his right. Sir John and William's valets were
to their right and left. The proceedings were as formal as
those upstairs even if the china and the cutlery were
cheaper and coarser. He was aware that he was being
carefully watched, and that judgement was being passed
upon him.

They were halfway through their somewhat frugal meal
when the door opened and Pandora walked in. She was
in her flyaway garb again, and appeared to be somewhat
distracted.

'Pray forgive me,' she said, her voice apologetic, 'for
troubling you at your meal, but Sir John and Mr Compton
have asked to speak to Mr Ritchie immediately. I visited
the schoolroom first and guessed where you might be
since Mr Galpin had informed me that the staff wished to
entertain Mr Ritchie some time soon. I'm afraid that Sir
John will become distressed if he delays his visit much
longer.'

Ritchie rose, wondering what in the world could be
occurring to account for his instant presence being required in the Holy of Holies, as Jack had facetiously nicknamed his grandfather's suite. He bowed his apologies in
Mrs Rimmington's direction, which had that good woman
comparing him favourably with 'that Sutton' who had always been disrespectful to her.

'I do apologise for this,' said Pandora, leading the way
upstairs. 'But my brother was most insistent and has quite
distressed Sir John—over what, I can't quite make out,
but it seems to concern you.'

'No matter,' said Ritchie. 'I am always at your grandfather's service.' He said nothing of William. What he
would have liked to say was a different matter.

As usual, a footman ceremoniously let them in, a service which was performed nowhere else in the house, and this, like his splendid suite, allowed Sir John to think that all was well at Compton Place.

Sir John was in his usual chair. William was standing by the window, glaring out at the neglected grounds. Sir John stared at Ritchie as though he had sprung out of nowhere and faltered out, 'What is this fellow doing here?'

Ritchie hoped to God that he was not going to start on his usual litany of the tutor really being a soldier! That would put paid to his mission and no mistake. Even William Compton might smell a rat if he did.

It was soon plain that William Compton thought that he had smelled a rat already. He waved at Pandora in his usual discourteous fashion when it appeared that she was about to leave the room.

'Stay,' he commanded, as though she were a dog he was training. 'I want you to be present when we question this fellow. Sir John, you may wish to begin.'

'If I knew what to say,' the old man quavered, 'I would.'

'Now, Grandfather,' William began impatiently. 'You surely can't have forgotten already…'

'I never forget anything,' said Sir John, loudly this time. 'It is unkind of you to say so. If you are so insistent on questioning this man, do it yourself. You may act on my behalf for once. After all, you are my heir, not Pandora or John.'

It was wonderful, all his hearers thought, how every now and then, the old man came out with some nuggets of sense, not necessarily always apropos, but sense all the same.

'Very well.'

William picked up some papers which lay on the table

beside Sir John's elbow. 'I have been examining your credentials. You have claimed that you tutored Henry Hayes at Castle Downing two years ago this summer. Now I was at Castle Downing then and I met young Henry's tutor, and he was certainly not you. This leads me to believe that you are not who you say you are, and if so, I shall advise my grandfather to dismiss you at once. Can you offer me any reason why he should not do so?'

'There is a perfectly sound explanation for your not having seen me then,' replied Ritchie, 'and it is this. I was young Henry's tutor during the late summer and early autumn for a brief period when his original tutor, Mr Shaw, I believe, was given leave to clear up his father's estate. I regret that by some mischance the letter setting out my terms of employment there was somehow omitted from the papers I handed over to Miss Compton. If you will allow one of the footmen to fetch my valise from my room, I shall be happy to hand it to you.'

He and Sidmouth had concocted this explanation in case any doubt was thrown upon his identity. It was what was called in the game of secrecy, 'a masterly ploy', which would serve to reinforce a person's identity if, by some ill chance, it were questioned.

William Compton threw himself angrily into a chair after ordering the footman to collect the valise, leaving Ritchie standing alone while the footman carried out his errand.

Sir John stared fretfully at Ritchie, trying to puzzle out why he was there at all. Pandora, furious at William's act of discourtesy to Ritchie, for once said nothing, fearing that to say anything at all might make bad worse. After a time the footman arrived and handed Ritchie his valise, which was locked.

Ritchie unlocked it and fished out the letter from an

inner compartment. He then handed it to Sir John, not William.

'What's this, eh? What's this? You have it, William. Makes no sense to me.'

William took the letter, written on the finest-laid paper, with a grandiose heading showing Castle Downing high on its hill, and written by Henry Hayes, senior, as a personal favour to Lord Sidmouth.

He read it, annoyance written on both his face and body, and flung it back at Sir John, saying, 'It is as the fellow claims. I'd know Henry Hayes's writing anywhere. You, sir,' he said to Ritchie, 'may go at once to the kitchen, and take your valise with you.'

Ritchie bowed, and silently picked up his valise. Pandora, unable to contain her anger any longer, said, in the direction of both Sir John and her half-brother, 'Are you not going to apologise, William, on your and Grandfather's behalf, for accusing Mr Ritchie of being an impostor and thus committing a fraud of which he is plainly innocent? You drag him here from his meal and then send him back downstairs as though he were at fault, not you.'

Now this was a truly splendid defence of him by Miss Compton. The only trouble about that, so far as Ritchie was concerned, was that William Compton was in the right! He *was* an impostor. As a man of honour he regretted this; as the useful agent of a beleaguered government he had to keep quiet and look like the wounded innocent which he wasn't.

'Really, sister, you exceed yourself. I had a duty to check whether this fellow was what he said he was. Having done so, I really see no need for apologies and wonder what your motives are for springing so constantly to his defence. I can think of a reason…but it is a disgraceful

one, as I am sure you must agree.' The jeering laugh
William gave was an ugly one.

Pandora's eyes filled with tears. For one mad second
Ritchie was on the verge of knocking the fellow down
and being ordered out of the house instanter as a consequence.

Reason, not honour, prevailed. He stood silent after the
veiled and vile insult to Pandora's reputation was made.
The only result of that was that William said, with another
laugh, 'I see that your hero stands there mumchance. He
does not care to defend you as nobly as you defend him.'

Ritchie, consumed with a rage which he dare not show,
said in as meek a voice as he could summon up, 'I am
sure that Miss Compton's honour does not need defending. Her innocence, her conduct and her tireless care for
this house, speak for themselves.'

Suddenly and surprisingly Sir John spoke up. 'Aye, that
they do. A good and noble girl is my dear granddaughter.
Will make some man a fine wife one day, I shouldn't
wonder!'

Pandora's tears were now those of gratitude. Ritchie
bowed in the direction of the three of them and took himself off before he committed some unforgivable act like
thrashing William Compton into unconsciousness, but not
before he had apologised on his knees to Pandora. Failing
that, he could ease matters by disappearing downstairs.
Not to the kitchen—for, at that moment, not only did he
fear that food would choke him, but he felt bitterly
ashamed that he was in such a false position that he could
not defend a slandered woman.

Chapter Three

What puzzled Ritchie was William Compton's so plainly expressed hatred of his half-sister. He could only conclude that her tireless devotion to her duty, so much in contrast to his own behaviour, was such a reproach to him that he felt the necessity to bring her down to his own base level.

He tried to avoid meeting the man, and Pandora as well, since William's nastiness was taking the form of using him to attack her. He spent the mornings in the schoolroom with Jack and then roamed the countryside with the lad in the afternoons, ostensibly painting, sketching and fossil hunting, but also keeping watch on anything untoward which might be happening.

He missed meeting Pandora: he had grown used to her cheerful frankness, but he was afraid that she would be punished by her half-brother's cruel tongue if he thought that she was seeking his company.

The staff at Compton Place, however, thought highly of him, despite the fact that he was that odd creature: a man who was neither servant nor master, who had no place in either class.

'Nice young fellow,' said Mrs Rimmington to Galpin.

'He'll be good for Master Jack. He needs someone to keep him in order and see that he learns his letters. That Sutton was no use.'

George, the groom, nodded his head. 'Taking Master Jack riding this afternoon, he is. T'other man couldn't sit on a horse. This fellow knows what's what, I'll give him that, even if he isn't what you'd call an experienced rider.'

'Mr William won't like him riding out with the young master, though,' said William's sly groom. 'Doesn't like the tutor at all, says he has ideas above his station and makes eyes at Miss Pandora.'

'Now that's a damned lie,' exclaimed the head footman, Galpin's nephew. 'He's a proper young chap, most considerate to us all, not like your fellow,' he flung at Brodribb. 'He does damn-all to help Sir John and flies at Miss Pandora for doing so. And where's his money coming from? Do you have any notion, since you seem to know so much about him.'

Brodribb looked indignant, but said nothing. Mr William wouldn't thank him for being loose-mouthed, that he wouldn't.

Later on that afternoon Ritchie and Jack were in the stables, making ready to go on an excursion along the nearby coast. Ritchie had his sketchbook and watercolours in his saddle bags, and Jack some paper and coloured chalks, when Pandora came in to the stable yard, wearing an elderly blue riding habit whose better days were long gone.

Ritchie busied himself with his horse. He was trying not to look knowledgeable in the stables, something difficult for an Army cavalry officer. Jack stared at his sister and said eagerly, 'If you're going riding, Pan, why don't you come with us? We're going fossil hunting, and Mr

Ritchie says that if we don't find any he'll help me to improve my drawing.'

Pandora said eagerly, 'Why not? It would be better than dragging George out into the country with me.'

She had been missing Mr Ritchie and it had saddened her to believe that he might have been avoiding her.

Sure enough he gave her his little bow and said gently, 'Do you think that would be wise, Miss Compton?'

'To ride with you and Jack? Why ever not? It would please me of all things and I am not, I repeat not, going to allow William to dictate my life to me when he is here. Besides, I want to see what happens when you go fossil hunting—do you chase them on horseback?'

'On horseback?' began Jack, and then, seeing her amused face, said reproachfully, 'Now you are bamming me, Pan,' while Ritchie gave her his rarely seen smile.

'That was meant to provoke you, Jack,' he said cheerfully, 'and it certainly succeeded. If you are determined to come with us, Miss Compton, then it will be our pleasure to escort you.'

'Excellent,' said Pandora, wondering why a smile from Jack's tutor seemed to brighten her day, while a smile from most men simply bored her. William had insisted that she accompany him to an afternoon fête at the Waters's place, the day before, and to placate him she had dressed in her only fine togs again and gone along. As she had expected she had found the whole business tiresome, what with simpering young women and young men talking nonsense to her, rather as though she were a backward child.

She could only wish that she had spent the afternoon in the schoolroom with Jack and Ritchie, talking about interesting things, or with old Rice doing something useful which would help Compton Place to avoid bankruptcy.

What could be better than to ride out on a fine spring day, knowing that she was going to enjoy herself, looking for fossils. And where were they to be found? Of all places, Mr Ritchie told her, they were in the stones in the walls of the church down in Old Compton village, which was a few miles from Compton Place.

She discovered that fossils were strange round things, looking rather like some of the shells she had gathered on the sea shore when she was a little girl.

A little girl who knew nothing about the cares involved in protecting a senile old man and trying to preserve his inheritance as well as worrying about an unsatisfactory half-brother. So why in the world should she find Jack's tutor, of all people, one of the most interesting men she had ever met?

To begin with, Mr Ritchie didn't patronise her. He showed her the fossils, explained them to her and then she sat happily sunning herself on the grass in the churchyard and watched him and Jack earnestly drawing them.

After that they all wandered into the church to look at the tombs of bygone Comptons, buried there since the Reformation. There was one which seemed to interest Mr Ritchie very much. He sat down sideways on one of the pews and began to draw it—not carefully as he had done with the fossils, but in quick bold strokes so that when she asked him if she might look at it she saw that the old monument was alive on the paper.

She thought that the knight's face looked very like her grandfather's must have done in youth.

'Oh, famous,' Jack said, peering over her shoulder, 'but you should see his watercolours. Do show them to her, Mr Ritchie.'

There was no avoiding it. Ritchie picked up the portfolio lying on the seat behind him and fetched from it the views of the downlands which he had spent the last fort-night depicting. Among them was the stretch of coast nearest to Compton Place, situated beneath some low cliffs. It was known as Baxter's Bay. Why Baxter? He had not cared to ask, though he thought that it was prob-ably a likely place for a ship to lie offshore while boats landed contraband to be carried to a cart or coach waiting at the cliff top. Once fully loaded they would most likely be driven to the turnpike road between Brighton and Lon-don by the nearest by-way. Someone named Baxter had probably used it as a good place for smuggling in the early eighteenth century when duties on drink had first made it profitable.

He had made such drawings and paintings of terrain for Wellington in Spain—although they had been much more meticulously laid out since men's lives might be at stake if they were inaccurate.

Pandora, wondering again why she found Mr Ritchie so fascinating, thought him more so when she looked at his delicate handiwork. 'Oh, these are beautiful,' she ex-claimed. 'I wonder why you have not tried to earn a living as a painter…they are so good. Do look at this one of Trottie Jordan's cottage, Jack. She's standing in the door-way as large as life.'

'Oh,' said Ritchie, as modestly as he could, but truthful for once. 'This is the extent of my talent. I have never tried my hand at oils. I had no time to waste on my in-terest in art,' he explained, beginning to bend truth once more. 'I was meant to be a scholar and those studies were more important than my minor gift.'

'Not minor,' she contradicted him. 'I think it a pity you did not carry on.'

He bowed to her muttering, 'Too kind, Miss Compton.'

'Not kind at all,' she replied, and led them out of the

church since the afternoon was wearing on and they had some distance to travel before they reached home again.

On reaching Compton Place, they found a man waiting for them in the stable yard, leaning against the wall. One of the lads was caring for his horse.

Pandora sighed at the sight of him. He watched them dismount before he strolled towards her. He was wearing a thick navy blue coat and cream trousers with heavy thigh-boots. He looked vaguely like a sailor.

'A word with you, Miss Compton, if I may.'

'What, again?' said Pandora sharply. 'If you must, I suppose.'

'Your loyal duty, mam,' he said. 'May I speak to you in the house?'

'Say what you have to say to me here, if you please,' she answered, showing a hauteur in her manner which Ritchie had never seen before. 'I would prefer that you spoke to me before a witness. This is my brother Jack's new tutor, Mr Ritchie. He may stay. Jack, run to the house and ask Cook to have a light collation and tea ready for us when we come in. She may serve it in the kitchen.'

She half-turned towards Ritchie. 'Mr Ritchie, this is Mr Jem Sadler, the local Riding Officer whose duty it is to catch smugglers, and who seems to think that it is his other duty to badger me about them when I really have nothing to tell him.'

Jem Sadler offered Ritchie a curt nod of the head, and the words, 'Mr Ritchie,' which was as short an acknowledgement as he could make.

'Now, Miss Compton,' he began, 'I find it difficult to believe that you know nothing about the large amount of smuggling and avoidance of Revenue duty which is going on in this part of Sussex. I would advise you that it is tantamount to treason to suppress such knowledge when questioned by an officer of the crown. It has come to my knowledge—'

At this point Pandora interrupted him in her most Amazonian mode.

'Treason, Mr Sadler? You really do surprise me. You know as well as I do that most of the wretched folk engaged in this trade do so to earn some sort of living. I cannot see that avoiding excise duties on brandy and silks constitutes treason.'

Jem Sadler stared sternly at her. 'Those duties, Miss Compton, as you must well know, help to pay for the war which we are waging against the Corsican ogre, Bonaparte. Even if you are prepared to defend those who smuggle drink and luxury goods *into* the country, how can you defend those who smuggle gold guineas *out* of the country, paying twenty-one shillings for them, to send them to Paris where they receive thirty shillings for them, seeing that these guineas are used by the French authorities to pay Napoleon's soldiers so that they may kill ours? The money they receive from this vile trade returns to the City of London to be secretly invested.'

Pandora turned so white on hearing this that the silent Ritchie thought that she might be about to faint. He had been listening to them both with great interest. Was that why Sidmouth sent me to Sussex? To try to find out who is smuggling gold coins to France to make a huge profit— and where they are doing it? Why he could not tell me of it when he briefed me I cannot think. Unless he wanted me to discover whether it was actually happening and, if so, who was organising it. There is more than one puzzle here.

'No,' Pandora said at last. 'I don't believe you. I don't

believe that anyone—even the Gentlemen—would do that.'

'No?' he answered, smiling savagely at her. 'But it is the truth. We, both the Board of Customs and the Excisemen, have been reliably informed that it is being run on the south coast. The profits are being collected not only by the smugglers, but also by several City bankers and business houses who finance the organisers of the trade. The only thing that our informants don't know is exactly which financiers and their counting houses are involved, and who is running the guineas out and bringing the profits in and where it is done. Now will you help me—and your country?'

'If I could, I would,' Pandora said. 'How many times do I have to tell you that my life is so busy, what with caring for Grandfather and the responsibilities of the estate, that I don't have time to take part in—or even gossip about—any of this?'

'No?' said Jem Sadler. It seemed to be his favourite word. 'If I find it difficult to believe you, you will forgive me. I would speak to your grandfather, only I understand that his mind is feeble these days.'

'No feebler than yours,' Pandora flashed back at him, 'if you believe that I am not telling you the truth. Mr Ritchie,' she said turning to him. 'You will escort me into the house. I have had enough of this.'

'A word with your fellow here,' said Jem, who had been intrigued by the silent tutor. Something about the man made him feel uneasy. Did *he* have anything to do with smuggling guineas and, if he did, was Miss Compton also in the know?

'Mr Ritchie, if you discover any evidence concerning the subject of my discussion with Miss Compton, I trust that you will see fit to inform me of it.'

'Most unlikely that I shall,' murmured Ritchie, 'seeing that my duties are mostly confined to the house.'

'But not this afternoon,' said Jem shrewdly. 'I gather that you have been riding far afield.'

'So we have,' said Ritchie, extending the portfolio which he was carrying in the Riding Officer's direction. 'I have been sketching and instructing Master Jack in drawing and in the identification of fossils. Miss Compton has been taking a break from her onerous duties by accompanying us and also being instructed on where and how to find fossils. You may examine my portfolio if you doubt my word.'

'No need,' grinned Jem. 'You impress me as a humble sort of fellow. I doubt that you would be one of the Gentlemen, or even help them.'

He was not speaking the strict truth when he said this, but best not to let the fellow know that he thought that there was something fishy about him. 'If you have any influence with your mistress,' he continued, 'try to persuade her that honesty is the best policy if she does know anything. I'll leave you with that.'

'One of my maxims, too,' said Ritchie dishonestly, watching the man ride away. Well, he knew who to go to now if the necessity to involve the Riding Officer ever rose.

All in all he had spent a most interesting afternoon!

It wasn't over. He joined Pandora and Jack in the kitchen and ate Sally Lunns and drank good tea which had almost certainly, he now thought, been smuggled into the country.

Pandora seemed distracted. She was uncommonly silent and left all the talking to Jack. He discoursed learnedly about fossils and Roman remains and Crusaders' tombs in the Old Compton church to the staff who kept exclaiming, 'Fancy that, Master Jack,' and 'Well, I never!' which fortunately gave Ritchie the opportunity to be silent himself.

He was wondering whether William Compton's sudden access to wealth was the result of smuggling and whether his great and good friends—for so the Waters seemed to be—were part of the game, too.

Tea over, he prepared to take Jack up to the schoolroom, but Pandora detained him, saying, 'Jack, run upstairs, there's a good boy. I wish to speak to Mr Ritchie.'

She was silent until Jack reached the turn of the stairs and disappeared from view before she turned to Ritchie and said, 'Mr Ritchie, I hope that you will believe me when I tell you that I spoke nothing but the truth to Mr Sadler.'

'Oh, I do,' he returned, bobbing her his small bow. 'I do not think that you would lie about such a matter to him or to me.'

'Which does not mean,' she went on, 'that I am stupid enough to believe that smuggling does not take place near here, and that some of my friends, and our staff, even, do not take part in it. I am shocked that we are helping to pay Napoleon's armies. It may be weak-minded of me, but I do see a difference between that and smuggling drink and luxuries.

'I shall not ask you if you have heard anything about the Gentlemen since you came here, it would not be proper, but if you have I believe that it would be your duty to tell Mr Sadler, or the company of Dragoons quartered near Lewes, or the local Yeomanry of what you might discover.'

'Oh, indeed,' he said, looking into her earnest and worried face and experiencing the maddest desire to kiss the worry away. 'You may depend upon me to do all that is proper.'

Now, it was his face which looked earnest and worried and Pandora who was feeling the strangest desire to put out a hand and stroke the worry away. Oh, dear, was William right when he had said the night before, after drinking too much, that 'she fancied the tutor'?

Did he dislike Mr Ritchie because he, William, was engaged in this treasonable trade? Was that why her half-brother had recently become so flush in the pocket? Did he fear that, by chance, the tutor might find out and conceive it to be his duty to inform the proper authorities? If so, did she really want Mr Ritchie, if he were to find out, to do his duty?

She was beginning to feel light-headed at the thought of all the complications which might follow if William were being so damnably foolish as to become a smuggler. They might even lose the house and the estate if he were caught committing what might be construed as treason. She was suddenly sure that Jem Sadler had good reason to question her so frequently if he thought that the Comptons were involved. Had he spoken to William? She would ask him this evening, after dinner. He was over at the Waters's house again, spending the day there, and that, too, had begun to worry her.

She must say something. Mr Ritchie would think her mad if she continued to stand there, staring at him. 'Oh, I am sure that you would always do your duty,' she offered him, and why she should say that she did not know. Except that she was sure that he would, just as surely as she knew that William had no notion what duty was.

Ritchie, for his part, thought that he knew why Pandora Compton was so distracted. She was no fool and he was certain that she had now begun to worry about her half-brother and what he might be getting up to.

She had quite enough things to worry about, and he must not add to them by hinting at William's possible involvement in treason, so he bowed to her again.

Before taking himself off to the schoolroom which was both his workplace and his refuge, he thought, wryly, that he seemed to be doing nothing else but bow obsequiously these days!

Pandora confronted William late that afternoon before dinner, which began around five of the clock. The Comptons still kept to old-fashioned times. Aunt Em was already there, waiting for them to arrive.

'William, I had that Riding Officer round again this afternoon,' Pandora began. 'He was questioning me in the most familiar fashion about whether or not I knew anything about the smuggling of guineas to France. Of course, I assured him that I knew nothing—which is the truth. He did not ask me about you, but I should be relieved to hear you assure me that you have nothing to do with this foul trade.'

'How dare you suggest that I might be involved,' he flashed at her. 'And so I told Sadler this morning when he had the damned impertinence to question me about it. He'll be after poor young Jack next, I shouldn't wonder. Since the French Revolution these fellows no longer know their place. It's time someone taught Jem Sadler a lesson.'

'He's only doing his duty, William.'

'Well, let him go somewhere else to do it. No wonder these fellows never catch anyone if they spend their time questioning the innocent!'

'Speaking of innocence,' Pandora said, 'I am troubled as to where, if you are not engaged in smuggling, you are finding the money to live so high. You rarely seem short of the ready these days—not that any of it is used to help the estate.'

'Oh, really, Pandora, you are such a child. I gamble, and I am good at it. I won a great deal in town this year, and I am spending it upon myself—and why not? It is my own efforts which have gained it for me.'

Could he be speaking the truth? Perhaps he was, but Pandora doubted it.

William, seeing the doubt, said jovially, 'Forget that. Let's go in to dinner.'

Ritchie, who had arrived in the drawing room in time to hear most of Pandora and William's dialogue, was strongly reminded of a line in Shakespeare's *Hamlet* which he had read as a boy. Slightly altered to fit the present occasion it described William's frenzied exclamations: 'The gentleman (not the lady) doth protest too much, methinks.'

William's anger certainly seemed out of proportion to the offence Pandora had committed by questioning him. As though he had read Ritchie's mind, William, once in the shabby dining room, swung round to glare at him. 'What are you staring at, may I ask? And why you are proposing to dine with us is beyond my comprehension.'

'You never objected to Mr Sutton dining with us once a week,' said Pandora angrily.

'Oh, but Sutton was a gentleman. Why you dismissed him is a mystery.'

'I didn't dismiss him. He chose to run away with one of the maids, which was hardly the action of a gentleman.'

'Well, at least he dressed better than this fellow,' muttered William.

'In that case you might care to contribute to Mr Ritchie's salary and, since you seem to have money to spend on frivolity, you might spare the few extra pounds which the estate cannot afford to see him outfitted more to your taste.'

This spirited interchange taking place before him while he sat there mumchance both distressed and amused Ritchie. He was beginning to picture himself as a rather large and juicy bone over which two bad-tempered dogs contended. Why that should be so was a mystery which he soon hoped to solve.

He decided to speak.

'Perhaps you might care for me to leave the room,' he offered.

'No, indeed,' Pandora shot at him, and, 'As soon as you possibly can,' ground out William.

Well, there was no pleasing both of them, so he might as well please himself. He rose, saying, 'I will find myself a meal in the kitchen and after that I have work to do in the library. So, if you will permit it, Miss Compton, I will leave at once.'

'No, it does not please me, Mr Ritchie, but yes, you have my permission to retire.'

Once Ritchie had left the room Aunt Em, who had been sitting there silent and shocked because this was the first time she had been a witness of William Compton's unpleasant treatment of the new tutor, took a hand in the game.

'William,' she said sharply, 'you may be Sir John's heir, and in effect the true master of this house, but you have no right to speak to Mr Ritchie so discourteously. He is a good and quiet gentleman who has been busy turning Jack into a gentleman himself, instead of an unpleasant rebel against convention.'

'Good and quiet lick-spittle you mean, Aunt,' sneered William. 'Haven't you noticed the considering and disapproving look which he constantly gives me? What's more, he's been casting sheep's eyes at Pandora ever since he walked into Compton Place.'

'No, I have not noticed either of those things,' exclaimed Aunt Em spiritedly. 'All I *have* seen is diligence in carrying out his duties. What's more, old Rice tells me that, in his spare time, Mr Ritchie has been helping him with the estates' books.'

Pandora looked sharply at her aunt on hearing this. Old Rice had said nothing of this to her—and nor had Mr Ritchie.

William, unmollified by this revelation, returned angrily, 'And that is what I complain of! He's a damned slippery upstart, worming his way into everyone's confidence but mine. I've a good mind to ask Sir John to dismiss him immediately.'

'No!' said Pandora, feeling helpless—a common sensation whenever she was with her half-brother. 'Think of Jack before you do any such thing.'

'Think of yourself, you mean! Knowing how much you favour him, I shall go to Grandfather once dinner is over. He, at least, will do me the honour of taking heed of what I have to say to him.'

'I beg of you—' began Pandora.

'Beg away and see where it gets you. You have been indulged far too long. What I have seen since I returned here has determined me on hiring an agent to run this place as soon as possible. After that, my girl, you will learn to behave as a lady should. You and Aunt Em may retire to the Dower House once I have had time to find a suitable man. Old Rice may be pensioned off, too. Now, let us eat dinner.'

Once the meal was over, William strode from the room,

his angry head held high. Pandora looked helplessly at her aunt.

'He means it,' she said. 'And what sort of man will he hire, do you think? Some wastrel like himself, no doubt, for we shall not be able to afford anything better. And if he does have the money to find someone competent, where does that money come from? I don't for one moment believe that he won it by gambling—he was always a hopeless card player.'

'My dear, perhaps it is all for the best. It is quite wrong that the running of the estate should have fallen on you, even if you have done splendidly by saving us from bankruptcy. But you need a husband…'

'Oh, no, Aunt, I don't! Think, he might be exactly like William, and my life would not be worth living if he were.'

With that she walked from the room, leaving her aunt seated, desolate at the table among the ruins of the meal—and her life at Compton Place.

Sir John had retired for the night when his grandson stormed in and ordered the footman and his valet, who had been assisting the old man, to leave the room until they were sent for.

'What's afoot?' the old man quavered at William, who had flung himself into a chair beside the great bed from which he began to try to dominate his grandfather.

'Sir John, I wish that you would tell that new tutor fellow, Ritchie, to pack his bags tomorrow morning and leave at once. He's a bad influence in this house.'

Sir John stared at him and said in something like his former voice before he had fallen ill, 'Oh, no, can't have that. No, not at all. Can't dismiss him.'

'Why ever not? Fellow's a nuisance.'

His grandfather shook his head, and said pathetically, 'No, no, there's a good reason why we ought not to dismiss him. I can't think what it is, though.' His old face brightened a little. 'He's damned good for Jack, that I do know—but that's not it, there's something else...'

William ground his teeth. 'Have you all run mad that you defend this...this...impostor, this supposed paragon as you all appear to think him?'

'That's him—a paragon.' Sir John thought for a moment, his face doubtful before he continued, 'But that's not it either—I wish my memory weren't so poor. I won't have him dismissed, though.'

'This beggars belief, that you all want to keep a fellow who's after Pandora—that I am sure of. Are you listening to me, Grandfather?'

'Yes, yes, I mean no, no. She's a good girl, Pandora, a sensible girl. She's safe with anyone, she is, and particularly with this young fellow, that I do know. As for why we shouldn't dismiss him...you've driven that out of my head with your nonsense. I do wish you'd leave me alone. An old fellow needs his rest.'

William stormed out of the room as furiously as he had entered it. The old fool was out of his head and ought to be committed to an asylum—except that the damned doctors wouldn't admit that he was senile.

Later that evening Ritchie left the library and walked into the entrance hall to climb the stairs to his bedroom next to the schoolroom. The door to the drawing room opened when he passed it and Pandora came out.

She stopped dead at the sight of him. Ritchie thought of acknowledging her by a small bow, but found the mere idea of performing yet another distasteful. He need not have troubled himself for, before he could do any such thing, Pandora said urgently, 'A word with you, Mr Ritchie,' and waved a hand at the door by which she had just left.

Ritchie followed her into the drawing room. She remained standing a moment before she said, still urgent, 'I think it only fair to you, Mr Ritchie, to tell you that this evening after dinner, Mr William Compton tried to persuade Sir John to dismiss you on the spot. Sir John refused to do any such thing which, I fear, has inflamed my half-brother against you more than ever. Sir John, my aunt Em and myself have no wish to lose you, you are doing such great things with Jack. On the other hand, in fairness to you I feel that you might like to consider obtaining another post where you might not be subjected to such unpleasantnesses as occurred this evening.'

Whatever could be the matter with her? On coming out with this last sentence Pandora felt her eyes fill with tears. She could hardly bear to look at Mr Ritchie's face which was becoming nearly as familiar to her as her own. It was always full of what could only be described as kind severity. Which might, she thought afterwards, serve to describe the manner in which he looked after Jack.

The thing of it was that *she* did not want to lose him, not for Jack's sake, but for her own! William, the devil, had been right about that. Perhaps it was because she knew so few men that she had begun to moon after the tutor. No, it wasn't that, either, she had met plenty of men, the squires from round about, William's grander friends, a few cousins, and not one of them had made her look after them as she found herself looking after—and for—Edward Ritchie.

Ritchie saw the tears in her eyes and was himself overcome by an emotion which he had never felt before for any woman. Was she crying for him? Was this hoydenish creature with her gallant face and body, who carried Compton Place, her grandfather and that worm, William, on her shoulders, really deeply concerned for his future?

He felt the most overwhelming wish to comfort her. Before he could stop himself and remember that she was the lady of Compton Place and he the newest servant in it, he moved towards her. He put his right hand into his coat pocket, took out his handkerchief—fortunately unused, he thought afterwards—and, putting his left arm around her shoulders, he wiped her tears away. All the time he was murmuring tenderly, 'Do not cry for me, dear Miss Compton, please.'

Oh, it was wonderful to have a man's strong arm around her, to hear his loving words in her ear. For one long happy minute Pandora allowed herself to rest on his broad chest, to lift her soft hand up to stroke his jaw and feel the stubble of the day's growth of his beard running along it.

Sanity and the thought of the cruel world broke in upon them. They sprang apart almost simultaneously, Ritchie thinking, What in the world am I doing? I am justifying that miserable creature's demeaning of me, while Pandora was busy thinking the same. Oh, what if William had come in upon us? He would have thought that all his vile insinuations were nothing less than the truth.

'Forgive me,' muttered Ritchie, while he sternly and silently reprimanded his errant body for becoming roused.

'Nothing to forgive,' whispered Pandora distractedly. 'You were merely comforting me, most natural.'

Very natural, thought Ritchie grimly, and had we continued being quite so natural we might have ended up on the carpet and where would Miss Pandora Compton's honour have been then—to say nothing of my mission!

It was that last anti-climatic thought which set his body

behaving again. Best, they both decided, that they pretended that nothing had happened.

They resumed being Mr Ritchie, the lowly tutor, and Miss Pandora Compton, his nominal employer, and went up to their lonely beds to sleep the broken sleep of the sexually frustrated.

Chapter Four

'**M**r Ritchie and I are going for a ride across country and then on to Baxter's Bay to try to find out whether there are any fossils there,' said Jack on the next afternoon. 'Why don't you come with us, Pan? You're looking a bit peaky.'

'I'm feeling a bit peaky, Jack my lad, and so would you if you'd had Grandfather on your back all morning.'

She was not about to tell him that Sir John had spent a long time complaining about William and his whim whams. 'Wants to dismiss poor Ritchie. Whatever for, the fellow's a treasure. If anyone needs to be dismissed, it's William.'

Aunt Em looked up from her ever-lasting embroidery. 'Yes, why don't you take a run with them, Pandora? The open air would do you good. If one of the stable lads went along with you as a chaperon, William couldn't make a fuss about you accompanying Mr Ritchie. Order a picnic, too, food always tastes better in the open.'

Oh, it was a tempting thought, was it not? To spend an afternoon looking for fossils with Mr Ritchie; and, being tempted, Pandora fell.

'If you think that he won't mind me going with you.'

'Mind, why should he mind?' exclaimed Jack. What noddies girls were, even the best of them!

Of course Mr Ritchie didn't mind. He was delighted. An afternoon with Pandora and a visit to Baxter's Bay would mean work and pleasure combined. He couldn't ask for more.

Yes, he could. Pandora beneath him for instance. He was sure that such a lively wench would be even livelier in that position... Oh, God, he was in danger of forgetting his mission because he couldn't forget Pandora in his arms yesterday—and that would never do. Besides, she was a lady and even though he was a true gentleman, which everyone at Compton Place thought he wasn't, he ought not to think about her in quite such earthy terms... She wasn't a barque of frailty for him to pursue at his leisure, but a young woman whose innocence was as strong as her sense of duty. He really must behave himself.

And behave himself he did, being even quieter than usual, so that Jack said anxiously when they dismounted on the cliff top at Baxter's Bay, 'Are you feeling ill, too, Mr Ritchie? Ought we to go down to the beach?'

His answer was a smile, a shake of the head, and, 'Oh, I'm A-one at Lloyds today, Jack.'

After that they tethered their ancient hacks to nearby trees before following the path down to the sands and to the caves inside the cliff face in which one could just stand up.

They had taken a candle and a tinderbox with them to look for fossils in the dark. Mr Ritchie possessed a little pick with which he prised fossils from the rocks and stones. He never used it on the church walls though, since that was sacred ground and the fossils had to be left there.

Fossil hunting over, all of them, including Rob, the stable lad, were having such fun enjoying themselves on the beach, the picnic food spread out before them on a large cloth, that they were unaware that two quite separate pairs of eyes were busy watching them.

One pair belonged to the Riding Officer, Jem Sadler, who had decided that Baxter's Bay might bear inspection that day. He had such a large territory to guard that it was difficult for him to decide which particular spot might be the next that the Gentlemen used to land contraband.

Well, well, Master Tutor is out with Miss Pandora Compton again, is he? And visiting Baxter's Bay, too. I wonder what the attraction is for him—apart from Miss P., that is.

He walked silently down the cliff path to give them no warning of his arrival and stood half-hidden for several moments listening to them chatter. The tutor had finished his *al fresco* meal and was seated on a boulder a little way from the others and was busy drawing them. Giving vent to a cough, Jem strolled forward, saying, 'A favourite place of yours, eh, Miss Compton? Any particular reason why?'

'No, Mr Sadler, it's Mr Ritchie's favourite place because there are fossils in the rocks in the cave,' exclaimed Jack before Pandora could say anything. 'He likes painting the Downs and the sea and the beach.'

'So long as that is all he likes,' drawled Jem walking over to where Ritchie sat and leaning over to inspect his drawings. He was a little surprised at their excellence. It seemed that Master Jack was right and that the tutor's trips to the Bay *were* innocent. Pandora, the lad and Jack were all living on the paper on the tutor's knee—and so was he in a rapid-fire caricature, done when he had been skulking before he revealed himself.

It was obvious that the tutor had sharp eyes, if nothing else.

Ritchie looked up and smiled at the Riding Office. 'Care to have it?' he asked cheerfully of the sketch. 'What did you think that we were doing, Mr Sadler? Waiting for the Gentlemen to arrive in order to help them to land their booty?'

'Nothing would surprise me,' said Jem, taking the proffered piece of paper. 'And yes, I'd like my portrait. Quite an artist, aren't we, sir.'

'Only an amateur,' said Ritchie.

'May I?' asked Jem, pointing at the portfolio on Ritchie's right side.

'Indeed.'

Once opened, the portfolio proved to contain the watercolours which Pandora had earlier admired, as well as some new ones. Jem stared at them. They reminded him of something, but at the time he couldn't think what. Later, riding home, he would remember where he had seen such meticulous work before. A Captain in the Dragoons whom he had met in the course of their joint duties in trying to trap smugglers had shown him the drawings he had done on campaign in Europe. They were to help his senior officers to decide what action to take before and during a battle, he had said.

Now why should Master Jack's tutor be recording the countryside so carefully? Another puzzle for a poor devil to solve.

Ritchie, aware of the Riding Officer's suspicions, was reasonably sure that someone else had been spying on them since they had left Compton Place. His experiences in Spain had given him an almost sixth sense in such matters.

'Have you another officer with you this afternoon?' he

said as casually as he could while continuing to draw. Jem had finished inspecting the portfolio and was now examining the little pile of drawings which Jack and Ritchie had made of the fossils in the cave.

'No, not this afternoon. Why do you ask?'

'Oh, I thought that I saw someone else showing an interest in us.'

'Did you, now? And what might cause that, do you think?'

'I've really no idea. Except that he might be more worthy of your curiosity than we are.'

Ritchie said this in such a mild voice, taking off his spectacles as he did so, that for a moment Jem did not immediately grasp the implied criticism in his quiet statement.

When he did he said, 'You may have a point there, Mr Ritchie. Did you see enough of him to be able to describe him to me?'

'Not really. He kept quite a distance behind us and my impression of him was a vague one.'

'Not very helpful, then. If you do see him again, and more clearly, then you might let me know. I believe I left my address with you when I visited Compton Place. As it is I must be off. I have a deal of coastline to guard and while I chat with you something suspicious may be taking place elsewhere. Bid Miss Compton goodbye for me.'

Ritchie nodded, and watched him climb up the cliff path, wondering what there was about him that could excite both William Compton and Riding Officer Sadler. It would be nice to know. Perhaps it was his very meekness which they found distressing. He found it distressing himself!

'I'm glad he's gone,' Jack volunteered. 'Always poking and prying about and asking silly questions.'

Ritchie found himself defending Sadler. 'That's his job,' he said mildly.

'Well, I wish he'd go somewhere else to do it,' snapped Pandora. For some reason she was feeling oddly restless. She looked across the beach at the tide rolling in.

'The day is hot, the water is cool,' she announced defiantly. 'I am going to paddle in the sea.'

Ritchie looked up from his drawing and exclaimed, 'Oh, Miss Compton, forgive me if I sound impertinent, but ought you to…?'

'Probably not, Mr Ritchie. But I am determined that for once I shall do as I wish and not as I ought. I shall remove my boots and stockings in the cave,' and she walked off, her naughty head held high.

Jack said, 'If you are determined to paddle, Pan, then I shall come with you.'

Ritchie, who had a sudden disturbing vision of the pair of them romping in the shallows—and the not so shallows—said, 'No! I have no authority over Miss Compton, but you are in my charge and I absolutely forbid it.'

'Spoilsport!' roared Jack, turning into the naughty child he had been in Mr Sutton's day.

'Not at all,' replied Ritchie. 'I have brought a cricket ball with me and while Miss Compton paddles we shall play Catch.'

It would be torture for him to sit there and watch Pandora playing in the sea. As it was when she walked towards him, barefoot, her eyes shining, and her skirts raised so that they should not touch the sand, he felt a pang of desire for her so strong and powerful that it shocked him.

And damn everything, she wasn't even the sort of woman he had always fancied. They had invariably been meek delicate little things, not tomboys who ran round barefoot and impudent, showing off their legs!

'I beg of you, Miss Compton,' was all that he could find to say, 'that you will be careful once you are in the water, and will not venture too far out. It may be dangerous.'

'Oh, I am sure, Mr Ritchie,' she returned, with a saucy smile, 'that if I do fall into danger, I may depend upon you to rescue me.'

Jack said kindly, 'I would help him, Pan, be sure of that.'

'I forbid that, too,' ordered Ritchie, desperate to control the unruly pair. 'Any assistance will come from me and me alone.'

'As I have no intention of doing anything other than paddle along the shore you may cease to bicker over an imaginary future where I am swept out to sea,' said Pandora grandly, raising her skirts to reveal even more of her legs before she walked into the water.

Ritchie's answer to that was a silent one. He ground his teeth in a mixture of annoyance, and lust, wondering at the same time what Rob, the stable lad, was making of all this and who he would favour with his gossip about Miss Pandora's goings-on. There was no doubt that it would be one more thing for William Compton to complain about when he learned of his half-sister's unladylike conduct.

'What happened to the game of Catch?' Jack called. He seemed to be learning impertinence towards his tutor from his sister. Ritchie gave a scarcely audible groan; rummaging in his bag, he pulled out the cricket ball which he threw at Jack, shouting, 'Catch!'

Jack caught it, shouting back, 'Bravo!' in joint praise of his own dexterity and Pandora's boldness, before throwing it towards Ritchie again. Ritchie was so busy trying to keep one eye on the ball and the other on Pandora lest she come to grief that, distracted, he dropped it.

'One to me!' shouted Jack joyfully, never having seen the tutor miss a catch before. Despite being such an apparent muff, Mr Ritchie had continued to be surprisingly adept with a cricket ball, making it turn and whizz when they played single-wicket on the lawn at Compton Place.

Meantime Pandora, prancing a little with joy at having defied convention *and* Mr Ritchie, proceeded along the beach, parallel with the cliff, enjoying the delightful sensation of the incoming waves rolling over her feet. Another equally delightful sensation was caused when she kicked the water so that it splashed high in a small fountain—never mind that it wetted her skirts, they would dry soon enough.

She could see Jack and Mr Ritchie apparently engrossed in their game, except that every now and then Mr Ritchie favoured her with a disapproving glare. After the third or fourth of them the Devil whispered naughty things in Pandora's ear.

True, she wasn't behaving in a particularly ladylike manner, but why in the world should *she* be expected always to be proper? She was doing a man's work at Compton Place, so why should she not be able to behave as freely as a man? Mr Ritchie deserved to have *his* priggish composure shaken—so why should she not shake it?

Pandora did not ask herself why she felt this continual desire to provoke Mr Ritchie. It seemed to be with her all the time. Isolated at Compton Place since childhood, innocent of the life of the senses, she was unaware that the strong attraction she was beginning to feel for him had no other outlet than this dreadful need to have his full attention on her. Even the caress they had exchanged had not told her that she felt for him as a woman feels for a man whom she is coming to love in the fullest sense of the word.

So, setting out to provoke him, she waited until his back was turned towards her and the sea before the Devil took over. When she saw Jack throw a curving and tricky ball at Ritchie, she shrieked at the top of her voice, 'Oh, help, please help me, I am losing my footing!'

Startled, Ritchie dropped the ball again and ran towards her to where she stood, waving her arms wildly, the water now up to her knees. All his instincts, so finely honed in war, had him reacting instantly when he thought that danger threatened. Behind him Jack crowed gleefully, 'Three to me, sir, and none to you!'

'Hold on, I'm coming,' Ritchie shouted commandingly at Pandora as he had once shouted at a young ensign who had wandered off into danger in the Spanish mountains. He reached her almost immediately, drenching himself thoroughly in the process, and lifted her into his arms. *Her* arms flew around his neck as he did so, and remained there while he carried her back to the beach, beyond the incoming tide.

'My hero!' she gasped at him when they reached safety and kissed him on the cheek. As though the kiss had stung him, Ritchie set her down. 'Goodness,' she added, smiling up at him. 'How strong you are. One would never have thought it.'

'Since you never stop to think, Miss Compton,' Ritchie snapped back at her, '*you* most certainly wouldn't!'

By her laughing, mischievous face he was suddenly sure that she had never been in any danger; that the whole thing was a hoax which had left her skirts wet and his trousers and elderly boots sodden.

She deserved…what did she deserve, the naughty, wild

thing that she was! She deserved a kiss, so she did. What was more, so did he—he wanted yet another to add to the one with which she had already gifted him.

To regain his moral and mental equilibrium rather than because he was actually angry with her, and because he couldn't kiss her, with Jack and Rob gaping at them, the most that he could do was to grind out hoarsely, 'Whatever would your brother think if you came back drowned?'

To Ritchie's private, and Jack's open, amusement, her merry answer was 'Well, ''Thank God for that,'' he would say, ''that's one worry the less for me.'''

Ritchie stepped slowly back and said, roughly now, 'I do believe that you were never in any danger at all.'

'Of course, she wasn't,' Jack said shrewdly. 'She was only funning. Pan loves to fun—when William isn't around, that is.'

Nevertheless, when she began to shiver Ritchie stripped off his cravat and handed it to her, saying, 'Go to the cave and dry your legs and feet. You must not catch a cold, richly though you might deserve to for frightening me so much.'

She said, looking a little remorseful, 'Were you really frightened?'

'Of course, I was. I never run into the water and carry a sea nymph out of the waves unless I am afraid that she might be drowning. Besides your cry for help was enough to wake the dead, let alone rouse one simple tutor.'

Ritchie immediately regretted the double meaning which lay in the word rouse, but it was plain that Pandora had not seen it. He knew, and in one sense it made him happy to know, that she was truly innocent. The admiring looks she threw at him were frank and open, there was no double, or knowing, meaning in them.

'I ought not to take your cravat from you,' she told him. 'Whatever would William think if he saw you without it when we reach home?'

'Oh, I have a clean kerchief with me, and I can knot that around my neck,' he said cheerfully. 'Now, for once, m'lady, be a good girl and do as you are told.'

Meekly she trotted into the cave, clutching his cravat in her left hand. A few minutes later she emerged, boots and stockings on again, but her wet skirts were still flapping around her.

'They'll dry on the way home,' Ritchie pronounced firmly. Out of long habit he had assumed the easy control of those around him which had been his for the last ten years. Both his hearers stared at him. He caught Jack's eye on him and reminded himself to resume being the humble tutor again.

There was an odd expression on Pandora's face, which was explained when she held her right hand out to him. A guinea lay on her palm.

'I found this in the sand in the cave,' she said. 'It looks as though Jem Sadler is correct in his supposition that they are being smuggled out of the country. How else would one arrive there?'

'How else, indeed?' said Ritchie, not wanting to say too much.

'I didn't quite believe him about the guineas,' she said mournfully. 'But it looks as though he was telling the truth. I knew that smuggling took place here, but this…' and she handed him the guinea '…is different. Shall we tell William—or the Riding Officer?'

All he could safely say was, 'That bears thinking about. You are Miss Compton of Compton Place and used to making such decisions. I am your humble servant and will do as you wish.'

'Not very humble lately,' was her cheeky reply to that.

Jack said, 'It doesn't do to peach on the Gentlemen, you know. The Dark Avenger will have you, if you do.'

'The Dark Avenger!' echoed Pandora and Ritchie as one. 'Who's that?'

'That's the legend,' said Jack smugly. 'The local people say that he may be seen wandering along this coast, threatening anyone who harms those of us who live and work here. He particularly protects the Gentlemen. They say he was a Compton lord who went to the Crusades and came home to find that marauders had burned down his castle and killed his wife and family. He pursued them to their deaths, but now haunts the coast, particularly Baxter's Bay, to make sure that the Revenue men never find out what is going on. Old Galpin claims to have seen him.'

'Why Dark?' asked Ritchie.

'Oh, he had sable in his arms and a black bear for a crest. He had been a Crusader and he always left a cross somewhere on his victims. To see him means death is nigh.'

'I thought that you said old Galpin saw him.'

'Oh, but *he* lives here. It's interfering strangers who are in danger.'

'I'm safe, then.' Pandora grinned. 'But Jem Sadler had better watch out.'

Ritchie listened with great interest to this variation of smuggler's lore. He had heard of men smearing their clothes with phosphorus and pretending to be ghosts to frighten off Revenue men and intruders, but the Dark Avenger was something else.

He decided to say nothing more and to leave Pandora to determine what action to take about the guinea she had found. One thing, though, was sure: Baxter's Bay was being used to smuggle contraband in and out of the country.

The rest of the afternoon passed without incident until they reached home again. William was waiting for them in the stable yard, his impatience as visible as his anger.

'Oh, there you are, Pandora. Out with *him* again, I see. I suppose you think that lad a sufficient chaperon. Next time take Brodribb with you,' and he waved at his groom, who was smiling impertinently at the three of them.

'You may leave us, Ritchie,' he ordered, 'and take your charge with you. I need to speak urgently to Miss Compton.'

'Well, what is it this time?' Pandora's voice was as weary as she could make it.

'I would like to entertain some friends for a few evenings in my own home for a change. To that end I would wish to see the house cleaned, rooms and beds aired, decent food and wine served at meals—if only for the duration of their visit.'

Pandora stared at him. 'How do you propose that we pay for all that, William? You know that the estate has little to spare for such junketing. We are only just managing to keep our heads above water.'

Her half-brother waved an impatient hand. 'No need for *you* to trouble about that. I told you that I had done well at the tables, and I am prepared to have extra servants brought in to clean the place, as well as a first-rate chef and plenty of good food from a grocer's in Brighton. It will only be for a week. I shall expect you to be my hostess, not that old trot, our aunt. I'm willing to arrange for you to borrow some decent *toilettes* to wear as well.'

Pandora flushed in anger. 'I have no intention of wearing any of your mistress's casts-off, William, and that's flat. I prefer to wear my own clothes. They may be old, but that reflects the true state of Compton lands, not the false one which you are proposing to foist on your guests.'

'I might have known that you would be awkward, but I cannot go on accepting other fellows' hospitality for ever—and that's flat, too. I expect that all will be ready in a fortnight, the first carriers' wagons will arrive to-morrow.'

Presented with such a *fait accompli*, Pandora could not argue further with him. It was a different thing, though, when as she turned to walk away he added, 'And by the by, you might as well know, I've arranged for a mad doctor to come to look at Sir John and decide whether it would be better for him to be sent to a madhouse. The old fool is beyond making sensible decisions. As heir I should undoubtedly be made Trustee of the Estate if he has to be committed.'

'No,' said Pandora, shocked. 'You cannot do that. He is not mad—far from it. His mind wanders a little, that's all.'

'Then it can wander in a madhouse where he can have some proper attendants, and we can arrange a suitable match for you at last before your wild behaviour makes you unmarriageable. Do not argue with me, my mind is quite made up.'

Useless to say anything further. William had a look on his face which Pandora knew well. She shivered, this time not because of cold, but because of the unwanted and unpleasant future which was opening up before her.

Oh, dear, she thought sadly, while walking to her room. If I were a character in a novel I could ask Mr Ritchie to run off with me! I'm sure that we would be able to manage to make some kind of living before I inherit mother's money.

Now where did that notion come from? Pandora asked herself, shocked, for once, by her own daring. *Particularly since, from what I have seen of Mr Ritchie, he is hardly the type of unprincipled scoundrel to do any such thing as run off with a future heiress. Except that this afternoon when I pretended to be drowning he was as brave and bold as I could wish any man to be—not at all like the meek man constantly bowing agreement at us all. He's taller than I am, too, so he makes me feel dainty.*

All in all though, I much prefer the bold man to the humble one!

If Pandora had thought that her conversation with William was the end of the bad feeling between them for that day, she was soon to find that she was mistaken.

After she had left him in the stable yard William had walked over to where Rob was helping George to unsaddle the horses on which Pandora's party had ridden that afternoon.

'A word with you,' he said peremptorily to Rob. 'Where did Miss Compton go today?'

'Why, to Baxter's Bay, Mr William—straight there and straight back. They was drawing—leastways Mr Ritchie and Master Jack were.'

'And what was Miss Compton doing while this was going on?'

Rob looked away, sniggering. 'Don't like to say, sir.'

'You'll either tell me, or I'll turn you away, so you'd better speak up, at once.'

Scared, Rob came out with the truth. 'She was paddling in the sea. Mr Ritchie told her not to, but she wouldn't listen to him—and then she got into difficulties and he had to rescue her.'

William's expression on hearing this, both George and Rob later agreed, was a sight to see.

'Paddled in the sea, got into difficulties! Are you making this up?'

'Gawd's truth, no, sir. Turned out that she was making a fool of Mr Ritchie. She wasn't in difficulties—just funning. Mr Ritchie was right cross. He told her what for, he did. After all, he'd had to carry her out, and she's no lightweight, but he made little of it.'

George rolled his eyes to heaven on hearing this frank account of Miss Pandora's folly. William's fury at this latest evidence of Pandora's lightmindedness knew no bounds. 'One more thing,' he said at last through gritted teeth. 'Did anyone else see Miss Compton paddling?'

Rob shook his head. 'No, sir. That Riding Officer came along a little earlier but he'd gone by then.'

'Sadler? You mean Sadler?'

'Aye.'

'What the devil was he doing there?'

Rob was looking scared by now and was wondering whether he had lost his job by telling the truth. 'Asking questions about smuggling of Miss Compton and Mr Ritchie, but they allowed as how they knew nothing.'

'And that's all?'

Inspiration struck Rob on the head. 'Not quite all. Miss Compton found a golden guinea in the cave when she was putting her stockings and boots back on again. That was all…I think.'

William's face altered. If anything, his expression grew even uglier. 'It's quite enough, *I* think,' he said at last, and stormed out of the stable yard. It seemed to be his usual mode of walking these days, what with all the provocation he was receiving.

Once he had gone, George seized Rob by the shoulder and spun him round.

'By the Lord, boy, do you never know when to keep your trap shut? Hasn't Miss Pandora enough to trouble her without you peaching on her and making her life even more difficult than it is? Yon nodcock will go straight to her now and read the Riot Act to her all over again.

'And then you had to prattle about the Riding Officer and guineas. Have you no sense? Want the Dark Avenger after you, do you?'

Rob's face turned a dirty yellow. 'Never say so! I ain't done anything.'

'No, but you've said enough. Now go and fetch me as many pails of water as you can carry before you have any supper.'

Pandora was combing her hair and dreaming about her happy afternoon on the beach with Jack and Mr Ritchie when someone started to bang loudly on her bedroom door.

'See who it is, Janet,' she called to her maid, but before Janet could reach it the door was flung open and William came in, his face like thunder. His anger over his half-sister's jaunt with Ritchie had grown when Brodribb, who had been following them at a distance, and whose spying on them Ritchie had sensed, had confirmed Rob's story.

'Leave us!' he bawled at Janet, then turned to Pandora, who stood there staring at him. He seemed to be afflicted by a worse case of the blue devils than ever before.

'What's this I've been hearing about you, madam? Paddling in the sea before that fellow Ritchie, to say nothing of Jack and Rob the stable lad! Have you taken leave of your senses? And what's all this about you tattling with the Riding Officer and finding guineas in caves?'

All Pandora could stammer out was, 'Who told you?'

'Never mind that. Is it the truth?'

'In a way, but…'

'*In a way,*' William shrieked at her. 'Have you no decorum? What if the county got to hear about it? Who would marry you then?'

'Well, since I don't want to marry, that worries me not at all. I thought that you didn't want me to marry, but preferred me to keep my inheritance in the family.'

'Roger Waters, my very good friend, has told me that he wants to marry you—which is partly why I'm arranging this house party so that you may get to know one another better. What would he think if he heard of this afternoon's goings on? And with the tutor *again*.'

'Well, if *you* don't tell Roger Waters I went for a paddle, then I'm sure *I* won't,' retorted Pandora spiritedly. 'Unless of course, he grows so importunate that that's the only way I can put him off.'

'You know,' said William thickly on hearing this piece of impertinence, 'I think that our grandparents made a great mistake when they stopped beating their impudent daughters. I'd like to order one for you. If you ever misbehave in such a fashion again, I might revive the custom.'

He began to leave her, but suddenly swung on his heel, saying, 'And that guinea you found. Do you still have it?'

'Of course,' said Pandora cheekily. 'I haven't had the opportunity to spend it yet.'

For one horrible moment she thought that he was about to strike her. Instead, he said menacingly, 'If you give it to me—at once—I'll try to forgive you for this afternoon's goings-on.'

'I don't want your forgiveness, and I won't give you the guinea. I shall give it to the Riding Officer and, if you take it from me, I shall still tell him where I found it. Baxter's Bay is being used to smuggle them out, isn't it?'

William controlled himself with difficulty. 'How the devil should I know? Have it your way, then. Keep the bloody thing and buy a faring for your fancy man with it. If it weren't for Grandfather, I'd have him out of the house on the double, and damme so I will, as soon as I can contrive it.'

He was gone. Pandora sat down on the bed and, despite all that she could do to stop them, the tears began to run down her face.

Marry Roger Waters! She could imagine no worse fate. She was beginning to think that he was involved in smuggling, which meant that William almost certainly was as well. The worst thing of all was that there was no one she could turn to for help and advice. She couldn't cold-bloodedly betray William and the Waters to the Riding Officer, even if she did have any hard evidence of what they were doing—but she didn't, only suspicions. Nor could she tell Mr Ritchie: she didn't want to put him in either trouble or danger, for she was sure that William would be even nastier to him if he thought that Mr Ritchie knew that he was smuggling guineas to Napoleon.

It was time to go down to dinner. It was Mr Ritchie and Jack's day for attending and she didn't like to think about how William would behave when he saw them. Badly, if the last quarter of an hour was any guide. On the other hand, however bold a face she had put on when talking to William, she knew as well as he did that the servants would tattle her folly around the county.

It was probably Rob who had given her away since she was sure that neither Jack nor Mr Ritchie would have said anything. It was hateful of William to have called him her fancy man, but why was it that she had done something so reckless and unladylike as to paddle in the sea before three members of the opposite sex? If she was honest with herself, it was because she wanted to tease Mr Ritchie, to shock him out of his humbly submissive and proper ways.

So what did that make her?

On top of that, why did Roger Waters wish to marry her, and why was William suddenly so eager to promote the marriage? Pandora's growing sense of the realities of the world in which she lived rapidly supplied her with an answer. Roger's father, Henry, was a city merchant who had risen in the world and had enriched himself. He had bought Milton House and the estate attached to it from its bankrupt previous owner. Of itself this was not enough to gain him complete respectability, but if his heir, Roger, married Miss Compton of Compton Place, a woman with a pedigree which went back to the Norman Conquest, then the Waters's position in society would be secure.

Roger, if not his father, would become a gentleman.

Chapter Five

Ritchie never enjoyed the weekly dinner-party with his supposed betters when William Compton was staying at Compton Place. What had been a jolly and informal occasion with Pandora, Aunt Em and Jack then became something of a misery. After his original expulsion from it, Aunt Em had been to Sir John and had seen him reinstated: a privilege which Ritchie could have done without.

William seemed to be in a worse temper than usual that evening. He snarled at Jack, at the elderly footman and was even rude to poor, harmless Aunt Em. Pandora he never spoke to at all, but glowered at her and at Ritchie alternately.

When Ritchie rose to leave at the end of the meal William said to him in a voice of ice, 'I want a word with you in the library, in ten minutes' time. Do not fail to be there, waiting for me.'

Ritchie inclined his head: remaining polite in the face of William's boorishness was growing daily more difficult. He saw Pandora's unhappy face and Aunt Em's worried one. Jack enlivened the occasion by asking, 'Do you wish me to attend you in the library, William?'

'Sir, to me,' ground out his half-brother. 'You grow a deal too familiar these days, young man, which doesn't say much for your tutor's success in training you. And, no, I don't want you. You may go to your room and try to improve your manners.'

Jack stuck out a mutinous lip, but was wise enough to say nothing more.

William's ten minutes stretched out to over half an hour before he walked into the library, his face reddened by all the port he had drunk while keeping Ritchie waiting. His manner was sullen and he immediately went on the attack.

'What do you mean by dragging Miss Compton all round the county and then encouraging her to paddle in the sea? If it weren't that it's become such a bore finding new tutors for young Jack on top of my grandfather's favouring of you, I'd have you dismissed on the spot for that.'

To defend himself by stating the truth, that Pandora had chosen to accompany him and Jack, and had disregarded his advice to her not to paddle, was something which Ritchie found distasteful.

'It is scarcely part of my duties and, indeed, might be considered an impertinence if I sought to treat Miss Compton after the fashion which I might use with Master Jack,' was all he could think to offer, while inwardly seething—his usual state of mind when with William Compton.

William could think of nothing to say in answer to this uncontrovertible piece of truth. As usual he had been outfoxed by the insolent swine in front of him, whose humility, in William's opinion, hid a nasty case of thinking himself better than his masters.

'Well, if she offers to accompany you again,' he finally achieved, 'then you will tell her that you have orders from me to the effect that you are not to be her escort, either in, or out of, Compton Place. Your duties are with Master Jack, and no one else.'

'I shall remember that in future,' said Ritchie, bowing his head, and promising himself that at some not-too-distant time in that future he might give William Compton the thrashing he richly deserved. He had no doubt that Pandora's unhappy and subdued face at dinner was the result of previous nastiness from William when he had discovered about her afternoon's adventure.

From Rob, the stable lad, no doubt, or possibly the unseen watcher whom he was sure had been spying on them.

In the meantime he must continue with his mission, and once Jack was safely abed he sat down and began to make plans in the same careful and conscientious way he had employed in the Spanish mountains. Once the plans were made and he was in action it would be a different matter. Boldness was all.

What Jack had told them that afternoon about the Dark Avenger had suggested something to him which, now that he was alone, set him smiling. The expression on his face would have surprised, if not shocked, the entire Compton family—other than Sir John, that was, for Sir John had seen in him the dedicated professional soldier which he had once been…and still was.

Before dinner, while Jack had been translating Caesar's *De Bello Gallico,* from the Latin, the only classic text in which he could be persuaded to take an interest because it was about the wars which the great Julius had fought for Rome, he had paid a visit to the attics. They lay next door to the schoolroom and were crammed with the discarded possessions of long-gone Comptons. Rummaging through them he had discovered a large old cloak, once navy blue, but now black with age, and a long and heavy moth-eaten black woollen scarf. Both of them, he decided, would be useful in the dark.

A crescent moon was rising in a clear sky and he was now ready to begin to reconnoitre the terrain round Compton Place all the way down to Baxter's Bay itself. It would be like old times again, and it would be amusing to revive the legend of the Dark Avenger, for that was who he intended to be. To impersonate the Avenger would allow him to perform two useful functions: it would enable him to scout around disguised and unknown, and the thought that the Dark Avenger was on the prowl again would frighten away the superstitious. All those who knew the legend would avoid the ghost which they would think that they were seeing.

He guessed, though he might be guessing wrongly, that William and his friend Roger intended to use the house party at Compton Place as a blind for some major piece of smuggling. Either the proceeds raised by selling the guineas in Paris were to be run ashore, hidden among more ordinary contraband such as liquor, tobacco or silks—or the guineas themselves were to be rowed out to a smuggling cutter for sale in France. He could not be sure which end of the operation he might discover.

William and Roger would thus be provided with a useful alibi: they would be junketing at Compton Place while their agents and servants were doing the dirty work. Sidmouth and his advisers were of the belief that a City magnate was behind this latest outbreak of smuggling and Henry Waters was a known and dubious merchant capable of being the head of such an organisation, and of knowing where to dispose of its illicit proceeds safely and secretly.

Ritchie thought that he might be wrong in his conjectures, but the same instinct that had made him one of

Wellington's most successful agents in the Spanish Peninsular War told him that he wasn't. He had spent his time since he had arrived at Compton Place in watching and thinking. The one thing which he did not know was how honest Jem Sadler was, and for that reason he had been careful in what he said to him.

All that he needed to do for the present was to be patient and wait for the night to come when he might skulk down the backstairs and add a new chapter to the folklore of the Sussex Downs and Baxter's Bay. Disguised as the Dark Avenger, he would be able to explore the district at will in the night hours, and with luck he might even come upon the Gentlemen at work elsewhere.

Gentlemen! he thought bitterly, what a name for those who are betraying their country when it was at war with the enemy.

As he had hoped, Ritchie found that there wasn't a cloud in the sky that night. After many days spent mostly indoors it was exhilarating to run through the neglected gardens, out into the Park, and through the gate which opened on to the Downs and the path which led to Baxter's Bay. He had wound the shawl round his head so that only his eyes showed. Occasionally he flapped the cloak behind him as though it were wings on which its wearer might fly.

A passing poacher on the Downs, looking for rabbits, saw him from a distance. He sank to his knees letting out a low moan and hiding his face in his hands. The Dark Avenger was abroad again after being absent for many months. He must warn the villagers and those of his friends who might fear the spectre's wrath. This part of the Downs must be shunned in future.

Unaware that his stratagem was already working,

Ritchie slowed down to a trot and began to enjoy the scene before him, which was very like the moonlit paintings of the Midlands painter, Wright of Derby. The light on the sea, the clear starlit sky, the blessed quiet all reminded him of his days in the mountains with the Spanish guerrillas. Although there were no French soldiers ready to kill him on sight as the laws of war allowed them to do, it was possible that if he were surprised by the Gentlemen they might be equally as savage with someone whom they believed would put a stop to their little game.

Finally he reached the beach where Pandora had paddled. The tide was high, and would be higher still on the nights of William's house party. He looked around him, all his soldierly instincts on the alert. He could see the path by which they had walked down, and up which the contraband would be carried to a waiting coach or cart.

From there it would either be driven on to a rutted byway which ultimately led on to the London to Brighton turnpike, or be stored in temporary hiding places to be carried away later.

How a guinea had come to be lost in the cave was something of a puzzle which was not worth the time he might spend trying to solve it. What it did bear witness to was that the Bay was most probably one of the places where they were loaded on to the waiting cutter.

For a time he sat on a rock and let the peace of the night envelop him before he made his way back to the Big House, as the locals called it. Another night owl, half-cut from a night's drinking in the inn at Old Compton village, saw him on the cliff and, like the poacher, drew the same conclusion from his presence.

The Dark Avenger was on the loose again!

He ran home, gibbering to wake his wife to tell her the news, only to be sourly informed that he was so drunk that he might have mistaken a lost pony for the Avenger, and if he didn't shut his gob at once she'd have his guts for garters, Avenger or no Avenger!

Not that it stopped him from telling half the neighbourhood the next morning what he had seen on the cliffs above Baxter's Bay in the moonlight.

Oh, what a hurry-scurry and a commotion there was when Compton Place was made reasonably ready to entertain William's friends! A haughty French chef arrived from London—hired by Roger Waters, William said. He promptly made enemies of everyone in the kitchen, and loudly announced, to Ritchie's amusement, that the tutor was the only person in the house who wasn't a savage. This was because Ritchie, for once acting without thinking, spoke to him in his beautiful accent-less French.

A flotilla of carts arrived, containing all the necessaries required for the guests such as new bed-linen and new furniture. After them came servants to clean the place, to shake down cobwebs which had existed for years and frighten every spider in the place, Jack said. The chandeliers were washed, new candles installed, new curtains were hung at the windows and even new carpets arrived, to be laid by another bevy of servants who left quite quickly, but only after driving the normal staff mad.

Galpin moaned at all the extra work which he was required to organise so William, glad of the chance to be rid of him for a time, brought in a new supercilious butler, borrowed from the Waters. He disliked everyone already installed at the Place, particularly Ritchie. 'Galpin can come back when the house-party is over,' William told an annoyed Pandora. 'I can't have that old fool embarrassing me in front of my friends,' he ended.

'What can all this be costing?' Pandora wailed to Ritchie one afternoon in the library—which had also been 'improved', William's favourite word these days. It was the only place where they could meet, what with William's prohibition of their jaunts and Ritchie's desire not to make Pandora's life more difficult than it already was.

'And to think,' she went on, 'that a fraction of this money would have meant that we need not have been in such a bad way with the bank, that we could have spent some of it on improving the running of the home farm, and a hundred other things which have been allowed to run down.

'And all for a few days' pleasure for William,' she ended.

Ritchie, who privately thought that there was more to it than that, agreed with her. He was becoming more besotted with her by the day, and perhaps William's prohibition was a good thing, what with his mission and his inability to control his errant body when he was with her.

I'm behaving as though I were eighteen again, and at the mercy of every female I saw, he thought savagely. Except that it's only Pandora who has this effect on me. I'm in no danger of debauching the entire female staff here, unlike the unlamented Mr Sutton.

'I shouldn't allow it to trouble you overmuch,' he told her gently, while longing to plant a kiss on her pretty mouth. 'Things have a way of solving themselves.'

'How they could solve this I can't imagine,' was her spirited reply. 'And on top of everything else, all of the staff and half of Old Compton village are frightening themselves to death because the Dark Avenger has reappeared.'

Ritchie thought it advisable to show ignorance here. 'The Dark Avenger?' he questioned.

'You remember. Jack talked about him that day we went to Baxter's Bay.'

'Oh, yes,' murmured Ritchie, 'forgetful of me, but surely they are mistaken. The result of a few drinks too many at the alehouse, one supposes. '

Pandora shook her red-gold head. 'I'm afraid not. George, who is a steady fellow and never drinks, saw him late last night. He'd been to visit his cousins at Orchard's Farm. He said that he was almost flying on the cliffs above Baxter's Bay. He thinks that some sort of doom may be upon us.'

'Dear, dear,' said Ritchie, putting on his glasses and looking more owlish than ever as he picked up an elderly copy of *The Gentleman's Magazine*. 'I do hope not.' He said this as much to assuage his own sense of guilt as to reassure Pandora whom, at the moment, he thought that nothing could reassure.

Except that she suddenly began to laugh. 'One of the things I most like about you,' she said at last, 'and I don't suppose I ought to talk like this to you—but since everyone around here is going mad and misbehaving, I might as well join in—is that you are so calm and controlled. Merely to be with you cools me down. Were you always like this? No, I shouldn't ask you.'

He gave her the oddest look. A look which made Pandora quiver all over. What was it about him? Why did she miss him so on those days when he was not to be seen save at the weekly dinner where he sat there so quietly that he might as well not have been present? Why did the slightest touch from him—accidental, of course—when he handed her something, have her trembling all over—and in the oddest places. Places which ladies should not know existed.

'I try to be,' he offered in his most controlled mode,

while thinking that when he was with her calm and controlled were scarcely words which could be used of him.

'I wish I were more like you,' she told him frankly.

Ritchie could not stop himself. 'I'm so glad you're not,' he murmured. 'For one thing, you would no longer be a young lady, but a young gentleman, and I much prefer you as a lady. For another thing, I like you because you're not calm and controlled. Perhaps I ought to add that I'm not always as controlled as I appear.'

This conversation was becoming most improper, both parties privately decided. The difficulty was that each of them was beginning to feel that it was not improper enough.

Pandora thought: What would it feel like if he kissed me?

In the library? Kiss one another in the library? Suppose William came in, suppose Jack came in, suppose the butler, the new chef, and old Uncle Tom Cobleigh and all came in, what would they think? If he were not Jack's tutor, severe but kind Mr Edward Ritchie, but was that awful Roger Waters, no one would mind if he kissed me—which just goes to show what a stupid world we live in.

Ritchie thought: How would she respond if I kissed her?

If I were not posing as Mr Edward Ritchie, Jack's humble tutor, but was present in my true self as Major Richard Chancellor, heir to a small fortune left to him by an old uncle who had taken a fancy to the quiet and studious boy I once was, no one would make too great a tohu-bohu if I kissed her.

They sighed together—and Jack came in. 'So there you are,' he exclaimed. 'Best not let William know, Pan. He wants you to marry ugly Roger Waters. I'd much prefer

for you to marry Mr Ritchie. If you did, I could talk about
soldiers to him all day.'

'Jack!' the guilty pair exclaimed together.

'I know, I know,' he said, unrepentantly. 'I shouldn't
say such things. You know, most of the people around us
never tell the truth. I always do, which is why I get into
such trouble.'

Ritchie murmured, 'Some things are best not said, Jack,
however truthful they might be. Since you have found me,
I think it best that we retire to the schoolroom and trans-
late a little more Caesar.'

Pandora smiled at them both as Ritchie walked Jack to
the door. She might have seen him for only a few moments, but those moments had brightened her day. And
tomorrow her day would be dimmed when William and
his dubious friends arrived and she would be compelled
to act as hostess in the unsuitable *toilettes* which William
had given her.

William's guests, she found were not dubious, at least
not totally so. They included, beside Roger Waters, four
young bachelors and three married couples who were fortunately so respectable that Pandora was happy to entertain them.

Unfortunately Jack and Ritchie had been told to stay
well away from the visitors so, for the time being, there
could be no quiet little meetings in the library—a place
where none of the guests ventured—but that was also out
of bounds to Jack and Ritchie during William's party.

'William's a beast,' Jack told Ritchie gloomily. 'For all
he knows, I like using the library.'

'He probably knows you too well,' said Ritchie with a
grin. Jack looked sharply at him. There were times when
old Ritchie came out with these barbed remarks, so unlike

his usual mild comments. He was acute enough to notice that old Ritchie never strayed far from being the subdued tutor when he was in company.

'Well, he can't ban us from the grounds,' Jack said, 'so long as we keep away from him and his cronies.'

Cronies was a good word, Ritchie thought. The ban kept him from seeing any of them on their first day. He played the Avenger that night, even though he thought it unlikely that the guineas would be moved on the first evening. On the third William was giving a grand ball to which, it being held on the night when the moon was full, half of the county's nobility and gentry were invited, and Ritchie was of the opinion that that night would be *the* night.

Mid-afternoon on the second day he and Jack had ridden on the Downs and gone fossil hunting in Baxter's Bay where they were lucky enough to find a splendid specimen, which looked exactly like one of the large prawns which Jack later caught in the sea.

They were walking back from the stables, Ritchie carrying his valise and Jack his net and the canvas bag full of the prawns which he intended to give to Cook for their supper—only later would he discover that the chef had confiscated them and they ended up as part of the guests' dinner, much to his annoyance.

They took the path which led to the back of the house in order to avoid trouble, but were unfortunate enough to meet William and four of the male guests strolling towards them.

Alas, there was no way in which they could dodge them. Jack said something rude under his breath and Ritchie put on his most cowed expression. He had practised it so often and had achieved such perfection with it that

William was beginning to think that he had misjudged the fellow.

Not that William looked particularly pleased to see him—or Jack for that matter.

'Why, if it isn't the tutor?' he exclaimed. 'And my brother Jack. What's the horrible smell of fish, eh? Thought you took him fossil hunting, Ritchie. Didn't know that fossils smelt bad.'

He was so busy making fun of Ritchie that he failed to notice that one member of his party was staring at the tutor with the most profound expression of shock on his face.

Ritchie was equally shocked at what he was seeing. Of all people his brother, Russell Chancellor, Viscount Hadleigh, was standing on William's right hand looking bored. Until he saw Ritchie, that was. Neither brother said anything. Russell was too stunned by what he was seeing and hearing to do anything but stare.

Fortunately, Jack, nettled by William's rude dismissal of them both as insignificant, growled, 'I caught some prawns in the Bay while Mr Ritchie drew the fossils in the cave wall. He said that they were unique and worth recording.'

'Did he, indeed?' sneered William. 'And pray, what marvels do you propose to engage in now?'

'With your permission,' said Ritchie, now at his most greasily humble, 'I should like to visit the library. At least I should; Master Jack wishes to deliver the prawns to the kitchen before having a good wash in order to remove the odour of fish from his person.'

He was keenly aware, and inwardly amused, by his brother's increasingly shocked face as he offered William his most cowed expression—something which was so foreign to Major the Honourable Richard Chancellor's normal one as to be a work of art in itself.

'The library, eh?' grinned William. 'Most suitable. You may use it, Jack may not, but may one ask what you hope to do there on this fine afternoon?'

'Oh, there are many good books in the library and one may find there explanations of many surprising things—if one knows how to look for them, that is.'

And if his brother didn't take that hint, Ritchie told himself sardonically, then he had changed alarmingly for the worst since they had been rowdy boys together. At least, Russell had been rowdy.

He thought that Russell gave him a slight inclination of the head when he had finished speaking. Which might mean anything—or nothing.

'Mustn't keep you, then. Wouldn't do to waste your valuable time. And, Jack, try to catch something a little less smelly next time—unless you wish to set up as a fishmonger.'

It took Ritchie all his powers of deception not to strike the unpleasant swine before them. Jack's face was working all the way back to the House.

'Why does he have to be such a beast to me?' he finally burst out when they had reached the safety of indoors and before he went to the kitchens with his trophies which William had mocked. 'And before strangers, too.'

'Because he's a beast himself. The best way to beat him, Jack, is not to let what he says to you spoil things for you. Show Cook your treasures and see how pleased she will be. Now I must be off to the library. I'll join you in the schoolroom before they bring us our supper.'

He did not have long to wait. With his notebook before him and several of the few worthwhile books from the shelves around him, he appeared to be engaged in solemn research when the door opened and his twin brother entered.

Ritchie rose to his feet. Russell stopped a few yards away from him but said nothing. It was left for Ritchie to speak. He said, abruptly for him, 'You keep poor company these days, brother.'

If he had thought Russell would immediately tax him as to why he was living at Compton Place under a false name and playing at being the poor tutor, he was mistaken. Russell shrugged and replied to Ritchie's comment equally abruptly, 'I am beginning to think so. I dislike the Waters fellow intensely. The *on dit* in London is that he and his father are involved in the smuggling business—hence the mansion in Sussex.'

'Then what does bring you here? Not to engage in smuggling, I trust.'

Russell shrugged again. 'Boredom, ennui, I am sick of everything, particularly myself.'

What answer could Ritchie make to that? Particularly when Russell was so studiously avoiding what *he* must want to know, which was, Why are *you* here and what are *you* doing?

Silence fell, until Russell gave way and asked his questions.

'And what brings you here, *Mister* Ritchie, to play the obsequious tutor? Are *you* so sick of yourself that you engage in such an odd masquerade?'

Ritchie replied enigmatically, 'One might think so.'

'Oh, but I don't think so, little brother. You always have some purpose in everything you do, unlike me. So why this? Have you always had a passion to bear-lead a boy and be insulted by his half-brother? What bee buzzes in *your* bonnet?'

It was Ritchie's turn to twit his brother. 'I might be finding life dull after Spain.'

Russell's laugh was humourless. 'Duller still here, I would have thought. And, by the by, what were you really doing in Spain? Someone said something to me the other night in London that made me think that you were more than a simple cavalry officer. Are you being more than simple here? No, don't answer me if you don't wish to. I promise not to give you away, but I don't promise to stifle a grin when I see you behaving so unlike yourself. For one moment out there I thought by the twitch of your lip that you might plant a facer on my oaf of a host for his insulting manner to you and the lad.'

'Most unwise of me if I were to do so,' said Ritchie with a grin of his own. 'I should be dismissed on the spot and that would never do.'

'I suppose it wouldn't. I won't give you away on condition that when your odd behaviour here is over you might tell me what you have been getting up to and will undoubtedly get up to in the future, if half of what I have heard about you is true.'

'Oh, never believe above half of what you hear, most unwise. And now I must leave you. Master Jack and I are having our supper in the schoolroom. I shan't ask you to join us.'

'No, indeed, although I would much prefer to. He looks a likely lad to me, better than brother William, though that wouldn't be difficult. Adieu, Ritchie, and mind your back—although from what I don't know.'

They smiled at one another. They had always been close friends from youth, despite the difference in their characters, and Ritchie took the memory of Russell's smile up to the schoolroom with him to banish the ugliness of William Compton's behaviour.

Russell had told him something useful when he had mentioned the rumours about the Waters which were running round London. He was sure that his brother knew nothing of what William and Roger Waters might be getting up to at the moment, and he had no intention of telling him. What Russell didn't know couldn't harm him.

'I hate all this,' said Jack the next morning. From first light Pandora, Mrs Rimmington and the rest of the staff had been busily preparing for the evening's junketing.

Ritchie looked up from his breakfast: a most unsatisfactory one since the staff were having their work cut out to look after all of William's guests in the manner to which they were accustomed.

'You mean the preparations for tonight's ball?'

Jack nodded. 'Hasn't Pandora enough to do without all this consequence? Does William never think of anyone but himself?'

'Probably not,' Ritchie told him, 'but try not to worry about it. Worry instead about that maths paper I set you.'

Which was all very fine of him since he was himself busy worrying about how he was to leave the house unseen and, while playing the Avenger, make his way to the cliffs so that he might check whether or not any contraband was either leaving or arriving in Baxter's Bay.

His plan was to collect his cloak and scarf which he had hidden inside a chest in a wooden folly in the Park. It was in such a decrepit condition that no one was likely to visit it. He had stowed it away there the previous night, wondering wryly what his brother might think of such odd conduct if he had been unlucky enough to meet him. Stupid really, to think such things, for he could not imagine Russell being a night prowler—he thought too much of his comfort for that.

Which was a harsh judgement but a true one.

Which didn't help him to decide how best to slip away while the ball was in full swing. It was quite possible that a number of the guests and the local visitors would wish to wander in the Park in the moonlight—some of them for reasons best not enquired into!

Meantime there was the day to get through.

He met Pandora on the first landing of the backstairs in the early afternoon. They stared at one another.

'I thought that you and Jack might be out riding on the Downs this afternoon,' Pandora said.

'No, it seems that William and some of his guests had the same idea and George told me that all the horses—including our old hacks—would be commandeered for them. We have been reading Shakespeare's *Hamlet* instead.'

'If I were not using the backstairs myself,' Pandora said, her expression as wry as Ritchie's thoughts, 'I might ask you why you were using them.'

'Oh, the word has come down from William that Jack and I are not to use the main stairs while the guests are here.'

'No!' exclaimed Pandora violently. 'How dare he…'

She was so distressed that Ritchie said gently, 'Do not trouble yourself. I am quite happy to avoid both them and him—which is, I suppose, why you are using them.'

'I am doing so from choice,' she replied energetically, 'but to inflict such a prohibition on you is the outside of enough!'

'True—fortunately though, William does not grasp that I see it as a boon conferred—but pray do not tell him so.'

Pandora began to laugh. 'You really are incomparable,' she said. 'My old nurse had a saying which she was fond of and which always amused me. She said that it was like water off a duck's back to try to put one over on me. I think that I like you so much because in our different ways we are very similar. Oh, dear,' she ended mournfully. 'I don't think that what I have just said makes very much sense.'

That did it! That royally did it, thought Ritchie ruefully. This time he lost all sense of what was proper and right. He leaned forward and, putting his arms around her, kissed her, not on the mouth—he thought that given his current roused condition that might not be safe—but on the cheek.

Then he growled, while still holding her, 'Everything you say makes good sense to me, my dear girl.'

At last she knew what it was like for him to kiss her, and oh, how sweet it was—and oh, how naughty! Old Sutton had seduced the servants, but young Ritchie was seducing the mistress—and she was enjoying herself mightily. Everything that William had been saying about them was true. The tutor *was* after his sister and his sister *was* enthusiastically co-operating with him instead of thrusting him away—for she immediately kissed him back, and on the mouth, too.

This had the opposite effect from the one which she intended. Ritchie, suddenly fearing that they might be caught at any moment with their arms around one another, drew away from her. To be found in such a compromising position would not only jeopardise his mission but would also destroy Pandora's reputation.

He had not reckoned on Pandora's determination. While he was inwardly cursing his own lack of control, she was trying to pull him back into her arms!

'No,' he said hoarsely. 'I shouldn't have done that.'

'Why not?' returned Pandora, shamelessly as she afterwards realised. 'I liked it and, if I'm not mistaken, so did you.'

'True,' Ritchie said. 'You must understand that it was quite wrong of me to kiss you, and the fact that we each enjoyed what we did is not to the point. I am a servant in this house and you are its mistress, which means that we are breaking all society's conventions if we begin to make love. Believe me, if things were different and I were your equal…even then, I ought not to have taken advantage of you by kissing you when we were alone. It was not the act of a gentleman. Forgive me and let us both forget the last few minutes.'

Pandora was as frank and free as ever. 'No, I cannot forget them, and nor can I forgive you. That would imply that what you—we—did was wrong, and—'

'And,' interrupted Ritchie, 'if we had continued, or were to do so in the future, where would it all end? Think of Mr Sutton and his shameless behaviour—mine just now was the more so.'

'I much prefer *not* to think of Mr Sutton and—' Pandora suddenly broke down.

What she was about to say was unsayable since it was to the effect that all her life she had been loveless and unloved and now she had found both love and the delight of being loved and could not bear to relinquish either condition. It would sound as though she were railing against life and chance, was a miserable creature reduced to finding comfort in a clandestine meeting on the back-stairs. On the other hand, if she said straight out what she really felt about him—which all the training she had received told her was an impossibility—what then?

Oh, to the devil with propriety! I shall speak the truth and shame the devil—as Nurse used to say, though I'm not sure that she meant it.

So she said, 'I think that I love you, Mr Ritchie—so what do I do now?'

'Nothing,' he replied, inwardly cursing his disguise, his mission, Sidmouth who had sent him here and even the God above who had landed him in such a pickle that he could not tell the woman who loved him that he loved her. Oh, to be Richard Chancellor again and be able to approach her honourably.

It had been so much easier deceiving people in Spain. There he had been helping the guerrillas to fight a war against a cruel invader and those whom he deceived were the invaders. Here he was deceiving not only the tricksters and traitors—which he was sure William Compton and Roger Waters were—but also the innocents like Pandora, Jack and Aunt Em. To say nothing of the servants who were being kind to him in their relief that he was so unlike Mr Sutton.

Pandora said, her face mournful, 'And that is all? Nothing?'

'As we are now,' Ritchie told her, and he was prevaricating, he knew, and speaking with a double tongue, 'there is nothing that we can do.'

She was intelligent enough to catch the possible underlying meaning in what he had just said. 'Do you mean that there could come a time when matters between us might stand differently?'

Oh, the clever creature that she was! He must be careful in future not to say anything which might put the pair of them at risk, for beneath her outward candour her understanding was as subtle as his.

He tried to laugh lightly, but thought that the sound he made was hollow.

'My dear, and you are my very dear, and this is the last time that I must call you so, we live in the here and now where you are mistress and I am servant and we must both do nothing which might dishonour us—however much we might desire to act otherwise.'

Pandora nodded her head gravely, thinking, That is why I love him. He possesses a sense of honour which is lacking in all of those around me—except for Sir John and Jack, and in the world as it stands they both count for nothing.

'I must not tease or tempt you,' was all that she could offer him, 'but that does not mean that my feelings towards you have changed. Only I must be fair to you. I must not do anything which could cause you to lose your employment here, and throw you out into the world where you might, after being subjected to William's spite, and possibly lacking proper references, be unable to earn a living. You must not starve because of me—that I do understand.'

So saying, she left him, after giving him a slight bow and a nod of the head—as dismissal, Ritchie supposed.

He winced again at the knowledge of his own duplicity. The only comfort he could gain from what Pandora had just said was of her own goodness in not selfishly pursuing him for her own pleasure, but considering instead the possible consequences for him if William thought that they were indulging in a clandestine *affaire*.

Pray God that this mission might soon be over so that he could approach her in his true name and condition—but what then might she think of a man who had so consistently lied to and tricked all those about him: however good his aims were. How hollow would his glib talk of honour sound when she knew the truth?

Chapter Six

'I hate missing all the fun,' said Jack crossly after they had finished their supper. 'When Papa was alive, Nurse was allowed to take me to the top of the stairs where I could see the visitors come. He used to send some of the good food upstairs, too, and all we have had this evening are the greasy leftovers from nuncheon.'

'I thought that you didn't like the fuss of the house-party,' said Ritchie, looking up from his book.

'I don't like being left out of it,' grumbled Jack.

He was about to begin complaining again when there was a knock on the door. He bellowed, 'Come in,' hoping against hope that some of the sweetmeats which he had seen being prepared earlier had been sent up from the kitchens. When the visitor proved to be Pandora he said ungraciously, 'Oh, it's you. What are you doing here?'

Pandora advanced into the room. Ritchie put his book down and rose to his feet.

'Miss Compton,' he said, his face stern. 'What may we do for you?'

'Oh, no,' she said sweetly, 'it is what *I* may do for *you*,' and she pulled her right arm from behind her back where she had hidden it and offered them a plate of chocolate sweetmeats—the very things which Jack had seen the chef preparing earlier.

'Oh, famous!' he exclaimed. 'What a brick you are, Pan. Everyone else had forgotten us.'

'Not quite,' she said. 'Mrs Rimmington smuggled them out. The kitchen had had orders, it seemed, that the schoolroom was to have nothing but nursery food while the guests were here, but she felt that that would be unfair to both of you. Since I had decided to visit you to show you my new *toilette*, I offered to bring it upstairs, because if I were caught no one could complain that I was disobeying orders.'

Ritchie had been aware of Pandora's new *toilette* from the moment that she had entered, but after what had passed earlier that afternoon he had decided that discretion was the better part of valour and compliments to his forbidden love were therefore out of order.

She was looking charming in a light green, high-waisted dress trimmed with cream lace so pale that it was almost white. Some lemon-coloured carnations, retrieved from Compton Place's ruined gardens, had been twisted into a coronet for her hair. She wore no jewellery—that had long gone during her efforts to save the estate from ruin. Her slippers were of cream kid and she had a tiny old-fashioned fan with tarnished ivory sticks—but pretty all the same.

'William told me that I look a fright,' she said, trying to avoid Ritchie's eye, 'because I refused to wear the horrid thing which he gave me. I looked like some lady of the night trying to be respectable. I wondered what you and Jack might make of it.'

'Oh, you always look splendid, Pan,' said Jack frankly, 'whatever you are wearing. Now I prefer you in that old blue riding habit you wear when you come with us, but I don't suppose that would do for a ball.'

Pandora and Ritchie began to laugh together. Pandora stopped, to say hesitantly to him, 'And you, Mr Ritchie, what do you think? Ought I to change into William's horror?'

Mr Ritchie's horror was quite different; with all this talk of clothes he was wildly remembering an old madrigal in which a man sang of his love and ended most daringly with, 'But beauty's self she is, When all her robes are gone.'

After this afternoon, and with Jack present he could hardly come out with *that*. Instead he said judicially, 'I like what you are wearing very much. But then, I always prefer ladies to wear simple clothes. Feathers and furbelows have no attraction for me.'

'Oh, excellent,' exclaimed Pandora. 'We are of the same mind again, I see. Now I must go before I get us all into trouble, first for smuggling in sweetmeats and secondly for visiting you. The schoolroom is out of bounds these days, I gather, but pooh to that. I am the lady of the house and shall do as I please. By the by, Aunt Em sends you both her love.'

She was gone in a pretty swirl of skirts.

Jack put out a hesitant hand towards the plate on the table. 'May I, Mr Ritchie?'

'Indeed, you may. You are most fortunate in your sister, Jack.'

'I know. What a pity she can't live in the schoolroom with us. We could all have such fun. Do take one of the sweetmeats, Mr Ritchie. I shall have finished them before you start, and that would never do. I'm sure that Pan would wish you to have your share.'

So they sat and ate the sweetmeats Pandora had brought

them. Jack dreamed of being given another plateful and Ritchie dreamed of Pandora in his arms both with, and without, her pretty frock, until Jack went to bed and he could start out on his odyssey to the cliffs overlooking Baxter's Bay.

The night was not so clear as it had been earlier. The moon rode in and out of the clouds, casting a fitful light on the land and the sea. Ritchie reached the top of the cliff which gave him a good view of Baxter's Bay and the sea beyond it.

He had crept down the backstairs and left the house behind him. The night was warm and all the glass doors and windows were open and for a time the strains of the music followed him, until he reached the neglected area of the Park where the little summer house stood.

Inside it was quite undisturbed and he found his cloak and scarf untouched in the chest. The sense of excitement which putting them on induced was strong in him that night since expectation rode on his shoulders. To reach the vantage point he had previously reconnoitred, he had to leave the path and cross the thick grass and scrub which ran toward the cliff edge.

Once there he lay down and fetched from his pocket the night-glass which had accompanied him in his Spanish wanderings and turned it on to the beach and then looked out to sea. For a time he could see nothing and began to think that he was on a fool's errand, but then a man ran on to the sand followed by another.

He could hear the distant sound of shouting. He turned the glass towards the land, and there, on the path at the entrance to the beach, was a coach and two. Nearby were several pack ponies accompanied by a mounted horseman.

His glass was an excellent one, but the light was so fitful that all that he could see of their faces was a white blur.

Ritchie turned his glass out to sea again, and squinting through it saw a ship, a cutter by its shape, slowly moving inshore. Even as he watched he saw a light flash from the cutter—it was signalling to the shore, and without doubt the shore was signalling back to it.

Several more men ran on to the sand, each of them carrying a box, and then a rowing boat appeared around the turn of the bay. The rowers sprang out and began unloading their cargo. The men who had been carrying the boxes stowed them on to the boat after which it began to row back to the cutter. Parallel to them, from the level strip of beach to Ritchie's right and beyond Baxter's Bay, another rowing boat was putting out to sea.

So, on this trip something was going out and contraband was certainly coming in. Only patience was needed now. The moon rode from behind the clouds and it was suddenly bright enough to read a book by which made his night-glass even more efficient. Ritchie swung it back towards the beach to see if he could identify one or more of the waiting men, but he knew only one of them: a groom from Henry Waters's place whom he had seen talking to George in the stable yard at Compton Place. He had given up hope of identifying any more when a new arrival walked up and began to harangue the watchers, pointing out to sea as he did so.

The moon was full on his face—and it was Brodribb, William's unpleasant groom, whom he was watching! Brodribb seemed agitated. He suddenly swung round and pointed up at the cliff where Ritchie lay. Ritchie lowered his night-glass and crouched down even further. When he cautiously lifted his head again an argument appeared to be in progress at the end of which a couple of the smug-

glers detached themselves from the main body and disappeared up the path from the beach, passing by the waiting coach and ponies.

For some reason Brodribb was sending them up to reconnoitre the cliff top where he was hiding. What to do?
Ritchie snapped his night-glass shut and looked around
him. He didn't wish to scurry back to the house until he
had seen the rowing boats return with another cargo for
which the men on the shore were obviously waiting. Besides, any attempt to do so might give his presence away
since the skies had cleared and the moon was so bright.

He knew that at a little distance from where he had
been hiding there was a dip in the ground: a deep sandy
hollow bordered by scrub and rocks. He crawled on hands
and knees towards it, for once cursing his cloak which
hampered him vilely, but he dare not stand up. At last he
rolled himself into the hollow with the cloak tucked beneath him and lay there, face down, thanking God as he
did so that the fickle moon had now sailed behind a stray
cloud.

He had hardly settled himself there when he heard
voices and the sound of two men approaching.

'Mind that damned dip, Wattie,' one of the men was
saying. 'Bart broke his leg in it running away from the
Avenger the other night. Broddie says that the Avenger's
out tonight—he was seen on the cliff top not long since.
He wants us to capture him—alive, if possible.'

'He ain't one of us, then?'

'Nay. No one knows who he is—unless he's the real
'un, that is. Broddie thinks he may still be hiding on the
Downs. He doesn't like someone unknown running
around among us. Particularly when word's come from
that Revenue feller that there's a spy from London been
sent here to inform on us.'

'Sadler?' interrupted Number One. 'Is he one of ours now?'

'No, not Sadler,' replied Number Two, impatiently. 'You know him, Jinkinson from Hove—he says as how there ain't anyone new among the Gentlemen that he knows on, so it may be all a hum. Any road, he sent Sadler up the coast tonight with word that there's a landing at Howell's End so's we'd be safe from him here.'

Their voices had started low, had increased while they carefully skirted the hollow in which Ritchie lay unseen, and then had died away when they walked further along the cliff parallel to the sea. Ritchie waited for some time before he clambered out of his hiding place in case they decided to come back along the cliff edge again, although he guessed, correctly, that they would return by the inland path, but he wasn't taking any chances.

He wasted no time in thinking about what he had heard, and what action he would take in consequence—that would come later.

Once he felt safe, he opened his night-glass in time to see the two boats return to the beach and begin unloading their cargo. Leather cases, barrels and boxes were hauled from the two craft and carried up to the waiting coach and ponies. They then rowed back to the cutter again, but Ritchie had seen—and, more importantly, had heard—enough to ensure that his vigil had not been a wasted one. William Compton was certainly involved in running contraband in and out of England. It was common gossip among the servants at Compton Place that Brodribb—whom they all agreed was an unpleasant fellow—was a favourite of William's and ran many dubious errands for him.

The coast seemed to be clear—figuratively as well as metaphorically! So he resumed his Avenger disguise and fled back towards Compton Place. He didn't mind being seen in the distance, and wondered sardonically whether there was yet another Dark Avenger abroad that night to frighten the innocent and keep them indoors.

Ritchie reached his room without further trouble. He had one difficult moment on the backstairs when he heard voices along the corridor which led to the last landing. Fortunately, as usual, he had slipped off his boots as soon as he entered the house, and was able to creep up the final flight without being heard.

Before he gratefully crawled into his bed—much more comfortable than the hollow—he found time to write out a plan of action, which he slipped under his pillow to keep safe from prying eyes. Morning would see it destroyed. Anyone who might wish to search Mr Edward Ritchie's room, for whatever reason, must not find anything there which might seem odd or incriminating.

He also wrote, and hid, a despatch to the accommodation address which Sidmouth had set up, telling him of what he had seen and heard that night. As a result he could pass on some hard evidence and a number of conjectures.

Item: that some person, either at the Home Office, or close to it, was in collusion with the gang which was using Baxter's Bay and that every effort should be made to find him since he knew of the existence of a spy.

Item: that one of the Riding Officers, Jinkinson of Hove, was in the pay of the smugglers. That an eye should be kept on him but no action against him ought to be taken until he, Ritchie, sent word that it should. He might be able to use him.

Item: he was of the opinion from what he had seen and heard that James Sadler, stationed at Brighton, was an honest servant of the Crown.

Item: that it was highly probable that the Sussex end of the operation which he had witnessed was organised by the Waters family of Milton House, Sussex, with the assistance of William Compton of Compton Place, Sussex. Henry Waters, being a London merchant, was well placed to collude with those in the City who were behind the trade in guineas. Unfortunately, he was unable to present Sidmouth with any hard evidence as to the guilt of Compton and the Waters which could be used against them. One of William Compton's servants was observed organising the movement of contraband but that was not necessarily evidence that Compton knew of his activities. Smuggling was certainly taking place, but all the evidence that he currently had as to who was responsible was circumstantial. Furthermore, he had no real evidence that guineas formed part of the contraband.

Item: that William Compton's sudden acquisition of wealth might suggest that it was the consequence of his friendship with the Waters and his collaboration with the smugglers—but this evidence was also purely circumstantial.

Item: that he would continue to keep watch over both the coast and those persons whom he thought were involved. Should he need assistance, he would ask for it.

Ritchie had not written to Sidmouth of the finding of the guinea for that might have been there as the result of chance, although he thought not. He had no wish to start hares which could not be caught: thinking so, he at last fell asleep, but not before dawn was breaking and the chorus of birds was beginning to be heard.

As usual, he was up betimes, and ate his breakfast in the schoolroom with Jack, who complained that he had been kept awake by the noise from the ball.

'I thought that you might have let me have a lie-in,' he grumbled, 'to make up for my lost sleep.'

Ritchie, who had barely slept at all, but looked reasonably fresh and lively—a trick which he had been compelled to learn in Spain when broken nights had been frequent—said cheerfully, 'But you haven't got a bad head, Jack, to plague you this morning, and what are the odds that most of the guests have?'

'So you say. I'll bet that they haven't been made to get up early, though.'

Nor had they. It was afternoon before most of them surfaced, yawning. Ritchie met his brother in the grounds. He had left Jack drawing the view of the house from the lower lawns—lawns being the name for the stretches of neglected grass which lay adjacent to the equally neglected lake.

Russell said, 'Oh, damme, Ritchie, how can you look so cheerful and wide awake—but since you weren't awake half the night, drinking and dancing, it's no wonder you look so spry.'

'Quite,' agreed Ritchie gravely, so gravely that Russell stared at him. He knew that gravity of old. 'I wasn't. I'm sure you'll be happy to learn that you didn't keep me awake, although poor young Jack is quite another matter.'

'Really, Ritchie, really? And why are you looking as if you are enjoying some damned great joke that only you can appreciate?'

Ritchie assumed an appearance of such holy piety that it plainly made his brother even more suspicious about what his twin was getting up to and why what he had just said about the previous night had so amused him. After all, thought Ritchie, Russell could not possibly have guessed that his past night, far from being one of divine peace, had been spent wide awake on this wretched mission of Sidmouth's.

'I assume,' he said, trying to conceal his secret amusement, 'that you are all too overset to need the services of Compton's stables, so I can safely conclude that I may commandeer one of his more elderly hacks for a safe outing, secure in the knowledge that I can stay on its back without danger of being thrown.'

Russell began to laugh. 'Dammit, Ritchie, why aren't I more like you? You make the best of everything. On the other hand, I can now have a quiet laugh at the thought of that major equestrian wonder, Wellington's pet cavalryman, quartering the countryside on a nag fit only for a maiden lady. Be off with you before we are caught talking together in this familiar fashion by one of Compton's more dubious friends—or even by Compton himself. I've only two more days here, so this may be adieu for the time being. Even Miss Pandora's undoubted charms can't keep me in Sussex any longer.'

And was that a spark of something like jealousy in his eyes when I mentioned Pandora? Russell asked himself when he walked back to the house. Is that what has brought him here? Surely not, he wouldn't need to play the tutor to catch Compton's sister—Compton would be only too willing to throw Pandora at him if he knew of Great-Uncle's legacy. So why *is* he here, and whatever can he be doing?

Ritchie duly claimed his nag from George. Brodribb,

yawning, was in the stable yard, his face plainly showing the evidence of his loss of a night's sleep.

'Decided to take a canter over the Downs, have we?' he sneered. 'Not that it'll be much of a canter on anything that's safe for you to sit on. Try Brutus, he'll give you a rocking-horse ride.'

'Oh, yes,' said Ritchie, all humility. 'I don't suppose I shall find Brutus too difficult, but perhaps I'm a little big for him.'

Brodribb looked him up and down.

'Come to think of it, perhaps you are. Could you manage Rufus? He might be a bit lively for you, though.'

Since Rufus had stopped being lively years ago this was the joke of the week. Ritchie's fear that he might be overdoing the humble bit flew away.

'Would you mind helping me up on to him?' he asked anxiously. 'I'm not very clever when it comes to horses.'

'Better at books, I suppose. Here we go, then.'

He threw Ritchie up with such vigour that only Ritchie's skill as a rider stopped him from landing on the ground on the other side of Rufus—as Brodribb had intended.

'Splendid!' he exclaimed when he was once safely up. 'No one's ever thrown me into the saddle like that before.'

Added to his pleasure at baiting a man who didn't know he was being baited was the knowledge that his despatch was on the inside pocket of his shabby riding jacket, ready to be posted in Far Compton in time for the evening mail-coach to pick it up, since the village was on the main London to Brighton Road.

I hope to God I didn't overdo that, he thought, riding out of the yard, by using my skill to stay on Rufus when he tried to upset me, but I was damned if I was going to take the chance of being crippled by a treacherous oaf like Brodribb.

Later, after his letter had been safely posted in a shop where he was unknown, Ritchie was walking through the gardens at the back of the house when he came upon Pandora. She was seated on one of the iron benches which had been part of the improvements recently brought about by William. This garden, too, had been much restored.

Pandora, however, was not there to admire it. Her head was bent and she had been crying. All Ritchie's protective instincts were immediately alerted. Regardless of wisdom, of common sense, of anything which propriety might demand, he walked up to her, and almost before she could register that he was there, asked, his voice tender, 'My dear, what is it? What has distressed you?'

What distressed him was that, knowing her as well as he did, something major in its importance must have occurred to reduce her to tears.

'I shouldn't tell you,' she muttered. 'It's not fair to you. We agreed to behave ourselves.'

'I didn't agree to stand by and allow you to be so distressed and do nothing about it,' was Ritchie's answer to that.

Her reply, through a muffled sob, was made with a touch of her old spirit. 'Then sit by me and endure it.'

'So I shall,' he said. 'But before I do, what about the rest of the house party—shall we not be disturbed?'

'They've all gone for a walk in the direction of Baxter's Bay, but I cried off. I didn't feel up to it.'

'Why not, Pandora? What has distressed you so?'

'It was Roger Waters,' she faltered, 'and then William. Roger proposed to me last night at the ball. We were in the drawing room, quite alone, away from the other guests. He said that he had William's permission to speak to me. I refused him as nicely as I could, and then…' and she began to sob again.

'And then?' said Ritchie, his voice as gentle as he could make it. 'What happened then?' But he thought that he knew, and how he sat there mumchance, he did not know.

'Then…then he tried to kiss and fondle me. He said that I was only refusing him because I was green and didn't know how pleasant love-making could be. It was horrible because I found that I couldn't bear him to touch me. I shouted at him and tried to push him away but he was too strong—until I kicked him…in the stomach, I think. He bent double, groaning and swearing, which allowed me to run out of the room. Except…'

'Except what, my darling? Tell me, you'll feel better when you have told me everything.'

He was sure that she had unwittingly struck Roger in a place more vital to him than his stomach and the thought pleased him mightily. It was all that the swine deserved. He could only hope that Pandora had emasculated him for life.

'Except that William was waiting for me in the ante-room. He had been there all the time. He had not come in to help me, even though he must have heard me shouting at Roger to stop. He said that I was to go back and accept him, and if I didn't, once the guests had gone I should be locked up in one of the attic bedrooms until I agreed to have him. I told him never, that I would appeal for help to Sir John, to anyone, even to that nice Lord Hadleigh who has been so kind to me. He swore at me, saying that I wouldn't and I said, try me.

'I must have convinced him, for the moment, anyway, for he allowed me to leave—but dare I trust him? I've nowhere to go. Aunt Em relies on our charity—her husband's little estate was entailed on a nephew and she has virtually nothing a year. His last threat was that he would turn her out if I continued to refuse Roger.'

'Oh, Mr Ritchie, I couldn't bear Roger Waters to touch me, so how could I agree to be his wife? Besides, it's you I love and I like you to touch me.'

What could he say to her?

His first duty was to Sidmouth and his mission. When he had agreed to come to Compton Place, he had no notion that when he arrived there he would find a woman whom he was coming to love in the best sense of the word—a good woman who needed a protector, and whom, in the normal course of events, he would have seen it as his first duty to protect.

This was not the normal course of events, however, but even so he found himself saying, his voice as calm as he could make it, for it was plain that Pandora, hitherto so gallant, was at the end of her tether and needed careful and loving handling if she were not to break down altogether, 'My dear, if that excuse for a man should try to trouble you again, you must come to me at once, and by one means or another I shall find a way to rescue you from your unfortunate situation.'

Given what he was about, had he even the right to say as much as that to her? The poet had written, 'I could not love thee, Dear, so much, Loved I not Honour more', but where was the honour in allowing a virtuous woman to be despoiled by a pair of villainous rogues who were apparently prepared to commit virtual rape as lightly as they were already committing treason?

Pandora looked at him. Her eyes were bright stars in her pale face. 'Do you really mean that, Mr Ritchie? That you would risk yourself for me?'

Oh, curse this masquerade, for had I met her in the

normal course I would already have offered for her and been happily accepted! Nothing for it but to continue as he had begun—with a little embroidery on the way.

'Don't think of that, my heart. And may we drop the mister? My friends call me Ritchie—and you are more than my friend.'

'Apart from Aunt Em my only friend, dear Ritchie. Oh, when I think of the happy future that I thought that I was looking forward to when I was a girl, only to see it disappear like all the family's fortunes, I am ready to give up hoping that things might be better. I have lived without hope for so long that I fear it is lost to me forever.'

Her voice faltered and stopped.

Ritchie went down on one knee beside her.

'Pandora, look at me. Remember the goddess whose name you bear. Remember the box she was given when she came down to earth and how all the good things in it flew away—as yours have done. But remember also that one thing was left in the box and that was hope. That hope is still there and when we are apart you must remember your faithful Ritchie and remember also that he assures you that if you continue to hope, then release from misery awaits you—as it awaited the original Pandora.

'More I cannot say—only hope and trust me. Come to me at once if you need help more than hope.'

Ritchie had never thought to say such things to any woman. He had long believed that women were either playthings or the convenient mothers of men's children. He had never dreamed that one day he might meet a woman who would be his other half, a woman who would lighten his darkness, who would bring joy and mirth into his serious life as Pandora had done ever since he had met her.

With her he was less dour, with her he could be himself

after a fashion that he had never been with anyone—even Russell. To think of her being ill-treated set him inwardly raving and how he would keep his fists off Compton and Waters when he next met them he couldn't think. Except that he must.

It was time for him to leave. They had had their moment out of time and must not be found together, either by friends or enemies. His other duty called, for now he had two, and for the life of him he could not think which was the more important.

He rose, took her hand and kissed its palm tenderly. He felt her shudder, and knew that the shudder was one of pleasure: but their pleasure must be deferred.

'We must part now, before anyone comes to mock or harm us. Be of good cheer, and be not afraid, for fear feeds on itself—which is easily said, I know, but there is great truth in it.'

Pandora's green eyes were more star-like than ever. Her cheeks were flushed now with the most delicate rose.

'I will remember all you have told me. I can only hope—like the original Pandora—that William will not pursue me further. Oh, Ritchie,' she suddenly exclaimed, 'you are so honest and true, why is it that I have never met anyone like you before?'

This outburst made poor Ritchie feel more of a cur than ever, but there was no help for it. He pressed her hand in his and murmured, 'Do not repine, my love, all may yet be well.' He could only pray God that he was right to reassure her of that but he could not bear to see her so distressed.

'Thank you,' she whispered in reply and watched him walk away from her, straight-backed for once, like the soldiers she had seen parading in Brighton on one of her few visits there. She blinked, because before he turned the corner he was the bent scholar again, the butt of William and his cronies.

Was it possible that there were two Ritchies? The one who consoled her so strongly and the other one who submitted so humbly to insult—and if there were, what was she to make of that?

Pandora shook herself. Was it not true that all men, aye, and women, too, were puzzles to others, and to themselves if it came to that. It was a puzzle that William resented her so much, and thinking so she walked back into the house, to discover that the walking party had returned, William leading them. All of them were exclaiming that their exertions, after the excesses of the night before, had overwhelmed them.

'You had the right of it, madam,' drawled Russell Hadleigh, coming over to where she sat and drawing up a chair to park himself opposite to her, 'to stay at home and rest after last night's junketing. I trust that you spent a lazy and restful and fruitful afternoon. I thought that you looked rather done up after breakfast, but no such thing now. Rosy would be the best word to apply to you.'

'I have,' lied Pandora who knew that it was Ritchie's presence which had revived her flagging spirits, 'been reading a most interesting book.' She had been carrying one with her as some excuse to be alone.

Russell raised his eyebrows at her. 'Indeed, madam, but you will allow me to say that I, personally, consider the book of life to be the most interesting book of all.'

'But failing that,' smiled Pandora, who thought correctly that Lord Hadleigh was no fool for all his indolent manner, 'paper, ink and binding make a most useful substitute.'

Paper, ink and binding did not put that look on your face, nor bring such a satisfied smile to that pretty mouth, thought Russell. I wonder if Mr Edward Ritchie has been spending a happy and fruitful afternoon with you. Only a man could bring about such a transformation in Miss Pandora Compton as must have occurred whilst I was out quartering Sussex!

Wait until I see Ritchie again. The rogue could do with some teasing.

Chapter Seven

I shan't have to endure many more nights of this, thought Pandora happily. While waiting in the Great Hall for dinner that evening she was carrying on a mindless conversation with two of the three wives whom she had already privately, and naughtily, nicknamed The Three Blind Mice. She thought the phrase apt because they appeared to be completely oblivious to what their husbands were getting up to with the chambermaids who had been brought in by William to accommodate the house party.

'Miss Compton,' asked Mrs Eleanor Gray. 'Who is the handsome young man I have seen about the place several times since I arrived here? He is not present at meal times. I believe that he was accompanied by your young brother.'

Ritchie! She must be talking about Ritchie. She had called him handsome. Pandora had not considered him to be particularly so; she loved him for other reasons than his looks. Now that she came to think of it, though, he was much better looking than all the other men staying at Compton Place—except Russell Hadleigh, that was.

'I believe you may be referring to Jack's tutor, Mr Edward Ritchie,' she replied carefully, trying not to look or sound too interested in him.

'Perhaps so—he was certainly not dressed in the last stare of fashion, but he had a most pleasant smile when he bowed to me.'

'Bowed to you?' enquired Pandora, overcome by a sudden fit of jealousy. 'Pray, how did that happen?'

'Oh, I was walking in the gardens yesterday afternoon and my hat blew off—it's a very light straw one—and he rescued it for me. Most gallant—he bowed when he handed it back to me.'

'Oh, I understand that his manners are excellent,' responded Pandora, happy to learn how brief his encounter with Mrs Gray had been. She had, it was whispered, despite being in early middle age, a taste for handsome young men which she did not hesitate to satisfy. The *on dits* also had it that she had engaged more than one brawny young footmen when willing young men in the *ton* were hard to find.

And now she had her eye on Ritchie.

'Is he married, do you know? To one of the women servants, perhaps?'

'No,' replied Pandora shortly. 'He comes, I understand, from a gentry family.'

Mrs Gray's expression told her that this was better and better—very few handsome young gentlemen had come her way lately. Before Pandora could think of a suitable reply, William came up to them, Roger Waters at his shoulder. 'You ladies seem to be having a most confidential coze,' he said jovially. 'May one enquire the subject of it?'

'Oh, I was merely asking your sister who the handsome young fellow was whom I have seen in the gardens. She was good enough to enlighten me.'

'You mean Ritchie? In the gardens—bear-leading Jack, I suppose.'

That William was not best pleased by her interest in the tutor completely escaped Mrs Gray's attention.

'I was surprised, on hearing that he is a gentleman, that he did not appear at dinner—but perhaps he is too busy looking after Master Jack.'

'Pray, who told you that Ritchie is a gentleman, if I may so ask you?' William bit back.

'Why, Pandora, Miss Compton, of course.'

'Then she knows more than I do—' He got no further with whatever he was about to say and thank goodness for that, thought Pandora, because his attention was drawn by the sight of the butler arguing with not one, but two Riding Officers who were demanding entry.

'What's that commotion in the entrance hall, Roger?' he roared. 'I hired that butler you recommended to me to be rid of old Galpin's incompetence and now he seems to be letting a pair of Excise flunkeys into the hall without consulting me first just as we are waiting to go into dinner. I'll have the pair of them out on their ear in no time, and no mistake.'

He strode to the door to find that the entrance hall was full of people among whom were the rest of the guests who were late arriving for dinner, and Mr Ritchie and Jack, who were at the bottom of the main staircase

Ritchie and Jack had been enjoying an early supper in the housekeeper's room to save the overworked servants from having to carry it up several awkward flights of the backstairs. On leaving, Jack had suddenly decided to rebel against being compelled to avoid the main staircase. He had surprised Ritchie by breaking away from him, shouting as he ran towards it, 'I'm Master Jack Compton of

Compton Place and I'm sick of sneaking up and down the backstairs since I've every right to use the front ones.'

Looking back at the whole episode, Ritchie thought that, although, at the time, he had been furious with Jack for his disobedience, it had resulted in the utmost benefit to his secret mission. They had arrived in the entrance hall, Jack first and Ritchie after him, at the same time as Jinkinson and Sadler. William appeared, with Roger on his heels, and Mrs Gray leading the other guests immediately behind him; an amused Pandora made up the rear.

Completely forgetting the presence of delicately minded females whose ears must not be assailed by men's coarser speech, William, infuriated, roared at the butler, 'What the devil's going on here? Why was I not properly informed of the presence of these upstarts? They should have been directed to the servants' hall to await my pleasure there.'

'Begging your pardon, sir, I tried to tell them that, but they insisted that the matter was urgent and demanded to see you at once. They would not take no for an answer and pushed by me, insisting that they could brook no delay.'

Before William could roar at them again, Sadler moved forward, saying, 'We are here on the King's business, sir, and are acting on the powers given to us by Parliament when our office was created. We have reason to believe that Baxter's Bay—which is on the edge of your land, Mr Compton, sir—was used last night to smuggle contraband into the country, which is against the law.

'We wish to question you, and the servants here, as to whether you have information or knowledge about this business.'

'What, here and now—when we are about to sit down to dinner? Fudge to that! Particularly since there's no need for any of this—I can tell you immediately that last night I entertained half the county into the small hours and I and my servants were far too busy to waste our time smuggling, either in Baxter's Bay—or anywhere else.'

'Begging your pardon, sir, but we had most reliable information this morning from a trusted source that the Bay had been used last night, and not for the first time. Is not that true, Mr Jinkinson?'

'Aye,' said Jinkinson morosely, something which did not surprise Ritchie, 'you received information and came to me for assistance.'

While Ritchie was busy wondering who Sadler's informant was, William began to roar again—it seemed his main mode of speech with those whom he considered his inferiors.

'I wonder at you, Jinkinson, I really do. I have given you every assistance in this wretched business and would help you if I could, but I suppose that Sadler has suborned you. He's in the habit of seeing a smuggler behind every bush on land and every rock on the seashore. I shall be making a complaint to the Home Office about the conduct of the pair of you. In the meantime, you may question any of my staff who are not engaged in preparing my dinner—including Ritchie here—in the servants' hall and nowhere else. I have to say that it's come to something when a man can't sit down to his meal because of the conduct of a pair of interfering flunkeys.'

He turned away, and then swung back again. 'And, Jack, you may go straight to your room. I don't suppose that you were rowing contraband out to sea—or hauling it up the beach for that matter. You,' he ordered the butler, 'may inform the outdoor staff that they are needed for questioning—not that I suppose that any of them will have anything useful to say.'

An amused Ritchie watched him climb the stairs before he joined Jinkinson and Sadler on their walk to the servants' hall, the disgruntled butler leading them. While they were waiting for the butler to round up everyone but the kitchen staff and the footmen serving the dinner, Sadler, who had refused a seat, said to Ritchie, 'I know that you ride about the countryside with your charge, Mr Ritchie, and I wondered whether you had seen anything untoward while you were doing so. There is talk that the Dark Avenger is abroad again. Have you seen, or heard, aught of him?'

'Yes, I have heard of him, but he always appears at night, Mr Sadler, and by then I am invariably confined to my room and my pupil's quarters.'

'True, but you might see, or hear, something odd in the future which might help us.'

'So far,' lied Ritchie, 'I have not come across any suspicious behaviour—but as I said, I am not in the habit of going out at night.'

Jinkinson, who was lounging in the butler's armchair, said sourly, 'I would have thought, Sadler, that you might gain more from questioning the informant you do have more severely—particularly when he always informs you after the event—and never before. Not too helpful, that.'

Sadler said, 'I am convinced that someone at Compton Place, and possibly from Milton House also, is helping to organise the smuggling which has suddenly become rife again in these parts. Finding proof is difficult—but it always seems to occur on the beaches near either the Waters's or Compton's lands. Mr Jinkinson here had some information fed to him last night that a landing was expected at Howell's End—but Howell's End turned out to be a Dead End.'

Sadler cheered up after making this mild joke, and Ritchie dutifully laughed at it.

He said, more to test the water as it were than in the hope of hearing anything substantive, 'Mr Jinkinson pointed out that your informant's information was always after the event. Have you no notion of why that might be?'

'None, but it is an oddity, I agree.'

Ritchie thought that he could guess why, but was determined not to appear to be too knowledgeable, and the arrival of the rest of the staff to be questioned stopped further private discussion. He listened intently to every word which was said, while giving off an impression of extreme boredom.

It was finally the grooms' turn to be questioned. They spent their time waiting by lounging about and making incomprehensible jokes, quite a few of them at Ritchie's expense. Brodribb had sniggeringly told them what a greenhorn the tutor was, which resulted in a series of comic tales about other Soapy Sams and their inability to ride anything more lively than the rocking horses with which he frequently taunted Ritchie.

After Brodribb's turn for interrogation, a squat, sturdy fellow who was Roger Waters's head stableman walked up and began to speak. Ritchie immediately knew that he had heard his voice before. He had been the knowing one of the pair he had overheard on the cliffs which meant that at least two of the smugglers at Baxter's Bay were connected with Milton House and Compton Place. He suspected that there were more.

George said quietly to him after his question time was over, 'You look tired, Mr Ritchie. Did you have a hard day—or perhaps a hard night?'

It was fortunate that Ritchie *was* tired. Had he not been

feeling so sluggish he might have been openly surprised by this odd question which seemed to reflect a suspicion that he was not spending all his nights quietly in bed. Was George trying to tell him something, or was he seeing and hearing a connection with smuggling in everything said and done before him?

'Not particularly,' he said, 'but I could have done without this nonsense tonight. Why the officers should think that anyone at Compton Place would be engaged in smuggling, I can't imagine.'

'Can't you, Mr Ritchie? I once heard it said that everyone in the county of Sussex is connected with it. What do you think of that?'

'That it is an exaggeration, George.'

'But all exaggerations have some truth in them, Mr Ritchie, as you must know.'

What Mr Ritchie was thinking was that George had the manners and speech of an educated man, so what was he doing working in William Compton's stable? More and more he was coming to think that George was sounding him out in some way. Sadler's interest in him was more diffuse. He probably thought that the tutor might be sharp enough to detect oddness, but nothing more than that, but George was obliquely challenging him.

He was also beginning to believe that George was Sadler's mysterious informant.

'Everyone at Compton Place is as innocent as a band of angels,' said Sadler dourly when the last man walked out of the back door. He had scarcely finished speaking when the door to the house opened and Pandora came in, still dressed in her dinner finery. She was followed by a couple of servants carrying trays bearing a tureen of soup, soup bowls, plates, cutlery, rolls, butter, a large cheese, slices of beef, fruitcake, and a great plate of biscuits which they put on the table in the centre of the room.

'Compton Place,' Pandora announced, 'was once a centre of hospitality. I would not like its name to be tarnished by any guests being ill treated—even self-invited ones. I suspect that you two Riding Officers and Mr Ritchie have had a hard day and so I cried off from dinner with the excuse of a headache and prefer to take my supper with you—if you will so allow.'

Ritchie would have liked to kiss her on the spot. The interrogations had been lengthy and his supper had been a meagre one. He suspected that it had been some time since the Riding Officers had eaten.

They all set to with a will, and when the servants returned a few minutes later with pewter tankards and jugs of ale, Jem Sadler toasted Miss Compton with the words 'To the giver of the feast'. Even Jinkinson had lost his sour look. Pandora saw them into the stable yard at its end so that they might not come across her brother again. She and Ritchie watched them ride off into the night.

'I shall not come in with you,' said Ritchie quietly. 'We must not give your brother any further cause to attack either of us.'

'True,' said Pandora sorrowfully, although her sorrow was a little lessened by Ritchie kissing her hand before she shot into the house to retire to her bedroom, using the backstairs so that no one should know that she had not spent her evening on a bed of pain.

Ritchie's night was not yet over. He allowed himself a few minutes' grace before he followed her. He was about to do so when George walked up to him and said quietly, 'How long were you a cavalryman, Mr Ritchie? And how is it that you are reduced to being a tutor?'

Ritchie said, equally quietly, 'I think that you are mistaken.'

George shook his head. 'Oh, no, I've had my suspicions for some time, particularly after I first saw you riding, but the way in which you dealt with Brodribb's little piece of nastiness could only have been done by a master horseman.'

'Circumstances brought me here, George, as I suspect they brought you.'

'Not quite, I think,' said George equably. 'I like to hope that you might rescue Miss Pandora. I also think that that is all I wish to say tonight. Goodnight, sir, and sleep better tonight than you did last night.'

He wandered away from Ritchie as quietly as he had wandered towards him, leaving the younger man musing half-humorously on the old saying, More know Tom Fool than Tom Fool knows.

Sadler was beginning to suspect everybody. He didn't just suspect that the Waters and William Compton were engaged in smuggling guineas to France, he knew that they were, but he couldn't prove it. He also suspected many others of being involved, but proof was equally lacking there. Mr Edward Ritchie he suspected of he knew not what. The man was too good to be true. He had kept a watch on him in the servants' hall and had observed, as he had done before, that Ritchie was undoubtedly taking the most careful note of all that was said without outwardly appearing to do so.

Perhaps it was simply the scholar's trick of paying attention to everything in case it came in useful, but Sadler did not think so. He thought that Mr Ritchie was deep, very deep, but that from what people said of him he was alone in his suspicions. Last night Brodribb had made a butt of him to the outdoor servants and it was plain by the laughter that this was not the first time he had mocked him.

He wanted to speak to the man again, and accordingly, on the very next afternoon he arrived at Compton Place and asked George if he might be able to interview Mr Ritchie without everyone in the house knowing.

George, who was alone there—the rest of the grooms were out with their masters enjoying an afternoon's riding on the Downs—stared at him and said, 'Why?'

Sadler shrugged. 'Because. I don't know. Or rather I think that he may know more than he knows—if you follow me—and that might be helpful.'

'No, I don't follow you—but you should know that he has no direct knowledge of the smuggling which is going on around here.'

'Unlike some,' said Sadler. It was his turn to stare at George. 'A little earlier warning about when it might be going on would be helpful—learning about it afterwards does not do much for me or my reputation.'

'Jinkinson got it wrong, too,' said George. 'The only thing you both found t'other night was a mare's nest.'

'True, but it was convenient for the smugglers that his informant was wrong, don't you think? His misinformed him and mine, as you well know, informed me the day after—both of them useless. Have you nothing further to say?'

'Only that chasing after Mr Ritchie would be another mare's nest—you're not likely to get anything from him—he's a tough nut for all his pretty ways.'

And thank you for that, if for nothing else, thought Sadler, watching George enter the house to find Ritchie and ask him to agree to meet Sadler in the stables.

Ritchie arrived some ten minutes later. He was wearing his spectacles and a harried look.

'What is it, Sadler? I thought I had finished with this wretched business after yesterday's inquisition.'

'But *I* haven't finished with it, Mr Ritchie, and for some reason I think that you may know more than you are telling me.'

Now, why should he think that? What can I have said or done to make him believe any such thing? Nothing, perhaps, the man is simply a terrier. He's also clutching at straws. The cream of the jest is that he's quite correct in his suppositions and even though the conversation I overheard the other night seemed to suggest that he, at least, is honest, I dare not confide in him yet.

'I cannot think why you should suppose any such thing. As you know, my interests are confined to fossil hunting and painting the delightful scenery which surrounds us.'

'But you might have seen something going on in that delightful scenery which might help me.'

Ritchie could not resist saying, 'But I rarely paint that delightful scenery in the middle of the night. No, I am more concerned with seeing that my charge's education is improved to the point where he is able to go to Harrow and Oxford without disgracing himself.'

'Most commendable of you, sir.'

They fenced with one another a little longer. As George had suggested, Sadler got nothing from Ritchie, and Ritchie learned nothing from Sadler that he did not already know.

He said at the end, pulling off his spectacles and earnestly cleaning them while he spoke, 'I was wondering why you were so sure that Mr William Compton is behind the smuggling which is going on here. Courts of law require very hard evidence, and so far as I could make out last night you have nothing which might prove his guilt except that Baxter's Bay is part of Compton land. From what was said, I gather that Mr Waters is also under suspicion. May one ask why?'

Sadler's expression was savage. 'Everyone around here knows that they are running the business, but no one will say anything because they are too busy profiting both directly and indirectly from it. Or they are too frightened of what the smugglers might do to them and their families if they inform on them. That is why hard evidence is so difficult to come by. Compton and Waters certainly provided themselves with a splendid alibi the other night, but you may be sure that many of their people, and a large number of the villagers around here, were helping to move contraband from Baxter's Bay.

'Now you are an outsider employed by Compton, a clever one, and are in a position to see if anything untoward is going on. All you need to do is to tell me and keep mum. I'm also informed that there is a government spy in the neighbourhood and I suspect that he may have been one of Compton's guests. I should like to know who he is, and you might keep your ears open for that.'

Ritchie replaced his spectacles and said, as mildly as he could, 'If he's a really good spy, then it is unlikely that he would give himself away. From what you say, his life might be in danger if he did.'

Sadler's smile was a weary one. 'All I want you to do is pass on anything suspicious, Mr Ritchie. I promise not to let anyone know that you have done so. Now I must go. I've a deal of coast to watch and a deal of work to do. Don't trouble to answer me. Good afternoon to you, sir.'

It was only when Sadler was riding along the London to Brighton turnpike that he suddenly had a notion so preposterous that at first he dismissed it scornfully, but it still persisted in popping up in his mind.

Deep Mr Ritchie with his owlish stare and his mild speech was the latest newcomer in the neighbourhood. Could it possibly be that *he* was the government spy. Were his tutoring of Jack Compton and his fossil hunting blinds? Were they simply pretexts for what he had really come to do?

Behind him, in the stables, George, who had overheard Sadler's conversation with Ritchie, was also asking himself some questions. He had once been a man of honour. Could a man of honour stand by and watch while what was virtually treason was being committed and do nothing about it?

George decided that he could not. The very next time that he overheard something that he should not he would inform Sadler of it beforehand—and be damned to the consequences.

After the excitement and commotion of the first few weeks, Ritchie's life at Compton Place suddenly became quiet, if not to say dull and boring. The house party broke up, Roger Waters went to London, doubtless to arrange for the disposal of the last lot of profits from selling guineas and to organise the details for the shipment of the next batch.

William Compton did not go with him but went to stay with friends at Hove for a few days, so the house became quiet and peaceful again once many of the furniture and fittings, and most of the staff, which had been brought in for his party, had been taken away. Nothing happened which might seem to suggest that Sidmouth had taken any action as a result of reading the admittedly sparse information which Ritchie had sent him.

In the intervals of being a genuine tutor to Jack and cementing his growing *affaire*—if that were the right word—with Pandora, Ritchie took stock of the situation and decided that he needed an aide if he were to discover any hard evidence which the Excisemen and Sidmouth could use. He thought that he knew where he might find one.

The day after the house party broke up he wrote a letter to Sergeant Joshua Bragg, who had nursed him devotedly after he had arrived at Wellington's camp an almost broken man, but armed with the information which was going to make his General's task of beating the French Army in the Spanish Peninsula less difficult than it might have been.

While doing so Bragg had alternated between cursing Ritchie for having engaged in secret intelligence work at all—he had known him since childhood—and praising him for the raw courage which had enabled him to survive and return with his news when it might have been easier for him to have lain down and died.

Once Ritchie had recovered enough to make the journey back to England in order to rest and recuperate there, Bragg, who had also been afflicted with an injury which had obstinately refused to heal, was ordered to accompany him and remain with him until they were recalled to active service again.

He had stayed with Ritchie in the post of batman, aide and head cook and bottle-washer, as he called it, until Sidmouth had given him his mission. Ritchie, saying nothing of his task, for he knew that Bragg would disapprove of his putting himself at risk again, had left him behind in his father's London home to await his return.

Now he sat down and wrote Bragg a cryptic letter, telling him that he was at Compton Place where a reliable groom was needed since William had decided that he could afford another.

'I could do with your presence here,' he wrote, 'so I would like you to come to Sussex and apply for the post. When you see me, remember Spain. Above all mum's the word, since we must not appear to know one another. We can find ways and means of meeting when and if you are appointed.'

With Bragg at his back, a reliable ally whom no one knew, he thought that his task might be easier. Trying to trap the smugglers on his own was proving almost impossible.

He was pretty certain that it might be some time before another shipment would leave for France. Meanwhile he would watch and wait.

Chapter Eight

R itchie was right in his belief that someone would be taken on before Bragg had time to reach Compton's Place. Someone was, but fortunately he proved to be so unsatisfactory that by the time that Bragg arrived at the servants' entrance George was only too delighted to hire a man who had once been in a cavalry regiment and had fallen on hard times—Bragg's excuse for needing the job.

'There's a new man in the stables, Mr Rice and George took him on,' announced Jack importantly one afternoon. 'George says that he's a cracker on a horse. That nasty Brodribb said that if he were he ought to give you some badly needed lessons on how to ride.'

Pandora, who had joined them in the schoolroom now that William was no longer there to harass her, looked up and said, 'I can't imagine why Brodribb thinks that Mr Ritchie needs any lessons, he seems a perfectly good horseman to me. I never worry about him when we're out together. I wish William had taken Brodribb with him when he left. He's a bad influence on the other servants. I find his manner to me most insolent. I told William so, but he simply said that Brodribb was one of the most useful men he has and I must learn to live with him.'

'Any idea what this new paragon's name is?' asked Ritchie idly.

'Bragg,' said Jack. 'What's a paragon, sir?'

'A person of supreme excellence,' said Ritchie. 'In this case, since he's a good rider, we might call him a centaur—you do remember what a centaur was, I hope?'

'Half-man, half-horse, sir, according to the Greeks,' returned Jack eagerly.

'Very good,' said Ritchie and Pandora together. They smiled at one another. Lately they had developed the habit of saying the same thing at the same time.

'We shall really have to stop doing this,' Ritchie had told her the last time they were alone and had already done it twice.

'Difficult that,' sighed Pandora, 'since it usually comes out without thinking.'

'True,' Ritchie had replied. He was busy feeling happy that Bragg had arrived and been taken on. The three of them had already agreed on a fossil-hunting expedition that afternoon now that William was no longer there to disapprove of them, so it would not be long before he met him again.

They arrived at the stable yard to find George there, with Rob who was filling buckets of water for the horses. William had left his curricle behind, which was one reason why he had decided that he needed another hand in the stables.

'Where's the new man?' asked Jack almost before George had had time to greet them and ask how far they proposed to go and which nags they wanted. 'Mr Ritchie wants to see the paragon,' he added.

George wasn't sure what a paragon was, but thought

that it might be something good, judging by Jack's excitement.

'He's taken that big stallion, Nero, that Mr William's just bought, for an outing,' he said. 'Brodribb can't manage him and I don't think that Mr William's quite up to it, either, but Bragg's a marvel on him. Here he comes.'

A subdued Nero was being ridden into the yard. Pandora stared at Bragg, who was thoroughly in control of him.

'Goodness,' she said. 'He must be a paragon if he can manage Nero. No one else can.'

Bragg stared at the little party in the yard and at Mr Ritchie, as well as George, Rob and Brodribb, who had emerged from the lad's quarters, yawning and stretching. He had been enjoying an afternoon nap while the new man exercised the disobedient stallion whom he feared.

'Back, are we?' he said to Bragg, who was now dismounting and handing him Nero's reins. 'You certainly seemed to have tamed him.'

'Only for now,' Bragg said. He was watching Mr Edward Ritchie, who was standing back and taking off his spectacles in order to examine that slow-moving animal, Rufus, which had been brought out for him to ride.

George decided to make Bragg known to the family and the tutor.

'Bragg, this is Miss Pandora Compton and Master Jack Compton. They are Sir John's grandchildren and Mr William's half-brother and sister. And this is Mr Edward Ritchie, their tutor. He is not very experienced as a rider and you must always be sure to saddle Rufus for him.'

Bragg grinned, showing a mouthful of strong yellow teeth. After bobbing his head at Pandora and Jack, he stared again at Ritchie, saying, 'Mr Edward Ritchie, is it?

Not very good with the hosses, eh. I'll be sure to remember that.'

'Needs a rocking horse, so he does,' sneered Brodribb. 'Good with a pen, but not much else.'

'Is that so?' commented Bragg gravely. 'I'll be sure to remember that, too. Like a leg up would you, sir? Don't be afeared, I'll be careful with you.'

Ritchie, not sure whether he wanted to compliment Bragg on his acting ability or give him a roasting for making such quiet elaborate fun of him, almost mewed at the wretch. 'You will be careful with me, won't you? Mr Brodribb almost had me off the other day.'

'Did he, sir? You may be sure that I shall always be tender with a novice. There, hup with you! Sitting comfortably, are we? Don't worry about falling off. Rufus is a gentle horse as I am sure you already appreciate.'

'Most kind,' faltered Ritchie, deciding to enjoy this charade since he couldn't control it. What he might say to Bragg later was another thing.

Pandora, annoyed at this demeaning of the man whom she had come to love and feeling that there was something wrong with this little scene, said reproachfully to George, 'Mr Ritchie has come on very strong as a rider since he arrived here as a complete novice.'

'Bit of a talent for it, has he?' offered Bragg.

How he controlled his facial muscles as Bragg continued to bait him indirectly Ritchie never knew. To avoid betraying his amusement he turned away to inform George that they were going to Howell's End—a rather longer run than usual. George said gravely, 'In that case, Mr Ritchie, I should be happier if I knew that someone was with you. Take Bragg—he might as well begin to learn the countryside. If aught went wrong he could always return post haste for help.'

'Went wrong…' faltered Ritchie, trying to avoid Bragg's eye. 'Why should you think that anything would go wrong?'

'Two of the Excisemen from Brighton were set upon the other day and one of them was left for dead. Yesterday someone tried to hold up the Brighton Mail Coach. Fortunately he made a botch of it but before he fled he shot one of the passengers in the arm. There's a deal of lawlessness abroad in Sussex these days and you need a strong arm with you. Look after your charges, Bragg, there's a good fellow.'

Bragg touched his forehead. 'I'll do my best, George.'

Pandora said crossly, 'Surely that's not necessary. Everyone round here knows who we are. I am sure that we shall be safe on our own.'

George shook his head. 'Mr William would never forgive me if you came to grief, Miss Pandora. Best take Bragg.'

Nothing, thought Ritchie, could be better than that Bragg should learn the lie of the land as soon as possible. He was amused and touched that Pandora should have taken Bragg in dislike because of his rudeness to him.

He and Pandora had taken to meeting one another in the library and in the schoolroom while William was away. Years later he was to look back at this time and wonder how they had managed to behave themselves. It was plain that Pandora was going to be as passionate in love as she was in everything else.

As for himself…he only had to be with her, as now, to be roused.

When they reached Howell's End and had unsaddled the horses and were ready to draw, Pandora decided to speak her mind. She said fiercely, 'I didn't like his manner to you, Ritchie. Just because you are not the most noisy of men there was no need for him to speak to you so harshly, except...' and she turned thoughtful eyes on him '...that there was something oddly familiar in the way he spoke to you. Have you, by chance, met him before?'

It pained Ritchie to lie to her, but he was compelled to be evasive. 'If so, it was not recently. You know that the stable lads all mock me for my lack of talent on a horse— but I don't mind that. I can comfort myself with the thought that they are equally useless with a pen.'

'All the same,' said Pandora, angrily drawing the perfect scene before them. 'It doesn't mean that I have to like it.'

Bragg had tethered their horses to trees at the top of the path which led down to the bay. He was sitting beside them, apparently at ease, but his eyes were watchful. After a time Ritchie put down his sketchbook and said, apparently absently, 'I've left my chalks in one of my saddle-bags and I find that I need them.'

Jack said helpfully, 'Let me go, sir. You need a rest after the ride.'

'Thank you, but no. The exercise will do me good. By the by, you need to concentrate on your shading if you are going to get the full effect of distance at sea. Like so.'

Ritchie left Jack and Pandora both busy with their work and walked up the path to where Bragg lay. He had purposely left his chalks behind to provide a useful excuse to talk to his sergeant privately. Bragg jumped to his feet and for one moment almost forgot himself by beginning to salute—and then stopped.

'At ease,' grinned Ritchie. 'Look disdainful while I speak to you. I shouldn't like to think that you had any respect for that pitiful pen-pusher, Edward Ritchie. I didn't intend to give you so much enjoyment when we first met, but on the other hand it will be useful for everyone to believe that you despise the poor creature which I appear to be. That way no one will think that we are working together.'

Bragg gave him an answering grin. 'Quite so, sir. I suppose that you've come up here to brief me on what the devil it is that you *are* up to.'

'Indeed. Now listen, and carefully, because I don't want to be away too long. I've only come to collect some chalks which I left behind.'

As succinctly as he could he told Bragg of his mission, his belief that William Compton and the Waters were involved, and his need to have someone who would back him up.

'The whole damned county seems to be working with the smugglers, as well as that Riding Officer Jinkinson, so go warily. You can listen to, and talk to, the servants in a way which I can't. You can also go to the inn and try to find out when and where the next cargo is coming in. But be wary. I saw the last lot arrive, but without help I can't collect sufficient evidence to allow Sidmouth to take action. Which is where you come in. We'll find ways and means to meet secretly to pass on information and plans.'

Bragg sniffed. 'I know it's my duty now that you've sent for me, but I can't say that I like peaching on a few poor devils who are only trying to make some extra pennies.'

'True,' said Ritchie, 'but remember, it's more than that here. They're busy selling gold to Boney's armies so that they can kill your and my comrades the more easily. That's treason in my book and it ought to be in yours. It's why Sidmouth has sent me here when he's not so urgent about snaffling those who confine themselves to bringing in liquor, baccy and silks.'

Bragg nodded his head. 'You're sure about the guineas, Major? I mean, sir—or should it be Mr Ritchie?'

'Anything, so long as it's not Major. Now I must go back.'

Pandora welcomed him, and showed him the little sketch she had been working on.

'I'd like to do some more fossil hunting,' she told him. 'There's a much bigger church at Far Compton than any we've looked at so far, and the cemetery there is surrounded by a very tall wall. I do believe that, from what I remember of it, there may be some fossils in its stones. Besides we could go for a walk before we return home. No one could complain about us being together if I can say that you and Bragg are keeping Jack and me safe.'

'Artful minx that you are,' murmured Ritchie, 'plotting for us to have a little privacy—although I don't suppose that Bragg will allow us to go wandering away on our own.'

'Well, he can guard us from the rear where he won't be able to hear what we are saying.'

So Bragg was meeting his match in Miss Pandora Compton when it came to cunning! What a pair of conniving wretches he had managed to attach to himself, to be sure. To be fair, though, he was a conniving wretch himself and the old adage had it that like called to like, so they were both probably all that he deserved.

Sure enough, when they reached Far Compton and walked to the church wall to examine the fossils which Pandora had rightly remembered as being there, Bragg followed behind them, while Jack pranced in front, completing a comical procession at which the villagers stared.

Bragg waited, yawning, while the three of them walked along the wall, occasionally stopping to draw the most interesting specimens in their notebooks. They had been doing this for some little time when Pandora turned to Bragg and said sweetly, 'You must be very bored by all this, Bragg. There's the alehouse. If I gave you a copper or two you could go and get yourself a pot instead of standing about, watching us.'

'Couldn't do that, Miss Compton,' returned Bragg cheerfully. 'Have to keep an eye on you and poor Mr Ritchie. Wouldn't do for either of you to come to harm if I was off a-drinking.'

So, the scaly bastard was bound and determined to prevent him from having a rendezvous with Pandora! Well, he knew a trick that might blow Bragg's boat out of the water.

'Now, Bragg,' he said as kindly as he could, although the eyes he turned on his old sergeant were as steely as those he had employed in Spain to curb recalcitrant private soldiers. 'I'm sure that if I gave you a shilling and asked you to take Master Jack and yourself into the alehouse where he could drink Adam's ale and you could enjoy the real stuff, you wouldn't argue with me, would you?'

Bragg's grin was an internal one. Trust the Major to get his way—there was no putting one over on him if that was what he didn't want.

'If you say so, sir—but you're sure that you feel able to look after Miss Compton, are you? Shouldn't like either of you to come to grief.'

The look Ritchie gave Bragg would have scorched water.

'You may depend upon me to do my best—and now be off with you. I'll send Jack to you. It would do him good to see how his tenants enjoy themselves when they're off duty.'

'Well!' exclaimed Pandora when Jack and Bragg had disappeared into the alehouse. 'How did you manage that? I thought that we were stuck with him for the afternoon.'

'I think that the shilling did it,' lied Ritchie.

'Can you afford it?' said Pandora, looking worried. 'If you can't, let me give it to you.'

'By no means. Count it as my offering to Venus,' said Ritchie with a grin.

'Venus? Oh, you mean the goddess of love. So that we can walk together and amuse ourselves without him behind us as an unwanted shadow.'

'Exactly. And now, my dear heart—note that I said that to you in such a cool fashion that no passing villager could imagine that I am about to shower you with endearments—what shall we talk of?'

'Sadly,' said Pandora, 'I have to inform you that Rice told me that he has had word that William would arrive back some time this afternoon, so this will be our last happy jaunt for some time.'

They had arrived at the end of the village's main street which was turning rapidly into a country lane. After a hundred yards they would be on their own, away from prying eyes. There was a stile in the hedge and Pandora sat on it, Ritchie by her.

'Now we may enjoy ourselves,' she said. 'Though the devil of it is that we have taken vows which compel us to behave ourselves. I hope that you don't mind me invoking the devil but living mostly among men has ruined my efforts to speak like a lady. What I shall do should I ever end up in polite society is beyond my wit to imagine. Aunt Em is always saying, ''Think before you speak, child'', but it always seems to me such a waste of time and energy.'

This was true Pandora, the plainly spoken tomboy whom he loved, and he would not have her different. Ritchie leaned sideways and planted a chaste kiss on her cheek.

'You may invoke him as much as you like when you are with me…' He checked himself. He had been about to say that a fellow living among rough soldiers was not easily shocked—and oh, what a gross mistake that would have been!

'Truly!' she said, smiling at him, hoping that if they married she might find herself in a society where her un-ladylike language might not matter.

If we married? What am I thinking of? What would we live on? My money, I suppose—but then, there are several years to go before I receive it, so how should we manage until then? And what a nodcock I am to think of marrying Ritchie when he hasn't even proposed to me, and because of his sense of honour I must believe that he would not do so if he thought that he was condemning me to poverty.

Unaware of all this speculation about him passing rapidly through his beloved's head, Ritchie rewarded her with a kiss—she looked so pretty when she was thinking.

Pandora turned her head towards him, and kissed him back—on his cheek, because that was all that they were allowing each other. Really, we ought to stop because every time he kisses me or I kiss him I want the kissing to go further than it did the last time we were out together. Where that would end I cannot think, because no one has ever told me what making love really means either when one is unmarried and should not be engaging in it, or when we are married and it is permitted. It must be very pleasant or why would men and women make love at all? Certainly these preliminaries are most enjoyable.

I wonder what it would be like to give him a real kiss on the mouth?

She remembered surprising one of the maids being embraced by a footman at the back of the stables. They had been kissing one another on the lips and had been making little moaning noises between kisses.

Well, if he won't kiss me on the lips, why should *I* not kiss him there? An experiment, that's all, just to discover what it's like.

So, Pandora turned again and this time kissed Ritchie on the lips before he could stop her!

Goodness, he gave a great moan, just like the footman, clutched her to him and kissed her back—fiercely—before letting go of her.

Now it was her turn to moan and to discover that the two kisses had had the most extraordinary effect on her since they seem to have set her whole body throbbing and vibrating in the nicest and most exciting way.

'Oh, don't stop,' she breathed. 'I liked that very much. Why don't we do it again?'

'Breaking the rules,' said Ritchie, whose breath had shortened in the most dangerous way, 'and I have the notion that that wretch, Bragg, will be following us here any moment under the pretext that we might be attacked by the Dark Avenger or some wandering smuggler who might think that we are keeping watch for him while pretending to make love.'

'We weren't pretending though, were we?' asked Pandora. 'I know that I wasn't.'

'I wasn't, either,' said Ritchie fervently. The effect on him of having been kissed by and then kissing Pandora on the mouth had electrified him nearly as much as Signor

Galvani's dead frogs when that eminent natural philosopher had experimented on them. 'But I meant what I said about Bragg.'

Sure enough, a moment later, Jack and Bragg could be heard talking noisily and making enough of a rumpus to awaken the dead, never mind disturb a guilty pair trying to engage in illicit, if chaste, love.

By the time that they arrived Pandora had hopped off the stile and was sitting on the grass and was making a daisy chain.

'There you are,' exclaimed Jack. 'I told Bragg that you would go back to the church to look at some more fossils, but he bet me that you wouldn't, that you would come in this direction, instead. Nice and secluded, away from the crowd he put it, though I told him that there's never much of a crowd at Far Compton.'

'Very astute of him,' remarked Ritchie drily. 'I think it's time that we went home, and made as little fuss as possible when we get there. I gather that your half-brother has returned, so we must all be very discreet about jolly little excursions to Howell's End and Far Compton. I can't afford to be turned away.'

Well, that was true enough, but not quite in the way which Jack and Pandora might assume he meant. Bragg's eye was on him again, and remained there all the way home—if that was what Compton Place could be called.

There was quite a tohu-bohu going on in the yard when they got back. William had returned and was about to take an impatient Nero for a run. Brodribb was standing somewhat fearfully by him, with George and Rob at a little distance. Roger Waters was waiting to be mounted—doubtless feeling happier at climbing on Cato once William and Nero had cleared the yard.

'So there you are,' exclaimed William, scarcely waiting

for them to dismount before he began to rant at Pandora. 'I thought that I told you to keep away from this fellow. When the cat's away the mouse will play, eh? Mind you do as I wish now that I am home again. And you must be Bragg, the new man George has hired. He says you're very good with the horses and I can only hope he's right. We could do with someone skilful round here for a change.'

Pandora, fuming, dismounted and allowed her mare and Jack's pony to be led away by Rob before answering him. Bragg handed his and Ritchie's nags over to George, who unsaddled them and took the opportunity to disappear by leading them out of the yard into the paddock at the back which looked out over Compton land, where they joined Rob's charges.

Rob behind him, he returned to find a fierce argument raging between Pandora, Jack and William over their outing with Ritchie. Bragg, looking vacant, stood to one side, ready to leave the yard while it was now Roger Waters's turn to fume at William.

'Oh, do come on, Compton,' he said testily. 'Can't stand here all afternoon while you read the Riot Act to Pan and Jack. Leave it until we return. Nero's growing impatient and you know what a devil of a fellow he is when he's annoyed.'

'Well, damn Pandora, and damn you and damn Nero, too,' snarled William. 'It's time Nero learned who's master here. I'll send for you later, Pandora, and you, too, Jack and Ritchie. You all need to learn who's master, too.'

Ritchie said nothing, merely inclined his head, wondering why William Compton was always in such an infernally bad temper. He also thought that it would be a gross mistake for him to vent that temper on a volatile stallion like Nero. Which was exactly what William proceeded to do; cursing beneath his breath, he allowed Brod-ribb to throw him up, whereat Nero tossed his head and began to dance about.

Determined to show the watchers that he would brook no defiance from a horse, however much human beings might cross him, William immediately struck Nero a mighty blow on his proud and thrusting neck. The result was catastrophic.

Nero gave a whinnying roar, reared himself up on his hind legs, his forelegs beating at the air and tossed William from his back to lie half stunned on the ground while he whirled and bellowed dangerously above him.

The whole yard sprang into a mixture of paralysis and mad and fearful activity. Pandora, the furthest away from the entrance to the yard, drew Jack to her and flattened them both against one of the closed stable doors. Rob ran out of the yard into the open, followed by Brodribb, both of them determined to be as far away as possible from the iron hooves of the maddened stallion.

George, the nearest to William, who had begun to scream, bent down and tried to drag him to safety, only to be pursued by Nero. Bragg, who had left the stables, returned on hearing what was going on inside, colliding with Brodribb and Rob who were running out.

Nero loose, and the Major in danger! Bragg ran immediately into the yard where Pandora had begun to pray for Ritchie who, like herself, had at first flattened himself against one of the doors and was now moving slowly forward.

Suddenly and improbably it was Ritchie, mild Mr Ritchie, who whirled into action. He flung the valise he had been carrying behind him, ran towards Nero and in one swift athletic leap he vaulted on Nero's back and was struggling to find the reins in order to control him.

'No, Ritchie, no!' screamed Pandora, while Jack stared at the horrible sight of Nero snorting, neighing and whirling, still trying to get at William to finish him off. At the same time he was trying to dislodge Ritchie who was grimly staying on his back. She saw Bragg, shouting something incomprehensible at Ritchie, run towards Nero, only to be forced to retreat before his flailing hooves lest he, too, be knocked to the ground to share William's fate.

Ritchie, as though he were the centaur of whom he had told Jack, somehow managed to control Nero sufficiently to turn him towards the entrance to the yard. The stallion fought him for a moment before giving way, until, under Ritchie's urgings, horse and man tore through the archway and out into the open.

George—forgetting William, who did not appear to be greatly injured and, with Nero gone, had staggered to his feet—joined Bragg in running after the swiftly disappearing horse and rider. Roger Waters, Brodribb, Rob, Pandora and Jack streamed after them.

They saw Nero galloping madly towards the fence at the far end of the paddock. Pandora screamed 'No!' again and put her hands over her eyes. She took them away to discover that Nero had flown over it, with Ritchie now obviously in complete control of him. Once the fence was behind them he gradually slowed the horse down, ending with a trot before bringing him to a stop. Nero's head drooped, as though the fury, which had gripped him after William's blow, had left him, banished by the will of his rider.

Ritchie, physically exhausted—this was the first time since he had arrived back in England that he had engaged in so much demanding exercise—dropped his own head. He had acted without thinking, without considering what such a feat of horsemanship as would be required to tame

Nero would do to his tale of being a novice rider. In his urge to control the lethal monster which Nero had become when he ran amok, all the instincts of a life spent in preserving and protecting those about him had made him forget that he was no longer Major Richard Chancellor, master equestrian.

What now? How was he going to explain this?

Bragg was the first to reach him, well before the others. Nero was now cropping the grass, oblivious to everything but his own hunger. Bragg looked up at Ritchie, at the exhaustion written on his face, and said, his voice devoid of the mockery which he had been employing with the Major ever since he had reached Compton Place, 'Well, sir, you have now well and truly given yourself away.'

Ritchie shook his head. 'Dammit, Bragg, what else could I have done, knowing that I could, if my strength lasted, control the wretched animal, and knowing that no one else would even try? You were too late on the scene to be of use.'

'Exactly, Major. But what now?'

'Now, you must help me down, and when you have me safely standing on the ground I shall faint ever so gracefully.'

He was amused at Bragg's surprised expression.

'Faint, sir…faint?'

'Yes, faint, nodcock. Do as I say, and quickly. The rest are on us.'

He was, he knew although very shaken, far from losing consciousness in earnest, but he had to do something to stop the immediate questioning which would follow his conquest of Nero. If he were believed to be comatose then that would checkmate that—at least for the time being.

He allowed Bragg to help him down, closed his eyes and collapsed most artistically to the ground. Kemble

would have been proud of me, he thought. He could hear
Bragg offering some muttered and muddled explanation
of his sad condition, ending with the words, 'I think that
he suddenly understood what a terrible risk he ran when
he got on Nero's back, and it was too much for him.'

Then he caught Pandora's sweet scent when she knelt
down beside him, careless of what any one might think
of her profound distress at seeing the man she had come
to love lying prostrate on the ground. He felt some com-
punction over deceiving her as well as everyone else, but
there was nothing for it but to go on.

'Oh, why did you run such a terrible risk?' she was
wailing. 'Do say that he isn't hurt, Bragg.'

'No, miss, he ain't. Just done in. Brodribb,' he exclaimed suddenly. 'Be of some use, for once. Take Nero
back to the stables and see him locked away before he
does anyone else a harm. Mr William won't want to be
riding him today, that's for sure. And you, Rob, fetch us
some water. A dash of it in Mr Ritchie's face might restore him.'

The thought of Bragg dashing water in my face is
enough to restore me straight away, thought Ritchie, deciding that it was time that he recovered as artistically as
he had fainted before Bragg thought of some even more
helpful means of reviving him!

He gave a slight moan and began to sit up, but decided
that it might be safer if he looked as though the effort
was too much for him and he lay down again. He seemed
to be surrounded by half of Compton Place's staff and all
of the family except Sir John—who would doubtless be
told of his astonishing performance as soon as the news
reached the house. William was standing above him, sup-
ported by George.

They were both staring at Ritchie as though he had sprouted two heads.

William said slowly, the words being wrenched from him almost against his will, seeing that he had spent his saviour's weeks at Compton Place taunting and demeaning him, 'George and the others tell me that you probably saved my life, so I offer you my heartfelt thanks. I thought that I was done for. How did you come to be able to ride like that?'

Ritchie sat up at last, as though sitting up hurt him. 'I saw someone control a horse like that once, and since everyone else was doing nothing I thought that I ought to do something. If I had had time to think, I should probably have done nothing, too.'

It was all that he dared to say. He did not wish to lie outright, and that explanation—which was no explanation at all—seemed to be as good as any. Keeping silent and looking modest would be his best bet. He dare not look at Bragg, who was now calling for a litter, damn him!

'Help me to stand,' he managed at last. 'I'm beginning to feel much better. I don't need to be carried.'

'Take my arm, sir,' said Bragg officiously, and leaning on it Ritchie walked slowly back to the house.

He could hear Jack behind him chattering away to Roger Waters who had reluctantly given up his ride. 'I've never seen anything like that before. Fancy Mr Ritchie being brave enough to ride Nero when we all know what a slow-coach he is on a horse.'

'Really?' said Roger Waters. 'He didn't look much like a slow-coach just now. I've seen worse tricks than that at Astley's.'

'At Astley's,' exclaimed Jack reverently. 'Oh, I should like to go there, but Pan says that we can't afford to go to London.'

'Well, you could if she married me,' said Roger. 'Why don't you have a word with her? She might listen to you.'

One would hope not, was Ritchie's silent comment. Trust young Jack in his innocence to say something damaging—but one good result was that he now knew that Roger Waters was a little suspicious of his sudden ability to ride, calm and control a dangerous stallion. He would be careful before him in future, but the damage had been done.

He refused to go straight to bed—another helpful suggestion of Bragg's—saying that he was virtually recovered. He was taken instead into that sacred place, the drawing room, where Pandora ordered tea and William, who could not stop staring at his rescuer, said brusquely, 'Brandy would be better for him first.'

It was apparent that he had no idea what to say, or how to behave, to the man who had saved him from death or mutilation.

'I think that you and I could do with a shot, too, Compton, if you don't mind,' said Roger Waters. 'A nasty business that. Sorry I was so surprised that I wasn't of more use, but I always did tell you that Nero was a bad buy. I should get rid of him if I were you.'

No one was saying anything which might suggest that William had almost brought his doom on himself by his pointless striking of his horse. Ritchie accepted the offered brandy gratefully. Drinking it would save him from talking. As would the promised tea when it arrived.

Pandora was hovering over Ritchie as much as she dare with William and Roger present. Her white face was a reproach to him since the blunt truth was that, although he had felt a little exhausted immediately after his taming of Nero, his appearance of great distress after that was a necessary pretence.

She was saying now, her voice anxious, and be damned to what William and the Waters brute might think of her for that, 'Are you sure that you would not like to rest—or perhaps have the doctor examine you? It would be of no trouble to send for him.'

Aunt Em's arrival immediately before that of the tea temporarily stopped her anxious quaverings. The only trouble then, so far as Ritchie was concerned, was that Aunt Em was even more worried about him than Pandora, if that were possible, and alternated commiserating with William with fussing over him.

She took the empty brandy glass from his hand, exclaiming to the assembled company, 'Is that the best you could do for him? Why has not someone fetched him a blanket or a shawl? A shocked patient needs warmth more than anything.' Her solicitude made poor Ritchie feel more of a lying cur than ever. It was only matched by her exclamations over his bravery when the details of what had passed in the stable yard were told to her.

It took the arrival of tea and several plates of Sally Lunns to silence her. This brought no relief for Ritchie since Galpin came in with them, saying portentously, 'The staff would like to add their compliments to Mr Ritchie for his gallant behaviour in the stable yard, and to trust that neither he nor Mr William has sustained any lasting injury in consequence of Nero's misbehaviour.'

'No, indeed,' said both men together; Ritchie and William Compton being in full agreement about something for the first time.

'I shall pass your good news on to the kitchen. In the meantime, Sir John, having been informed of the trouble with Nero, wishes both Mr William and Mr Ritchie to visit him as soon as they feel able to make the journey upstairs.'

'Convey our compliments to Sir John and tell him that we shall visit him when we have done justice to the kitchen's excellent food,' was William's answer to that.

Now there's a thing, thought Ritchie, astonished, that's the first time that I've heard William Compton being even halfway civil to any of his family, friends or servants. Nero might have done him a good turn by putting him in fear of death for the first time—though it probably won't last once the first shock has worn off.

William was even civil to him on the way up to Sir John's suite, asking him if he felt able to manage the stairs and waving him into Sir John's sitting room instead of preceding him.

'So there you are,' exclaimed Sir John, indicating that they should sit. 'Now, I wish to know exactly what happened when that damned horse ran riot. I told you that buying him was a mistake.'

William gave him a brief and truthful account of Nero's misbehaviour and Ritchie's salvation of him when he was lying on the ground in fear of his life.

'You owe him a debt which you cannot repay,' said Sir John at the end. 'He's a gentleman so he can't take money—what he deserves in future is your courtesy and your consideration.'

To say that both his hearers were surprised to learn that Sir John was well aware of William's rude demeaning of Jack's tutor on virtually every occasion on which they had met would be an understatement. Astonishment would have been a better word.

William coloured and mumbled something.

'I hope that was gratitude,' said Sir John sharply. 'And now you may leave us, sir, but not before you assure me that you will dispose of that stallion as soon as possible. Shoot it or sell it, but tell any damned fool who might wish to buy it of its murderous disposition. Mr Ritchie, you will stay. I have something which I wish to say to you.'

Yet another surprise. William did not argue about his *congé*, although until now he would have done, but left immediately. Sir John motioned to Ritchie to remain seated.

'My grandson is in a state of shock, but you, sir, are not. I will say no more of that now. For the present I have something to give you.'

He rang the bell on his side table and the footman who attended to all of his wants came in. 'You may bring the parcel which stands on the whatnot in my bedroom and hand it to Mr Ritchie—and then you will leave us.'

The parcel duly presented, Ritchie stared at it.

'Open it, sir, open it,' said Sir John testily.

Ritchie did so, to find a small golden bowl, with some odd markings underneath the rim, wrapped inside tissue paper beneath a coarse brown cloth covering. By its appearance it was extremely old.

'That,' said Sir John, 'is for you. It's the luck of the Comptons, not that its brought us much lately. That's because I should have passed it on to my son when he reached twenty-one, but alas, he was not fit to own it. Nor is William. Only when the holder is a true man and either a Compton himself, or married to a Compton, does it bring the family luck. Now, since you are going to marry my granddaughter, Pandora, I give it to you.'

'Marry Pandora, sir?' said a dazed Ritchie.

'Well, you are going to ask her, aren't you? And from what I hear her answer will undoubtedly be yes—or so I have been reliably informed.'

'I undoubtedly wish to marry her—but you know nothing of me.'

'Know nothing of you! Why, sir, I suspected that you were a brave soldier, and your conduct this afternoon has verified that beyond a doubt. You were, I suppose, a cavalryman. You are a gentleman, too, and a scholar who is busy transforming Jack into the man he ought to be. What you are doing playing about here I do not know, nor do I wish to—although I might guess. When you are ready to inform me you will do so, and I suppose that that is when you will offer for Pandora.'

'I must remind you, Sir John, that you know nothing of my financial affairs. I might, after all, be simply an adventurer after Miss Compton for her inheritance.'

'Oh, pooh to that. I know you, sir, you would not offer for her unless you could support her. Now, take that with you, hide it away and good luck will go with you. You must pass it on in your turn, either to your heir, or young Jack or his heir.'

'Supposing I do not marry Miss Compton, what then?'

'Then, sir, you will hand it back to me, but I have every faith that your—and my granddaughter's—good sense will render that unnecessary. I trust that from now on you will take every care to ensure that none of my grandchildren come to grief. You have rescued Jack and Pandora, so William must be your next charge however much you might wish to leave him to go to the devil on his own. Now you may leave me—but pray do not inform anyone that I have entrusted you with the Compton's luck. Not that anyone knows of its existence, mark you, and I would wish to keep it that way.'

Slightly stunned by what had passed, and with the bowl stuffed in one of his coat pockets Ritchie walked downstairs. It seemed that, although Sir John might be an invalid, his mind was still in perfect working order despite the odd fashion in which he occasionally behaved.

Was he aware of the dubious venture, or ventures, in which William was almost certainly engaged? Or was he simply worried because he thought that his grandson's obvious moral weaknesses might lead him into trouble? Whatever the reason, he had picked on the stranger to the house as the saviour of the house's family—and on what evidence Ritchie could not imagine.

Unless—at this juncture he encountered Pandora on the landing outside the schoolroom's quarters and lost his train of thought.

'Oh, thank God, you look better already,' she exclaimed. 'How was Sir John taking the news? I hope that he wasn't overset by William's near accident.'

'On the contrary. He was only too pleased that he had escaped injury. He told him to sell Nero, of course, but that was to be expected.'

'And you, what did he have to say to you? I hope that he was properly grateful for what you did.'

'He was very generous, Pandora. I also have to say that he seemed in perfect command of himself, his mind didn't wander once.'

Pandora's smile was a sad one. 'Oh, his illness seems to be capricious. Do invite me into the schoolroom, Ritchie. I think that in future William is going to have much less to say to you about what you may or may not do.'

'Certainly.' He held the door open and they walked in, Pandora slipping her hand into his as though she had been doing this for years. Jack, it appeared, was still downstairs, enjoying his tea in the kitchen where Bragg was also being fêted, she said.

'I think we have acquired a treasure there,' she said, putting one finger on the big old globe which stood in a corner of the room and setting it spinning. 'George says that Bragg seems most capable and wonders why he needs to find such menial work.'

'Oh, old soldiers often have difficulty in settling down when they leave the Army,' he told her. 'But I agree with you and George—he's a regular treasure, is Bragg.'

There was something odd in the way in which Ritchie said that, Pandora thought. It was not the first time that she had noticed that before Ritchie came out with something two-edged his mouth and his eyebrow curled up a little at the left.

'George says that he was a cavalryman. I wonder if he fought in Spain—and why the Army let him go. I would have thought that Wellington's army couldn't afford to lose anyone as competent as he is.'

Now this was shrewd of her given that Bragg, like Ritchie, was still in the army, but on prolonged furlough. Best to say nothing, but look wise, something at which Ritchie was becoming extraordinarily competent. Besides, it was perhaps time, now that he had Sir John's approval, that he began to make some gentle love with Pandora—the phrase in society for such innocent goings-on was making a leg.

Alas, he had no sooner taken her hand in his and had begun to kiss it in an almost absent-minded fashion, than Jack burst in. 'Oh, there you are. I wondered where you had both got to. You're looking much better, sir, almost like your old self.'

I should have been looking better still if you had delayed your arrival by another quarter of an hour, was Ritchie's disgruntled mental reaction to that. Pandora said swiftly, and untruthfully, 'I was just going. Is William making a commotion about me being missing?'

'No, not at all. *He*'s been most unlike himself since

Nero went mad,' said Jack, showing something of his sister's shrewdness. 'Much nicer, in fact. I hope that it lasts.'

'So do I,' said Pandora fervently, 'but best to show myself downstairs I think. He might be quite like his old self any moment now.'

Jack and Ritchie laughed together at this mild joke.

'What I would like to know, sir,' Jack said, 'is why you've been having such trouble riding all those hacks and then were able to leap on to Nero's back and get that great brute to behave himself even when Brodribb and the rest were almost too frightened to walk him.'

'Now, there I can't help you,' Ritchie said. 'It's just that someone had to do something and since everyone else was paralysed I thought that I might as well try to tame him.'

'Well, it was jolly brave of you, I must say.'

Brave it might have been, Ritchie thought, but not very wise. He could only imagine some of the other conversations which might be going on…

Chapter Nine

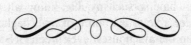

'Do you know anything about this tutor of Jack's, anything at all?' Roger Waters was bullying William later that same afternoon. 'Where he came from, for instance, or who recommended him?'

'Of course we know about him. Lady Leominster recommended him to Pandora and Aunt Em. Said he was a thundering good chap, and I have to admit that he's transformed Jack. He's still as cheeky as ever but is working hard and doesn't make a nuisance of himself at all hours. Why do you ask?'

'Because I understood from Brodribb and George that the man was a novice on a horse and a regular bookworm. Yet this afternoon your so-called bookworm gave a display of horsemanship I've never seen equalled—and I don't believe that it was some sort of divine accident. The man's an accomplished rider. What else is he accomplished at? And why is he here, tutoring Jack? Do I smell something fishy?'

'I can't say that I like the man. I agree there's something odd about him. But Brodribb's been keeping an eye on him for me—says that he's never done anything untoward or been where he shouldn't. Until this afternoon, that is, and I can't complain about a man who saved me from injury—possibly saved my life.'

'There is that,' agreed Roger. 'All the same, best keep an even firmer eye on him in future. I'm off to London tomorrow to make arrangements for the next shipment and the last thing we need is anyone nosing about looking for trouble. If you do find he's up to anything that might suggest he's some sort of spy, you know what to do.'

'Oh, we don't want any more of that,' sighed William. 'There's been too much already. Someone's bound to take notice, soon.'

'Better safe than sorry, is my motto. I'll see you next week.'

There were times when William Compton wished that he had never lost so much money at cards to Roger Waters that he had been unable to honour his IOUs. Roger's suggestion to him that if he helped him and his father in their smuggling ventures he would not only be able to pay his debts, but would make enough money from them to ease his almost bankrupt situation had seduced him into breaking the law. What he had not counted on was how dangerous the whole business was.

It was too late now to repine: he was in no position to withdraw without incurring the wrath of the two Waters. He had not thought of Ritchie as being a spy—but suppose he was? The pickle he now found himself in was enough to send a man mad, what with having got himself involved in treason and with Roger Waters blackmailing him in order to make Pandora agree to marry him.

God send that Sir John never found out what he had been doing!

It had been a really good notion to send for Bragg, Ritchie found. Two days later he went down to the stables to order them to have horses ready for himself, Pandora and Jack immediately after nuncheon. Fortunately George was busy and Brodribb was off on an errand for William—or so he had said. Consequently it was Bragg who came out to deal with him.

'I have some news for you, sir,' he whispered confidentially to Ritchie. 'Some I can tell you now, some later when you return. We mustn't be seen to be talking too long together—that ass Rob follows me around asking my advice about everything.

'Any road, all the servants know that Mr William is in league with the Waters, but, apart from Brodribb, no one here is involved in it. They're either too old, like Galpin, or too cowardly. George knows more than he should but isn't saying anything. Brodribb is a weak link, I would say—being a right lily-livered fellow. On the nights when the lodge-keeper, Haines, comes to the house to play whist with Galpin, Rice and the housekeeper, Brodribb sneaks out to share Haines's wife's bed. Quite a joke it is with the staff since the keeper has no notion of what's going on. I wonder if the Dark Avenger could have a go at him—a coward is always ready to save his bacon by talking.

'Here comes Rob, more later. I'll have the hosses ready for you by two of the clock, Mr Ritchie, sir, that I will,' he ended loudly for Rob's benefit. 'Rob can go with you. George needs me here.'

Two riders clattered into the yard. Bragg stared at them. 'Who the devil are they?'

'Excisemen, Bragg. Riding Officers Jinkinson and Sadler. You may remember me speaking to you of them.'

'Aye, sir. Both will bear watching, I'll be bound.'

Jinkinson was the first to dismount. He returned Bragg's stare, saying brusquely, 'Who may you be?'

'Bragg, sir. New groom here. Mr Ritchie tells me that you are Riding Officers. What may we do for you?'

'*You* may do nothing,' returned Jinkinson roughly. 'It's Mr William Compton we wish to speak to. You'll look after our mounts while we go in to see him.'

'Oh, aye, sir. Prime piece of horseflesh you have there, sir. Cost you a pretty penny, I'll be bound.'

'Bought from a fool who didn't know what he was selling. Mr Sadler and I are busy men. Mr Ritchie can show us into the house, eh, Sadler?'

'Nay,' said Bragg. 'Rob can do that. Mr Ritchie is here to help me with Nero. He's off to be sold tomorrow.'

'I heard as how he'd misbehaved himself,' said Sadler. 'I understand that Mr Ritchie did a brave thing for a man who's by no means a first-class rider. Congratulations, sir.'

'Oh, as to that,' replied Ritchie with a modest half-laugh. 'I still frighten myself by thinking about it—as Bragg, here, will verify. I was lucky to get away unscathed.'

'Oh, I'm sure you were,' said Sadler. 'By the by, have you anything you might wish to tell us before we see Mr Compton?'

'No more than before, I fear. Too busy otherwise.'

'So I suppose,' said Sadler, and he and Jinkinson followed Rob through the back entrance into the house.

'Sadler obviously thinks that you're a fraud of sorts, sir,' said Bragg. 'The other man didn't say enough to prove that he thinks anything—has to be careful, perhaps, if he's on the take, not to say something which might betray him.'

'True,' said Ritchie. 'Now Rob's gone, tell me the rest of your news.'

'I think that you may have guessed it already. Roger

Waters will be going to London shortly to pick up the next load of guineas to be sent to France—or that's what the staff think. They wouldn't bear witness, though. Smuggling's a holy thing round here, even if it helps Boney—I suppose you know that, too.'

Ritchie nodded. 'About the Dark Avenger and Brodribb—that's a useful suggestion. When does the next whist party take place?'

'Tomorrow night as ever is. Want any back-up, sir?'

This time Ritchie shook his head. 'Thanks. But better not. The Avenger is a lone creature, or so legend says. If I ever do need you, I'll let you know. I must be off now, duty calls, and as you said we must not be seen too much together.'

'Point taken, sir. See you later.'

Later never came. Pandora was on her way upstairs that afternoon to change into her riding habit, when William sent a maid servant up after her.

'Miss Pandora,' she said breathlessly when she caught Pandora on the first landing. 'Mr William has had word that Lady Leominster is coming over from Lancings, where she is staying, to visit Sir John, who was a great friend of her father's. She will expect both you and Master Jack to be presented to her, so he has sent me to assist you to dress.'

'And Mr Ritchie, what of him?' asked Pandora, sad that her ride with him would now be cancelled, but still hoping to see him that afternoon.

'Oh, he will be present, too, Miss Pandora. He and Master Jack have already been informed.'

What should she wear? Pandora's wardrobe was scanty in the extreme, but she did possess one good afternoon dress in pale blue muslin, trimmed with cream lace around a high neck and small puffed sleeves. It was somewhat out of date, but would have to do. With light kid shoes and a straw bonnet, she would even be ready for a walk, if that were the lady's pleasure.

She arrived in the drawing room to find the rest of the party there. William was dressed to kill. Jack was also kitted out for once in clothes suitable for a young gentleman of fashion. They included a giant stock which he obviously found confining since he kept running an impatient finger around it. Aunt Em was resplendent in old rose and was carrying a large fan since the day was hot. She had been conversing with Ritchie about Jack's education. Mr Rice, looking uncomfortable in his best clothes, was also present.

Ritchie was his usual calm and ordered self in his threadbare best. His stock was splendid also, and was the smartest thing about him. His calm self was a lie. He had met Lady Leominster once, fleetingly, when he had been little more than a boy, and he sincerely hoped that she had forgotten him.

William said abruptly, 'You are just in time, Pandora. Lady Leominster and her companion have already arrived and are at present with Sir John. She asked to speak to him alone, goodness knows why. I have ordered tea to be served when I ring for it, and can only pray that it arrives on time and not before or after.'

'I had no warning that the lady was coming,' said Pandora a trifle sharply.

'Nor had I,' retorted William, looking harassed. 'The messenger saying that she was on her way reached us only half an hour before she arrived. The *on dit* is that she is a law unto herself, and this simply proves that rumour, for once, is true.'

He had barely had time to finish speaking when the double doors were thrown open with a flourish and Galpin quavered out, 'Her Ladyship of Leominster and her companion, Miss Honoria Cheadle.'

The assembled company all sprang to their feet like jack-in-boxes, and made their reverences to Her Magnificence, as irreverent Mr Ritchie later nicknamed her to Jack and Pandora.

'Sit, sit,' she exclaimed, advancing majestically into the room, her companion creeping behind her. 'Mr Compton,' she continued. 'You may introduce the company to me.'

She was so majestic and so sure of herself and everything that she said and did that Pandora had a desperate wish to say or do something out of place to see what her reaction to such *lèse-majesté* might be.

'Charming!' the lady exclaimed, turning her tortoise-shell-handled lorgnette on Pandora, 'and your brother, Jack, such a manly little fellow, too.'

Jack did not take this as praise since he was several inches taller than the lady. He said nothing but stuck out a mutinous lower lip at her Ladyship, who now strongly resembled a frigate in full sail across an ocean of her own making.

'And this is your tutor, Mr Ritchie. Of course, I remember you, sir, not that we have met, I think, but when I heard that my old friend, Sir John Compton had a grandson who needed a reliable fellow to bear-lead him, I asked among all my dear friends if they knew of anyone reliable. It was you who my cousin, Lady Lomax, recommended to me. Has he been reliable, sir?' she demanded of William.

William allowed that Mr Ritchie had been most reliable.

'Splendid! One likes to know that one has been of use

to one's friends. Now you must tell me all your news. I understand from my cousin Pollard at Lancings that the most exciting news in Sussex centres around the exploits of the Gentlemen—as I believe smugglers are called. Such stories! Our London lives are quite eclipsed by the goings-on here. Have you encountered any of these people?' she finished, waving her lorgnette at William, Ritchie and Jack in turn.

In turn they all confessed ignorance.

'What a bore!' she exclaimed. Exclamation, combined with monologue, seemed to be her usual mode of conversation, both Ritchie and Pandora separately thought. 'Cheadle, did you hear that? I should have liked to meet a smuggler—few in society have done so. Ah, well, but I've also heard about a spectre called the Dark Avenger who is supposed to haunt these parts, and who, I am told, has recently been seen again.

'Mr Ritchie, you are a scholar, I understand. Pray tell me, do you believe that such a creature exists and, if I were fortunate, or unfortunate enough, to encounter one, what should I say to it—if anything?'

Privately Ritchie thought that her mode of speech was enough to silence, if not frighten off, any Dark Avenger she might meet, but he did not care to tell her so. Avoiding Pandora's amused eye—he seemed to be doing a lot of eye-avoiding lately—he said smoothly, 'Oh, I am sure that any Dark Avenger unfortunate enough to meet such a strong-minded person as your good self would flee the spot immediately if you turned your lorgnette and a disapproving stare on him.'

To his surprise, the lady burst into loud laughter at what she took to be a compliment.

'Oh, Mr Ritchie, you are an original, are you not?' she exclaimed, before lifting her lorgnette and turning her basilisk eye on him. 'You might not believe this, sir, but I have the distinct impression that we have met before, and that you had an original turn of speech then. Have we, sir? Met before?'

She was correct. It had been years ago when she had visited his father and his late mother and he and Russell had been sent for from the schoolroom. She had said something ridiculous to him and, curling his lip and his left eyebrow, he had made a quietly uttered two-edged reply to her—he could not remember exactly what.

The lady had, however, been clever enough to know what he was doing, and had bellowed at him, 'Oh, what a naughty boy you are, but I like you. What a charmer you will be when you reach your majority.'

Nothing for it now but to look surprised and say, 'I am sure, Lady Leominster, that if I had met you before, I would not have forgotten you.'

Her response to that was similar to the one she had made all those years ago when he had been an impudent schoolboy waiting to go to Oxford.

'Splendid, sir! You will go far in life if you can make such an apropos remark at such short notice. Miss Compton, I must enquire of you—does he tease you and his pupil as he has just teased me, twice? No, don't answer, for I am sure that he does. We shall meet again at dinner, young man, and you may entertain me there. I might then remember where we have met before because I am sure that we did.'

'It's a good thing that she's old enough to be your mother,' Pandora was later to murmur to Ritchie, 'or I fear that she might run off with you.'

'I don't think,' he murmured back, 'that *I* should wish to run off with *her*.'

'Oh, she would leave you with no choice. I am certain

that she is determined enough to tuck you under her arm and carry you off to Gretna Green or somewhere else equally unwholesome.'

'Wretch!' he had exclaimed back in an excellent imitation of her ladyship.

That afternoon, though, they were behaving themselves and conversation became general. M'lady sank into a chair, fanned herself and announced that she and Cheadle wished to be shown the gardens by Pandora. Told that they were something of a wilderness, she informed them she liked wildernesses best, rose immediately, tucked Pandora's arm in hers and led her off through the glass doors to inspect them.

'Phew!' exclaimed William, and Ritchie thought that exclaiming must be catching. 'Thank God she's leaving us after dinner—more than a day of her and I should be fit for Bedlam.'

Dinner was as fraught as one might have expected. After the lady's comment Ritchie had been invited to be present but Jack dined on schoolroom fare. Once it was over, the lady dominated the conversation again before, replete with food and self-satisfaction, she set off for Lancings immediately the meal was over.

'Tomorrow afternoon,' Pandora told Ritchie before he retreated upstairs again, 'I would like the three of us to ride to Little Compton. The village has gone—they say that it died when my family moved to Compton Place in the early eighteenth century when the old manor house there was burned down. But the church is still in existence and contains the tombs of all the early Comptons.

'They are very fine, being carved in alabaster, and in-

clude one which tradition says is that of the Dark
Avenger—I think that you would like to see them.'

'Very much,' replied Ritchie, who was eager to see
what the Dark Avenger was supposed to look like.

Consequently, the following afternoon found them riding to Little Compton, Bragg in attendance, armed with
their notebooks, drawing paper and pencils.

Little Compton church was as fine as Pandora had
promised. True, it was dark and dusty, but the glass in the
windows and the tombs were rare examples of medieval
workmanship.

'We were lucky,' Pandora explained. 'Cromwell's
troops never passed through here so neither the windows
nor the tombs were smashed, but were saved only to be
neglected by my ancestors, I fear.'

Jack sat down in one of the old pews, which had the
heads of the apostles on its ends, while Ritchie examined
the remains of soldiers of an earlier day than his own.
Most of the medieval Comptons had been knights in the
service of their king and, carved in pale pink alabaster,
were lying at rest in full armour on top of their tombs.

Sir Aymery de Compton, the Crusader supposed to be
the Dark Avenger, was soon found. He was, if his statue
told true, a tall man for his time and was lying with his
feet, not on a pillow, but what looked suspiciously like a
lion cub. A lion rampant raged across a stone shield which
hung dangerously above him.

'There is no longer a lion on our arms,' said Pandora,
'only three trees. Why trees I have never discovered, but
the Comptons have not been soldiers since the Wars of
the Roses.'

'I want to be a soldier,' Jack called from his seat in the
pew. 'If the French Wars go on much longer I should like

to fight in them and be a Dark Avenger, too. Our cousin Jocelyn was killed at Badajoz.'

'Oh, I think that Wellington will make short work of the French before you become a soldier, Jack,' Ritchie said, 'but there may be other wars.'

Pandora said earnestly, 'Oh, I do hope not. We deserve some peace after all these years of fighting, do we not, Mr Ritchie?' She was always careful to use Ritchie's formal name before Jack.

'Yes,' said Ritchie simply, thinking of his dead comrades and of Talavera, Badajoz, and Salamanca, a particularly bloody battle in which he had taken part before he had been captured on reconnaissance, and after escaping had hovered between life and death, saved only by Bragg's fierce determination to keep him alive.

The sight of the bold Sir Aymery, though, served to confirm his decision to make sure that the Dark Avenger would quarter the countryside that night. As was customary with him, the thought of action made him quieter than ever as he considered ways and means and girded himself for the task.

He was so quiet on their way home, and after they had reached Compton Place, that Pandora began to fear that he was sickening for something. His face was so grave that in the few minutes which they spent alone before going their separate ways, she asked anxiously, 'Are you well, Ritchie? Is something troubling you today?'

'Oh, no,' he said, shaking himself out of his almost trance-like state. 'I was thinking about Sir Aymery and the others who lie in the church and wondering what they would make of us.'

'Not much, I suppose,' returned Pandora seriously. 'I expect that they would think of us as a pampered collection of namby-pambies. Their life must have been a very hard one compared with ours.'

Which was only partly true, Ritchie told himself that evening, while he lay hidden in the overgrown shrubbery dressed in his Dark Avenger costume, waiting for Brodribb to leave the house by the back door on his way to his assignation with the lodge-keeper's wife. It was surprising how this mission in supposedly tranquil rural England kept putting him in some damned uncomfortable situations, both physical and mental!

A gentle rain had begun before Brodribb emerged into the open, trotting briskly in the direction of the lodge. He kept to the path which led to the main drive. Ritchie tracked him by walking through the trees which ran parallel with the path and then the drive itself.

Halfway to the main gates the trees became particularly dense. Ritchie made ready to catch his prey and drag him into their shadow where he would be hidden from anyone passing—although few used the drive after nightfall.

He had brought with him one of his black silk stocks which he had twisted to make a stout, if short, rope. The Spaniards used such a rope, or cord, to strangle criminals and Ritchie had seen it employed by the guerrillas in Spain against hapless French soldiers whom they had kidnapped and wished to question.

Silently—for he was in his stockinged feet—he ran up behind the unheeding Brodribb, seized him round the neck with his stock and, careful not to strangle him to death, dragged him into the trees, coughing and choking. He then slammed him up against the stoutest tree trunk he could find and thrust his masked face into Brodribb's purple and scared one.

'Hear me, hear me,' he cried hoarsely. 'I would know

why you help my country's enemies, the French.' At this
point to confuse Brodribb even further he threw in some
muttered Spanish phrases, before adding, 'Answer me,
lest worse befall you.'

'No,' shrieked Brodribb. 'I haven't helped the Frenchies, I never would.'

'Liar,' intoned Ritchie, now fully in the skin of the
long-dead Sir Aymery, 'you send gold to France to help
their armies. Now confess your treason before me and my
God. Tell me when the boats arrive to collect it.'

'Drink and baccy,' moaned Brodribb, 'drink and baccy,
that's all we deal in, as God's my witness.'

Ritchie tightened the garrotte around his neck. 'Don't
lie to me, or you shall, this night, meet your maker and
confess your sins to him, not me. You have shared in the
money which the gold brings, have you not?'

Brodribb gasped something unintelligible, so Ritchie
loosened the garrotte again. 'What's that, churl? What are
you trying to tell me?'

'Next Friday week, at Howell's End this time,' Brodribb howled. 'Young Waters has gone to arrange it, but I
swear to God I didn't know that gold was being smuggled.'

He might be speaking the truth or he might be lying,
but Ritchie thought that fear had forced from him the date
of the next consignment. After he had pulled away the
garrotte, his voice still hoarse, he recited over Brodribb,
who had now sunk to the ground, a few words in garbled
Latin, saying at the end, 'With this I have purged thy
soul.'

'Don't want my soul purged,' Brodribb moaned and,
pulling himself to his feet, launched himself desperately
on his tormentor, to be met again with the garrotte, pulled
tight. This time he slumped to the ground, barely con-

scious. Ritchie knelt over him, pulled off the garrotte and used it to tie Brodribb's hands behind his back.

'Foolish serf,' he roared in a thunderous voice. 'Thank your God that the Dark Avenger has spared your worthless life. Live and change your ways lest I return to finish the task I have just begun.'

He turned and ran at full speed through the trees which thinned out the nearer he drew to the house. Once he was sure that no one was following him, he pulled off his cloak and mask, making a crude parcel of them before he left them in the folly. That done, he walked slowly back to the house, waiting in the shrubbery until he thought that the whist party had broken up and gone to bed before he entered it, through a window next to the pantry, to emerge near the backstairs.

He could hear footsteps and laughter on the flight above him so he hid himself in a doorway while the thoughts in his brain scurried round inside his skull like rats in a cage.

If Brodribb could be believed, he had at last found some hard evidence to share with Bragg and decide what to do with it. Could he trust Sadler to arrange for the smugglers to be caught in the act? Or would he insist on informing Jinkinson, with the inevitable result that the venue would be changed?

Sir John had also given him another problem to solve. He had asked him to save William from the consequences of his folly. Whether or not he knew that William was engaged in smuggling guineas to France was beside the point. For Ritchie to act without consideration for William would be easy—but if he did so then William would be accused of committing fraud and treason. After that he would be arrested and tried and his inevitable punishment would not only be hanging, but also the sequestration to the Crown of all the Compton estates and the ruin of the

Compton family, including Pandora and Jack, who were innocent of all wrongdoing.

He was trapped inside an enigma which left him in a position in which every course of action he might choose could be the wrong one. He was thinking hard about this apparently insoluble problem when he ran into Bragg, who had just emerged from the door to the kitchens.

They stared at one another. Bragg said, 'Well, well, sir, you're soon back. Did Brodribb cough up anything?'

'I've no time to bandy words with you tonight, Bragg. Listen to me, carefully, Sergeant—and that is an order. The Dark Avenger was out tonight and wrenched from Brodribb the date and venue of the next delivery of guineas on Friday week. I'm telling you this in case anything untoward happens to me, since, if so, you must take my place and inform Lord Sidmouth, the Customs House at Brighton and Sadler of it in any order you please.'

That, Ritchie knew, would not save William, only he could do that, and for that he needed to live: dead he could not help him.

'Sah,' hissed Bragg, saluting his superior officer in proper form for once.

'Stow that,' ordered Ritchie. 'Now, be off about your business, and I will try to reach my room without being seen.'

Alas, he had not progressed further than the bottom of the backstairs than it was Pandora he encountered, coming from the housekeeper's room. It was the first time on his secret forays as the Dark Avenger that he had ever encountered anyone and it was cursed luck that he should do so on the first night that he had played the spectre to some effect!

'Ritchie!' she exclaimed. 'I thought you abed long ago.'

Only impudence might pay here. 'I had thought the same of you,' he countered.

'I was sent for by Mrs Rimmington,' said Pandora, immediately deflected. 'It seems that not one, but two of the maids fell ill suddenly. Besides that, Brodribb is missing. It is thought that he went to the stables during tonight's whist game. He usually returns by the time it breaks up, but didn't tonight. Galpin sent George to look for him in the stables, fearing that he might have met with some mischance, but he wasn't there.'

Of course he wasn't in the stables. He might have been with the lodge-keeper's wife and been detained, but he hadn't, the Dark Avenger had nabbed him on the way to her. Ritchie thought it best not to confess to knowing either piece of information. Instead, he confined himself to looking as concerned as a man ought to be who had been constantly and brutally insulted by the missing Brodribb.

'Probably went down to the alehouse in Nether Compton,' he offered.

'Galpin thought not. Too far to walk for Brodribb's liking and William won't permit him to take one of the horses in order to go drinking. These recent attacks on solitary walkers have worried the staff so George, Galpin and Haines, the lodge-keeper, are searching the grounds for him. By the by, what were you doing down here?'

'Oh, I couldn't sleep, so I was on my way to the library where I had left one of the books which I was using to prepare Jack's lesson in Roman history. I only found it the other day: it seems to have been overlooked in the general clear-out.'

He had thought this excuse up while Pandora had been telling him about Brodribb's disappearance. It wouldn't do for him to be suspected of being out and about at the time that Brodribb had disappeared.

'Don't let me keep you,' Pandora said. 'You need your rest—what with teaching Jack, fossil hunting and coping with Grandfather. He complained that you hadn't taken Jack for his weekly visit today: I do believe that he likes you.'

'True, and we haven't had one of our rides lately, what with Lady Leominster's visit and your Aunt Em being poorly. How is she today?'

'Much better.'

During this brief and impersonal interchange Pandora and Ritchie had been moving nearer and nearer together. Pandora was wondering distractedly if she dared to try to make him kiss her, but was worried by the thought that if they did kiss they might be caught in the act by any servant who was late going to bed.

Ritchie was nobly resisting the temptation to kiss her for exactly the same reason. What was it about her which attracted him so? He hadn't felt like this about a woman since his late teens when their lure had become irresistible. He had assumed that age had inoculated him against feminine temptation—but perhaps it was because Pandora *didn't* try to practise any of the female arts on him that he was so drawn to her, that to see her was to be roused.

As he was now.

Perhaps a light kiss on that graceful neck…?

Fortunately common sense took over at that point for there was a loud commotion outside. The noise of men's voices, George being the loudest, heralded the return of the party which had gone to look for Brodribb. By the sound of it they had been successful.

Both Ritchie and Pandora thought it best to find out what was going on. Pandora because it was her duty as

Compton Place's chatelaine, and Ritchie because it would be unnatural not to be curious.

They arrived in the servants' hall to find that Brodribb had indeed been found and has been ensconced in Galpin's great armchair. Bruised and battered, he was moaning distractedly about ghosts and spectres having attacked him, although, George said, it seemed that only one of them had laid him low. William had been sent for since it was thought that, Brodribb being his particular servant, he ought to know that he had been assaulted.

'The Dark Avenger threatened me, he did,' Brodribb was wailing. "Orrible it was, 'orrible. He was so strong and so fearsome—he was like to strangle me. I fought like a tiger, but it was no use.'

Bragg, drawn by the commotion, leaned forward and said, 'Tried to strangle you, did he? But why did he threaten you, Brodribb?'

'It were a mistake. He said that I was a traitor, but I've allus been a good Englishman. God bless the King, I say, and all the Royal Family.'

'Do you think that the Dark Avenger might still be roaming around?' asked Haines, his face anxious. 'I don't like the thought of going home if he is—seeing as how Brodribb was found so near to the lodge.'

'Near to the lodge?' said Pandora. 'What were you doing there, Brodribb?'

'Dragged there I was,' moaned Brodribb, determined not to give away the secret of his assignations with Haines's wife while Haines was present. 'Knocked me about he did before he disappeared.'

Pandora said doubtfully, 'Can spectres attack human beings—and then drag them away? Mr Ritchie, being a scholar, you must know of such things. Is it possible?'

'Opinions vary,' said Ritchie in his most pedantic

mode, trying to avoid Bragg's eye again. 'Different people who have encountered them have told different tales. There is a belief that they can take over the bodies of human beings for a short time and then leave them when an attack is over.'

'Best cut the cackle and get him to bed,' said Bragg, disrespectful, but practical, 'and let the doctor see him in the morning, eh, Mr Galpin, sir?'

'That's right,' said the agitated Galpin. 'Lord knows what's come over the world these days. Spectres and smugglers and Boney wanting to invade us. It weren't like this when I were a lad.'

Several of the older heads nodded agreement. Haines and Bragg offered to carry him upstairs, but Brodribb said that with their help he could walk.

Before they could perform this charitable office, William burst into the hall.

'What the devil's all this about Brodribb being attacked? Good God, man, who has done this to you and where?'

Brodribb's explanations being somewhat muddled, it was left to Galpin and George to tell his sad tale.

'But what the devil were you doing out in the grounds at that hour?' exploded William. 'Knowing how lawless the Downs have become these days, you should have had more sense. The gates are in such disrepair that anyone could enter the grounds, anyone. As soon as I have a little cash to spare I'll have them mended.'

No one was tactless enough to tell William what he did not know—that Brodribb was on his way to an assignation with Haines's wife, something of which all the servants were aware…except Haines, of course.

Brodribb mumbled an unhappy explanation. 'I was in the stables, sir, and I heard a noise, an 'orrid noise, like someone wailing. I went out to see what was what—and saw the Dark Avenger who set about me at once. I think that he thought that he'd left me for dead.'

'Dark Avengers don't exist, Brodribb,' said William. 'I expect that he's a common thief who runs around knocking people about and stealing from them. Have you lost anything?'

'No, sir. He *said* as how he was the Dark Avenger. That's all I can tell you.'

'And a traitor,' said George helpfully. 'He called you a traitor, you said. Though the Lord knows why he should say that.'

'A traitor,' said William sharply. He looked to be somewhat alarmed by this. He promptly stopped questioning Brodribb, and before he went upstairs merely ordered the others to see him to bed, and arrange for the doctor to visit him in the morning.

Later Pandora accompanied Ritchie up the backstairs to the first landing before he left her to make the final steep ascent on his own.

'Like William,' she said, 'I'm a little troubled about what Brodribb was up to in the grounds at night. But I gained the impression that the servants weren't surprised that he was. As for Dark Avengers, like William I think that they're imaginary—despite your scholarly explanation of their behaviour. Do you think that he was on his way to meet some of the local smugglers? I know that George believes that he is in league with them.'

'Apparently the Dark Avenger thought so, too,' Ritchie could not resist saying.

'It's my opinion—and I know that something similar has been done elsewhere—that the Dark Avenger is a smuggler himself, and runs round the countryside in disguise in order to frighten honest people into staying in bed. There's probably more than one of them since I know that he's been seen near Brighton on nights when he's been sighted here—and I doubt that even a spectre could be in two places at once. But why on earth should he attack Brodribb?'

'Difficult to explain, I agree,' sighed Ritchie, who was busy silently admiring Pandora's usual down-to-earth brisk understanding of what went on around her. 'So you wouldn't scream if, by some ill chance, you saw him?'

'Oh, I suppose I should. Common sense would be sure to desert me if I were alone in the night and saw a creature running around where he ought not to be. We are all brave when we contemplate our possible actions in a dangerous future, are we not? It's a different matter when we arrive there.'

Ritchie thought of himself, and of how often he had needed to 'screw your courage to the sticking-place', as Lady Macbeth had said, in order to carry out some of the exploits which had brought him fame and which had seemed easy enough to carry out beforehand but had proved hard in the doing.

'Yes,' he said, and the manner of his saying that simple word had Pandora looking sharply at him, his face was suddenly so grave and so thoughtful. 'Yes, you are right as usual. Tell me, Pandora, how do you manage to grasp such essential truths when you have lived a quiet life in the country, while those whose lives should have been eventful enough to be able to understand them, so often don't?'

Pandora said slowly, 'I suppose that, living alone so much with only Aunt Em, Jack and a reclusive grandfather as companions, I have had a great deal of time to read and to think. But I'm sure that you overestimate my powers of understanding.'

Ritchie thought not, but he did not contradict her. They had been alone together quite long enough and by the laws of unkind chance they were likely to be discovered if they continued to stay talking on the landing—even if their conversation had been far from that known to the scandalous newspapers, and the law, as 'criminal'—criminal conversation being a polite way of describing illicit sexual relationships between men and women.

The same thought must have occurred to Pandora since she said, a trifle wistfully, 'I think that we ought to separate now. We have been so good and chaste that it would be a pity for anyone to come across us and think quite otherwise.'

'Agreed, but allow me to be a little forward,' and Ritchie took her hand in his to kiss it. 'And do not have dreams about Dark Avengers or ghosts of any kind—they are but spectres of the imagination and you must not allow them to haunt you.'

'I won't,' said Pandora in a voice which could only be described as manful, 'but if we are to part now, you must allow me to return your favour,' and she leaned forward, took his hand and kissed its back.

Oh, what a fatal thing to do! Ritchie, for once acting without thinking, leaned forward in his turn to kiss her again, not on the hand this time, but on the lips, fiercely and demandingly. His was the kiss of a warrior who had found his mate and wished to seal her to himself, to prevent any other from claiming her.

Pandora responded as the mate of a warrior should— as fierce and demanding as he. Mouth to mouth, body to body, they were lost to everything but the power of the attraction between them. Time and space disappeared: caution, self-control and convention disappeared, too. What would have happened, Ritchie asked himself afterwards, if there had not been noise from above and the sound of feet descending? It was a question he dare not answer.

They pulled apart as rapidly as they had come together. Pandora exclaimed, 'Oh, dear!' and dashed in the direction of the door which led to the main part of the house and to her bedroom. Whatever had come over them both? she asked herself agitatedly. Nothing which had passed before between her and Ritchie had resembled in the least the brute power of the passion which had overwhelmed them in an instant.

Ritchie, indeed, had been so strongly affected that for one mad moment he began to dart after Pandora in order to claim her, to… Only for reason and common sense to return to him once more and compel him to stop. He waited for the footsteps to draw near and stood back to allow their owner to pass by him.

It was one of the footmen from Sir John's suite, come down for some reason or other. He stared at Ritchie when they met. Ritchie gave him a nod and ran lightly up the stairs, away from Pandora, away from temptation—and towards duty and honour.

He damned them, damned fate, himself, Sidmouth and the mission which had brought him to Compton Place. Except that had he not done so he would never have met Pandora and discovered what true love was. A paradox to end all paradoxes, he told himself, and spent a sleepless night trying to work out the unsolvable equation with which the clash between love and duty had presented him.

Chapter Ten

Pandora arrived in the schoolroom on the next afternoon to discover that Ritchie and Jack were not there. She hoped that they had not decided to go for a ride without her, but finally concluded that Ritchie would not have neglected to take her on an excursion where they could have been together with only Jack and a groom to accompany them so that they could enjoy themselves more freely than when they were in the house.

Perhaps they were playing cricket in the grounds—she knew that they often did in the afternoon. Recently they had taken to asking Rob, one of the footmen and the kitchen boy to join them in order to make the game more exciting for Jack. Before she went down to discover whether her supposition was correct, she decided to explore the schoolroom which looked a very different place from when Mr Sutton had been tutor there.

Jack's primers and exercise books were laid neatly out on the table in front of his chair, with a pencil, two newly sharpened quills and an inkpot beside them. Ritchie's books and writing equipment were on the other side of the table with his spectacles lying on top of an open book.

Pandora examined it to find out what they had been working on. It was Livy's *History of Rome*.

Some unexplainable instinct of curiosity led her to pick up Ritchie's spectacles and put them on. To her surprise, unlike the time when she had tried on her grandfather's, the world she saw through them was as clear as the one she normally viewed. The only explanation she could think of was that the glass in them must be plain and that Ritchie did not really need them in order to be able to see properly.

So why was he wearing them? Pandora could think of no logical explanation. It suddenly occurred to her that it was not the only thing about Ritchie's behaviour which was odd. There was also his sudden ability to ride when he had been acting like a novice on horseback—and his remarkable talent for bending all the servants to his will without upsetting or distressing them.

Her walk downstairs was a thoughtful and somewhat troubled one. For the first time she asked herself what he was doing at Compton Place when he was apparently able enough to hold down a much better post. She recalled his original explanation for his decision to be Jack's tutor—but was that good enough?

On the other hand, he had said and done nothing really suspicious. He was obviously not involved in the smuggling which was rife locally, and to be fair to him he was not only making Jack study, but had also improved his manners and his will to work to a remarkable degree when she remembered what he had been like under Mr Sutton's careless regime.

Her arrival in the park convinced her that her sudden doubts about him were baseless. The players of the game of cricket which he had arranged for that afternoon had been enlarged by the inclusion of two of the gardeners, one middle-aged and one young, as well as three of the older lads from the Dame's School at Nether Compton.

They were all so busy enjoying themselves that they did not see her arrive, so she stood and watched them without making her presence known. What impressed her was the care which Ritchie was taking to instruct them in the best way to play so that pleasure and learning were artfully combined. He seemed to know what to say and do to encourage them to give of their utmost, and his patience appeared to be inexhaustible.

A wave of love for him swept over her. Not the love of the body which is simply passion, but something deeper, a mixture of understanding and admiration for his warmth of feeling which was so different from the fashion in which most of the men she knew treated those whom they regarded as their inferiors.

How stupid she was to think that there was something deceitful about him and his behaviour! His goodness and honesty were patent in everything he did. At a pause in the game she smiled and waved to them.

They all turned to greet her. Jack shouted gleefully from his position as fielder, 'Come and join us, Pan!'

'Why not?' she called back to him, and ran forward. Her shabby old working day dress was high above her ankles and would thus allow her to field, or to wield a bat. She had seen the pleasure on Ritchie's face when she had responded to Jack, but all the same, he said when she reached mid-wicket, 'I don't wish to spoil your enjoyment, Miss Compton, but do you think that this is wise?'

'Wise!' she exclaimed joyfully. 'What has being wise to do with my playing cricket on a sunny afternoon? Pray tell me where to stand to catch the ball and when I may go in to bat.'

Ritchie could not resist smiling back at her happy face. 'All the same,' he said, 'what would Mr William say if—?'

'Pooh to that,' she interrupted, tossing her head. 'There is no one here to see us. I'm sure that playing cricket is a more innocent pastime than many which ladies and gentlemen enjoy in the afternoon.'

Well, he had no answer to that, and what with Rob grinning, and Jack egging his sister on, Ritchie thought it best not to make too much of a fuss about what William would certainly see as most inappropriate and unladylike behaviour.

'Very well,' he said, and tossed her the ball as lightly and gently as he could. Pandora caught it and threw it back.

'I've caught harder throws than that,' she boasted, 'when I used to play single-wicket with the Vicar's son.'

'You're not playing with the Vicar's son today,' shouted Jack. 'Just shut up, Pan, and let us get on with the game. It's your turn to bowl, sir, and mind—not too many twisters.'

The game began again. Pandora joined in enthusiastically, running after the ball when it came her way. The kitchen boy, Jack's particular friend, was at the wicket and was soon out, and after him Rob was the next victim. Finally Ritchie announced, 'Right, Miss Compton, your turn to bat, and no sending the ball into the next county, if you please.'

'I'll try to remember that,' she called back to him before taking up her stance before the wicket—which was a single stump set firmly into the ground.

Oh, dear, Ritchie himself was going to bowl to her, but no need to worry. He was kind and sent down what was called a dolly-drop, so Pandora ran gleefully forward to hit it hard and high over his head before scampering along to where Ritchie's battered top hat stood on the turf to mark where the batsman ended his run.

'I'll have no mercy on you after that,' he told her, his face one grin. 'I can see that you've been playing with the Hambledon masters, or at the Marylebone Club, so watch out for my twister.'

Pandora waved her bat at him. 'Send your best men against me,' she cried, 'and I'll make mincemeat of them all.'

Oh, how Ritchie wanted to kiss the charmingly impudent face his love was tempting him with, and what pleasure it was to joust with her in the sweet scents of an early summer afternoon—even if he were having to do so in company with several other men and boys.

Down came his twister and how Pandora did not lose her wicket she never knew. She blocked the ball, which trickled slowly to Jack's feet—and put out her tongue at Ritchie. She could almost feel the desire which was consuming her.

His next ball was a slower one and Pandora went forward to blast it into the next county. It rose high into the air, towards Ritchie and slightly to his right. He began to run for it at the same time that Jack did. They collided, fell to the ground—and the ball dropped between them. Pandora was laughing so hard at this merry sight that she forgot to run. The fielders all began to clap and cheer, and Rob forgot himself and shouted, 'Come on, Miss Pandora, show him what's what!'

Man and boy rose, smiling ruefully. Ritchie picked up the ball, and called to the triumphant wench at the other end of the impromptu pitch, 'You'll pay for that, madam.'

Her response was to stick out her tongue at him again, at which all the fielders laughed even louder.

His next ball was another dolly-drop, though, and Pandora, drunk with power, mistimed it completely, and it hit her wicket with a resounding bang. She threw down her bat in disgust.

'I wasn't ready for that,' she explained untruthfully.

'Oh, what a fib,' shouted Jack. 'It's my turn to bat now, Pan—and you may bowl. I'm sick of his twisters and fliers.'

After that was something of an anti-climax. Pandora sent down a few balls, was followed by Rob, and then Ritchie again—who had been showing Rob how to bowl what Jack called his twisters.

The game came to an end when Mrs Rimmington and a maid-servant came out carrying a tray full of mugs of lemonade and ale. She stared at Pandora, saying disapprovingly, 'Oh, Miss Pandora, I had no notion that you were playing cricket, too. I haven't brought you a mug.'

'No matter, she shall have mine,' said Ritchie, handing it to her. 'It's not ale, Miss Compton, so you are safe to drink it as a reward for trouncing my first ball so severely, and for surviving my first twister.'

'Not many have done that,' said Jack approvingly before downing his lemonade. 'Did you really play cricket with the Vicar's son, Pan? Or was that all a hum?'

'Yes, I did,' said Pandora her eyes twinkling, 'but don't remind him. He's a most sober, reverend gentleman these days and might not like to have his wild youth recalled. Mama never knew what I got up to, for I used to climb out of the kitchen window to join in the game on the Vicarage's back lawn. I was most miffed when he went off to Harrow School and cricket stopped for good.'

Ritchie had a sudden heart-stirring vision of a chestnut-haired and green-eyed little girl romping round the Vicarage lawn. The vision was so strong that he almost choked over the pot of ale which Mrs Rimmington had sent out for him because he had given his lemonade to Pandora. His reward was to have Pandora pat his back gently and say, 'Now, now, take a deep breath.'

What Ritchie really wanted to take was something quite different, and he had the distinct impression that while Pandora knew little of the actual mechanics of love she did know how to be a great tease.

Once the patting was over, she put her mug regretfully back on the tray. 'I really should go in now. Rice left the estate account books with me this morning and since we are not going for a ride this afternoon I ought to go through them.'

Ritchie wanted to say 'Don't leave us yet,' but he ought not to, so he didn't. He watched her trot merrily back to the house and her disappearance dimmed a little the brightness of the afternoon. So much so that Jack accused him of wool-gathering and not paying attention when a ball from Rob, which he should have caught, flew past him…

William accosted Pandora when she tried to slip, unseen, into the house.

'Where have you been? I have been looking for you. Roger Waters is here.'

'In the grounds. I needed exercise,' Pandora improvised. 'And I have no wish to meet Roger Waters, so do not ask me to.'

'No, no,' said William hurriedly. 'I don't want you to meet him. I was looking for you to tell you to hide in your room. I told him that you were visiting cottagers with Aunt Em.'

Pandora stared at him. 'Do I hear you aright? I thought that it was your dearest wish that I should marry him.'

'I've changed my mind,' said William stiffly. 'And Sir John does not approve of the notion.'

Since when had what Sir John thought of anything have any influence on William's behaviour? Pandora asked herself, bemused. But best to leave at once, lest William change his mind again and decide that he wished her to marry Roger after all.

Up the stairs she went with yet another mystery to occupy her mind. Her life, which had been running for so long on an even keel in a sea of deadly boredom, had suddenly become unpredictable, exciting and a little uncomfortable. Not that she minded that. It had brought her Ritchie and a whole new world had opened up before her: an avenue to a future which she dared not anticipate.

In the meantime there were Rice's books to check.

William, his head in a whirl and suddenly becoming aware that his own folly had brought him to this sorry pass, was also for the first time facing his true feelings about his half-sister and why he resented her so much. Pandora had suffered his undeserved dislike because, he thought glumly, she is such a reproach to me. She is everything which I ought to be and am not in her selfless devotion to the family and the house.

He slowly made his way back to the drawing room where Roger Waters had helped himself to sherry from the decanter on the sideboard.

'Thought you was never coming back,' he grunted.

'Problem with one of the grooms,' improvised William in his turn.

'Thought Brodribb looked after that for you. Pandora not back yet?'

'No.' William hesitated before pouring himself a glass of sherry. 'There's something I have to say to you, Waters. I want to withdraw from our arrangement. I'm most unhappy about it.'

'Can't be done,' said Roger. 'I told you that when you agreed to join us.'

'When you blackmailed me into joining you in this risky business, you mean.'

'Now, Compton, you know as well as I do that you had no option but to join us. You owed me a vast sum in gambling debts and I was generous enough to allow you to become a member of our little syndicate in lieu of payment and take a share in the profits. You gained. We didn't.'

'But you did, you gained a great deal—access to the part of the coast you needed, where landing from a row-boat, or picking up kegs, can easily be done. You needed Baxter's Bay and my co-operation there. When I agreed to your proposition I thought that it was drink, baccy and silks you were bringing in—only later did you tell me of the sale of guineas to the French government.'

'What of that? It's all of a piece. Smuggling's smuggling whatever the cargo.'

'It's treason,' said William heavily. 'You are as well aware of that as I am.'

'No, I'm not, but it's too late to change your mind. You know too much. Can't do it, old chap. Too dangerous. Dangerous for you if you renege.'

William, white to the lips, whispered, 'You're threatening me.'

'No, telling you what you ought to be aware of.'

'I could inform the Customs—'

Roger interrupted him. 'You're a bigger fool than I thought, Compton. Half of them are in our pay and you've no notion which half is and which half isn't. No, you'll stay with us—or take the consequences.'

This was no idle threat. William knew only too well what had happened to those who had tried to cross the Waters.

'I could...go to the Home Office,' faltered William, but he knew that he was whistling in the dark.

Roger laughed. 'Same problem there, old chap. Sidmouth isn't on the take, but there are those there who are and who would be quick to warn us. As well as that, my father has a number of MPs in his pocket and half the City's dealers in currency and gold. Checkmate—or should I call it Fool's Mate, Compton, seeing what a noodle you are?'

His grin was infuriating. 'Two more things,' he offered chattily. 'I hear that man of yours, Brodribb, was the victim of the Dark Avenger last night. Now since I don't believe in ghosts I'd be relieved to hear that you had a stiff word with him to discover whether he had been blabbing about our arrangements. If he has, you know what to do—and quickly.

'Oh, and t'other thing. I'm still determined to wed Pandora. My father has a mind for me to be a gentleman since he can't be one himself and marrying your hoyden of a sister would do that for me. Be a pleasure to tame her, too, and teach her to speak politely to me when we've tied the knot. That's all, and no more nonsense about wanting to withdraw.

'Finally, as proof of your good faith, I want you down on the beach at Howell's End next week when the next consignment arrives—time you dirtied your hands a little like the rest of us.

'Good day—and watch where you walk.'

Ritchie knew that Sadler would arrive at Compton Place some time that day. One of the Riding Officer's mistakes was to be entirely predictable in his behaviour by following the same route of inspection every fortnight. A wiser man would have been more erratic. As it was, all those in the district who were engaged in smuggling knew exactly where he would be on any given day. This made it easier for them to decide which part of the coast to use when planning a new consignment. This was partly due to the fact that Sadler had to fill in a daily written diary for his superiors and to keep to the same routes made that task easier.

Of course, there were times when reports that a consignment had come in meant that he had, as on the occasion when he had arrived at Compton Place on the day after William's ball, broken the pattern.

Thus Ritchie asked Bragg to let him know as soon as Sadler arrived at the stables so that he might have the opportunity to speak to him now that Brodribb had given him some advance information of the date, place and time of the arrival of the Waters's next consignment. He would have to take the risk that Sadler was honest, would not give him away to Waters or Compton, and would be able to follow the plan of action which Ritchie would suggest to him.

The game of cricket over, he was walking back to the house with Jack when Bragg came up to him.

'A word with you, Mr Ritchie, if you would be so good.'

'If you wish.' Ritchie turned to Jack. 'Why don't you run ahead and ask Cook to have some tea and Sally Lunns waiting for us when we've had time to tidy ourselves.'

'Oh, splendid,' said Jack eagerly, and set off at the run. He was of an age when he ran everywhere.

'It's Sadler, isn't it?' asked Ritchie.

'As ever was. He's drinking ale with George. If you

nip along now, you'll catch him. I'll disappear for a bit so's no one shall think we're together. I made up some tale about needing to talk to Galpin about my future here.'

'Excellent. I have the excuse that I wish to have a word with George about arranging another excursion tomorrow afternoon, weather, and available horses permitting.'

Sadler was alone in the stable yard when Ritchie reached it. He was obviously ready to mount and leave, so Ritchie's excuse was not immediately needed. Sadler waved a cheery hand at him. 'Still here, sir. I heard as how your appointment as tutor was temporary.'

'So it is—for the summer—to be kept on if I satisfy.'

'No doubt about that, I shouldn't think,' returned Sadler. 'I have the notion that you wish to have a word with me.'

'Acute of you,' said Ritchie, 'because I do. You asked me once to inform you if I heard of anything which might help you in your duties. Look bored when I tell you what I have learned, as though we're engaging in idle chit-chat in case any one comes in suddenly.'

'Oh, aye, sir. Fire away.'

'Roger Waters, who seems to be the ringleader locally, with his father as the man behind the scenes, as it were, is expecting a consignment of contraband on Friday week at Howell's End. Not only that, he is almost certainly sending back to the cutter, which brings the contraband in, a consignment of guineas to be sold in France—the money for them to be brought in at a later date, mixed in with drink, tobacco and silk. There may even be some in this consignment.

'This information comes from a most reliable source so I expect you to inform your superiors, particularly since, if you capture those who engage in it, you will, at one stroke, be able to arrest the two Waters and destroy the biggest organisation engaged in smuggling on this coast. Think of what your masters will say to that—and how pleased they will be with you!'

Sadler stared at him. 'How in the world have you found this out? More to the point, sir, dare I believe you?'

'I assure you that you may believe me. Believe me also when I ask you to take this news, not to your immediate superiors in the Customs Service, since some of them are in the Waters's pay, but to the headquarters of the Sussex Yeomanry. I must particularly ask you not to reveal any of this to your colleague, Jinkinson, who is also in the pay of Waters and his friends. He will certainly inform them that the Customs Office has had wind of a planned landing and it will be cancelled. Best to say nothing to anyone in the district. As you must know, the majority of folk round here are either smugglers themselves, or their sympathisers.'

Sadler's jaw dropped again. 'You seem very sure of yourself, Mr Ritchie, but I still have difficulty in understanding how you came by such detailed information—if it is true, that is.'

He had always thought that there was something strange about Mr Ritchie, but this beat everything.

Ritchie sighed. 'Sadler, what can you lose by acting on my information? It may seem extreme to involve the Yeomanry, but you must have had previous occasions when you were ready to catch the smugglers at their game and the weather then changed and landing became impossible. Or your information was proved to be wrong, or the smugglers had been informed that the military or the Excisemen would be waiting. Why not take a chance that I am telling you nothing but the truth?'

If it had not been for Sir John's wish that he would try to save William he might have trusted Sadler with his true identity, but at this point the less official he was in this business, the more freedom of action he retained. He was so troubled over this that, while he had been speaking, he had unconsciously dropped into the voice he had used in the Army when speaking to his subordinates. It was a voice which Sadler recognised and which spurred him on to action.

'True,' he said. 'The only thing which surprises me is that you have not told me how you have managed to discover this after such a short time when I and my more honest colleagues have not discovered anything so detailed in our whole term of office.'

'Don't ask,' said Ritchie with a grin, showing Sadler a face which belonged to someone quite different from the mild tutor which he claimed to be. 'Just act as I suggest. I promise you that, if matters do go awry and this proves to be a mare's nest, I shall make it my business to see that you don't suffer by it.'

Now, how would you do that, Mr Ritchie? Sadler asked himself, after assuring Ritchie that he would carry out his instructions to the letter.

In the hope that he would, Ritchie returned to the house to write a despatch to Sidmouth, telling him of these latest developments, and then arranged to post it to him as soon as possible.

Another pair of conspirators were having a conversation that evening. Henry Waters, that well-known India merchant and financier who had a finger in every pie in the City, was talking to his son after dinner.

'Being a nuisance, is he?'

Roger knew to whom his father was referring. 'Of course, the man's a greedy fool and a coward, too. Time we put the frighteners on him. He's dallying over his sister's marriage to me, and he's now canting about withdrawing from our arrangement with him. I scared him a little this afternoon—but not enough.'

'Hmm.' Henry drew on his pipe. 'A little lesson for him might do us the world of good. Tell Joss to shoot the hat off his head the next time he goes walking, or riding, alone—since you warned him to be careful he should have the wit to grasp why it was only his hat which flew off, and not his head.

'If he still carries on with his nonsense about wanting to cut line, then we might consider taking his head next time. With him gone, Compton Place virtually bankrupt and the next heir an under-age lad, Miss Pandora Compton might not be so haughty if you turned up as her saviour. For the moment we'll leave it as a warning—but for the future the real thing might be better.'

'Done carefully,' was Roger's only comment.

'True, but what with all the discontent and Radicalism about these days one careless squire, shot dead by some disappointed peasant, wouldn't be much of a surprise.'

Roger nodded an agreement. 'But not yet. Let me try to secure the termagant in marriage first.'

They left it at that. Father and son in perfect agreement—as usual.

'Pandora, a word with you.'

It was William. He had been in the library, a place he rarely visited and on the way out he had met Pandora carrying Rice's account books.

His manner to her was so completely different from that which he had been using to her recently that Pandora stared at him. It was not very long ago that he had been so unkind to her that only Ritchie's sympathy had prevented her from breaking down completely. There was no fathoming him.

'Yes, William. What is it?'

He led her into the library, sat her down opposite to him and said, 'I have been thinking. I am not sure that I would wish you to marry Roger Waters after all. The man is something of an oaf—he still reeks of the City back streets from which he and his father have sprung. Miss Compton of Compton Place could surely do better. I thought that Lord Hadleigh was quite taken by you. Would it please you if I invited him here again?'

'Is something wrong with you, William?' exclaimed Pandora bluntly. 'It is not long since Roger Waters virtually tried to ravish me, and even after that you were urging me to marry him. What has happened to persuade you to change your mind? I am sure it is nothing which I have said.'

'A man is surely permitted to change his mind without being the subject of an inquisition,' said William stiffly. 'Suffice it that I have done so. If you do not wish me to send for Lord Hadleigh, then I propose that you and Aunt Em visit London for what remains of the Season where you might meet someone who attracts you more than Roger Waters. I have just about enough of the ready to support you there for some weeks. You are, after all, due to be an heiress in a few years, which should ensure you a measure of popularity.'

To say that Pandora was stunned on hearing this offer would be to put it mildly. The worst thing of all about William's proposal was that, if he had made it before Mr Edward Ritchie had arrived at Compton Place, she would have been up in the boughs immediately, prepared to run upstairs to pack her trunks in order to leave as soon as possible.

Instead she said, 'I don't wish to leave home yet, William. I am fulfilling so many responsibilities to do with the running of the house and the estate that you would find it difficult to replace me at such short notice. For one thing, although Rice is nominally our agent-cum-steward, it is I who am really doing his work, he has become so incompetent.'

Frustrated, William said, 'Why are you being so contrary?' He broke off. He could scarcely tell her the real reason that he wished her to leave: that he wanted her as far away from Roger Waters as possible. He was not so thick-skinned that he had not been filled with horror at the manner in which Roger had spoken of Pandora. Nor was he so far gone in villainy that he was prepared to hand her over to him now that Roger had revealed himself on several occasions to be the coarse brute which he truly was.

No, he could not tell Pandora any of this. Instead he said, so desperately that Pandora wondered what was the matter with him, 'You are sure that you will not change your mind?'

'Quite sure,' returned Pandora.

'It's Ritchie, isn't it? It's Ritchie that you want to stay for. Good God, girl, the man's only a poverty-stricken usher! Still, I suppose that you've seen so few men while you've been cooped up in the country that even he might seem attractive.'

'For shame, William! Remember that this poverty-stricken usher saved your life.'

'I haven't forgotten that, but my gratitude doesn't extend to allowing him to marry my sister.'

'Half-sister, William. Half-sister if we are to be precise.'

'I bloody well don't want to be precise,' exclaimed the

goaded William in accents which were more familiar to Pandora than his recent ones had been. Couldn't the silly woman see that he had only her best interests at heart? 'I bloody well want you to do as I ask you for once.'

'Bad language won't help,' replied Pandora, rising in her most dignified manner—one which she seldom used. She would not allow herself to descend to William's level. He was well and truly back to his old self. If she was doing him an injustice by thinking this, she was not to know it.

'So, you won't oblige me?' wailed William, reverting to his recent civility.

'You heard what I said, William. I have no wish to visit London at the moment—next year, perhaps. As for Lord Hadleigh, you may invite him, but I am making no promises. I found him a pleasant man, no more than that. I am sorry to disoblige you, but there it is.'

She did not add that William had spent his life disobliging her and the rest of his family, and that his sudden change of heart was most puzzling. She felt a desperate need to find Ritchie and ask him if he could fathom her half-brother's remarkable behaviour. She knew that he would be in the schoolroom at this hour, teaching Jack the fundamentals of mathematics and/or natural philosophy, both of which disciplines Jack found more interesting than Latin or Greek, even if they did deal with soldiers and battles.

Still clutching Rice's account books to her, she ran up the main stairway in the most unladylike fashion. Marry Lord Hadleigh? Why would she wish to do that? He was a nice enough man, but compared to Ritchie he was like flat ale after good wine. If she couldn't have Ritchie she wouldn't have anyone, but once she had inherited her money she would do as she pleased and live and die a spinster. She would have a borzoi for a companion, not a pug, and the reputation of being a downright old beldame.

As she expected, Ritchie was in the schoolroom. He and Jack were obviously enjoying themselves. She could hear them laughing when she opened the door. Well, at least someone was happy! They looked up when she burst in. Burst being the only appropriate word to describe her entrance.

'Jack,' she exclaimed breathlessly—the run up three steep flights of stairs had taxed even her strength. 'I wonder if you would allow me to consult Mr Ritchie privately on—' and she improvised recklessly, waving Rice's account books at them '—on some problem I have discovered with Rice's arithmetic—or perhaps it's mine,' she finished wildly.

'Oh, I could help you with that, Pan,' said Jack, ever willing to demonstrate his new mathematical prowess.

'No, no, it's Mr Ritchie I really need.' Pandora's expression was so desperate that Ritchie, knowing that something was badly wrong, rose and walked over to her.

He said, his voice as quiet and calm as though he were gentling a frightened mare, 'I am only too willing to assist you, Miss Compton. Jack, go downstairs and ask the kitchen to send some lemonade and biscuits up to the schoolroom. Your sister is feeling a little under the weather.'

Jack opened his mouth to argue, but the look which Ritchie gave him was one he had come to recognise. It meant that he would brook no argument. Once Jack was gone, Ritchie took Pandora by the arm, still gentle, and sat her down. 'What is it, my dearest love?' he said. 'What has distressed you?'

'It's William,' she told him. 'He's behaving most peculiarly. Not at all like himself. I wonder if I ought to tell Sir John. He may be having one of his good days.'

Privately Ritchie wondered if Sir John ever really had a bad one.

'In what way is he being peculiar?'

'He's being so kind. After trying to bully me into marrying Roger Waters, he now says that he does not want me to marry Roger after all. He called him an oaf, implied that he was a jumped-up cit, and said that I ought to marry Lord Hadleigh instead. He wishes to invite him here. Then he offered to send me to London with Aunt Em to find a husband if Lord Hadleigh didn't suit. This is all so different from his old behaviour.

'Except that when I said that I wasn't happy with either of his proposals he…he…' she faltered. Could she really tell Ritchie what William had said about him?

'He what? Did he threaten you?' In the face of Pandora's very real distress Ritchie was beginning to feel distressed himself. Particularly since William had suggested his brother as a possible husband for Pandora. A wave of the most violent jealousy ran over him and nearly swamped his reason.

'Not really. He was unkind about you,' said Pandora. 'I had to remind him that you had saved him in the stable yard, and then he became reasonable again. In fact, he was almost in tears. Whatever can be the matter with him?'

All that Ritchie could find to say was—most inappropriately, he afterwards thought—'And you don't really wish to marry Lord Hadleigh?'

'Who? Oh, Lord Hadleigh. No, certainly not, after you he's a bit lightweight. Very handsome, of course, but that's not enough.'

She had no idea how much she had pleased Ritchie,

who had lived in the shadow of his brother's good looks all his life. No need to be jealous after all. The all-conquering Lord Hadleigh had failed to capture his darling's heart.

He thought that he might know what was wrong with William, but it was not something which he could yet share with Pandora. For some reason William was beginning to regret his alliance with the Waters—and he could not imagine what that reason was. It was plain to him that William was trying to move Pandora out of the Waters's orbit. He was also of the opinion that William had belatedly decided that honey might be more effective than gall in trying to bend Pandora to his will. All he had done by that was to succeed in confusing her.

He must answer her—but what was he to say? He did not want Pandora to leave Compton Place. On the other hand, if William was so anxious to make her do so, might it not be because he was concerned for her safety? Or was he concerned for his own? Perhaps for both reasons.

'I can't immediately fathom the reason for his behaviour,' he said, lying as usual. 'I'm relieved to learn that he doesn't wish you to marry Roger Waters—the *on dits* are that his reputation is not good.'

Pandora was too worried to notice that Ritchie had made a slip—how did he, the poor tutor, know what Roger Waters's reputation was?

'Well, I have good reason to know that—after the way he treated me. Since William didn't mind that then, why is he so exercised about Roger marrying me now?'

'I agree that is a puzzle. On the other hand, if he is prepared to treat you more kindly, that must make your life easier. Allow me to think about this for some time. And now let us open Rice's books and be examining them with serious expressions on our faces so that Jack will find us behaving irreproachably when he returns. I fear that he is getting to an age when he will begin to be suspicious of a man and a woman who are always manoeuvring to be alone.'

'This wasn't a manoeuvre, Ritchie. I really did wish to speak to you most urgently on a serious matter.'

He laughed gently at her indignant face. 'Now you know that, and I know that, but would an impartial observer of either sex believe us? I fear not.'

Pandora was mutinous. 'Then they must have nasty minds.'

'They're human, Pandora, as we are.'

'Sometimes I doubt that of you, Ritchie, you are so very good.'

'Alas, Pandora, I fear that I must correct you. I am not good at all. I am as sinful as the next man.'

'Well, if you are, then *I* must say that you make a good fist of trying not to be.'

Ritchie had never felt more of a hypocrite. Here he was with a false name and a false identity and like to put her half-brother into prison and do away with her and Jack's inheritance as well. Unless, of course, he compounded his villainy by somehow getting William off!

'The Gospel teaches us that we are all, to some extent, sinners,' was all that he could find to say in reply. Pandora's shining face told him that it was of no avail. He gave up. All that he could say to comfort himself was that his masquerade might soon be safely over.

And then what?

Chapter Eleven

William Compton did not know which way to turn. His life had become so wretched that for the first time he was compelled to admit that it was his own shortcomings which had brought him to this pass. This conclusion was of no help to him: it merely added to his misery.

He took himself to the stables and ordered George to saddle a not-too-frisky horse for him. Since Nero had turned on him he had become suspicious of every nag in the stables, even the ones only fit for novices and frightened women. He rode out alone, ignoring the warning which Roger Waters had given him and also ignoring Brodribb who had been living in a bog of misery ever since the Dark Avenger had frightened him so much that he had become a shadow of his old aggressive self.

Once he was out on the Downs William began to feel a little better. He did have the common sense to keep near the by-ways which led between the smaller villages, and it was when he was trotting along one of these that he met Lady Leominster in her open landau. She was being driven to Bayview, the home of Lady Larkin.

As soon as she saw William, she gave her driver an

imperious blow on his shoulder with her stick, shouting, 'Stop, man, stop,' with great vigour.

Oh, God, the old cow was going to start bullying him again! It was more than a fellow ought to be asked to endure. Like her unfortunate driver, however, he stopped and removed his hat.

'Lady Leominster, how pleasant to see you. You are still staying in the district?'

As usual Lady Leominster took no note of what the other party said to her. She had her own list of priorities and firmly kept to it, happen what would.

'Oh, I come upon you most apropos!' she roared at him. 'I have just remembered, this very morning, where and when I met your half-brother's bear-leader, Mr Ritchie. Pray tell me, sir, are you unaware of what the naughty fellow is up to, pretending to be a tutor? Or, perhaps, you sly thing, you already know that he is Major Richard Chancellor, a cavalryman in the Army, Bretford's younger son and Hadleigh's clever brother, come home from Spain to recover from his injuries. You've a fine catch for Miss Pandora there, you lucky dog—I suppose that's why you're mum. His bachelor uncle left him all his money and a fine old manor house to boot.'

William stared at her, his jaw dropping. 'Richard Chancellor, Hadleigh's brother…impossible,' he croaked. 'You must be mistaken. After all, you vouched for him being a tutor.'

Lady Leominster bridled like a turkey cock and raised haughty eyebrows at him.

'Now, now, young Compton, don't you try to put me down with that piece of information! I was told of him by a friend of a friend who I had to suppose was informing me correctly, and I never actually saw him myself. Besides, you know quite well that I never forget a face, or a fact. I'm famous for it. I was sure that I'd seen him before, but couldn't remember when. And I was right! I met him when he was a lad—he was an artful rogue then, and I don't suppose he's changed much since. He'd make a splendid brother-in-law for you—he'd keep you on the straight and narrow.'

William scarcely knew what he ought to say. Should he admit to knowing who Ritchie really was—or not? The lady was grinning triumphantly at him. If she were correct in her assumption, then what in blazes was Major Richard Chancellor—of whom even William had heard of as something of a hero—doing pretending to be a tutor? His ability to control that wretched beast Nero was suddenly explained. No miracle had occurred—the damned mountebank had simply been using his equestrian skills.

'I trust, Lady Leominster,' he said, as coolly as he could, 'that, seeing that I have not thought it fit to make public Major Chancellor's visit to Compton Place, that you will also see fit not to bruit the matter abroad. I should not wish it to appear that I have breached his confidence.'

The lady let out a merry trill. 'Of course, of course. I know when to keep a secret, none better. At some time in the future you will do me the honour of explaining this delightful mystery to me, but for the moment, mum's the word, eh? Drive on,' she roared at the coachman. 'Give my regards to Major Chancellor and to your pretty sister,' were the last words William heard from her while her landau disappeared up the by-way.

Inwardly William was seething. What the devil was all that about? What explanation could there possibly be for Chancellor's presence as a poverty-stricken tutor? Oh, he had been a good one, no doubt of that, the improvement in young Jack over the summer had been remarkable. Nevertheless, once he reached home again, he would have the damned mountebank sent for immediately. He could only hope that when the explanation came it would be sufficient to make up for the shock which the old cow had just given him.

It was not the only shock which he was to receive that afternoon. He was ambling along, minding his own business on the road which ran by Larkin's Wood, when, for the second time in a fortnight, he was thrown from his horse. A shot had been fired from the trees, a shot which took the hat off his head and frightened Crusoe into the bargain. He bolted madly down the by-way, having first shaken William off his offended back.

'What the devil!' exclaimed William, picking himself up and trudging back to where his hat lay…to find that there was a bullet hole in it. Either the marksman had aimed at his head and hit his hat instead—or the hat had been his chosen target. Whoever had fired at him must have done so at close range and, once he had missed—or hit—as the case might be, he had presumably run away through the trees because William could detect no signs of anyone having been present there.

Shocked and bruised, he walked towards Crusoe who, having recovered from *his* shock, had slowed to a stop and was now standing placidly waiting for him over two hundred yards away.

What in the world was coming over everything? The fates themselves seemed to be conspiring against William Compton. Or had Roger Waters's threat been a serious one? If so, then he was in deep water, very deep water, indeed. It did not bear thinking of that a man could not ride safely through the sweet Sussex countryside.

Well, one thing was sure, once he was safely home again he would send for that lying swine Chancellor and let him know what William Compton thought of him!

* * *

Ritchie and Pandora had been deep in Rice's books when Jack returned, quite disappointed to find them behaving themselves. He still had a faint hope that, somehow, Mr Ritchie might yet be able to marry Pandora, thus keeping him in the family. He could be both his brother-in-law *and* his tutor, Jack told himself optimistically.

The lemonade and biscuits arrived shortly after Jack and were greatly enjoyed by the three of them since it gave Pandora an excuse to remain with Ritchie. After their little snack she persuaded him to allow her to stay for the rest of Jack's lesson, giving as an excuse that her mathematical skills were not so good as she might wish.

'Girls don't need them,' Jack told her scornfully.

'Now, Jack,' said Ritchie. 'If Miss Pandora wishes to sharpen her numbering, who are we to deter her? I must warn her, however, that I shall be as severe in keeping her nose to the grindstone as I am with you.'

So he was. Pandora found his teaching as invigorating as Jack did, and she could see at once why Jack's education had progressed so rapidly since Ritchie's arrival.

At last, regretfully, the lesson came to an end, and Pandora left them, clutching Rice's books to her heart and now able to check them more quickly and accurately than she had ever done before.

Ritchie watched her leave. The afternoon light always seemed to dim a little when she was not with him. He and Jack continued to work together until Galpin arrived to inform Ritchie that Mr William wanted to see him at once. 'In the library,' he said, ' and I ought to warn you that he's in a rare old taking.'

'I'll leave at once then,' Ritchie said, wondering what bee could be buzzing so insistently round William Compton's empty head that his presence was demanded at such short notice.

He was soon to find out.

William was seated behind the battered desk, his face one frown. Since this was his normal expression when talking to his half-brother's tutor, that alone did not warn Ritchie of what was coming.

'So there you are,' William exclaimed as though he had been compelled to wait for half an hour for Ritchie to arrive rather than a few minutes. 'I have some urgent questions to ask of you, and by God I want some civil and truthful answers. That silly old bitch, her lunatic Ladyship of Leominster, has been twitting me this afternoon on the grounds that you are not Mr Edward Ritchie, a poverty-stricken tutor, at all but are, on the contrary, one Major Richard Chancellor, cavalryman, Hadfield's brother and damned nearly as rich as he is. If she is correct, what the devil are you doing in my home, pretending to be someone you are not?'

Ritchie's worst fears when he had set eyes on Lady Leominster the other day had come back to haunt him— nay, to trip him up. What to say? How to extricate himself successfully from this pickle without compromising his mission?

'It's a long and complicated story,' he began, trying to give himself time to come up with something halfway convincing.

'Oh, God,' moaned William who had never previously invoked the deity quite so often, 'try to make it short. One way or another I've had a damned unpleasant afternoon.'

'It would be difficult to make it short, but I'll try. I was bored, you see, when I was sent home after being wounded in Spain—'

'Never tell me that you're one of our heroes,' wailed William. 'That silly old woman hinted as much.'

'It's not my heroism I am telling you about,' replied

Ritchie, grateful for any diversion, however temporary, which would give him time to improvise, 'but of my boredom. Civilian life is so dull, you see, and I grew tired of pushing a pen in Whitehall…'

'So you came to push a pen in Sussex and bear-lead my brother into the bargain. That's the most unlikely story I ever heard. Do go on, time's wasting—'

'It wouldn't if you didn't keep interrupting me,' said Ritchie with a self-righteous smirk which he thought might annoy William to the point of losing his self-control. He had heard of people gnashing their teeth, but had never seen anyone do so. He thought that William was about to begin.

William's patience finally cracked. The strain he was under now that he knew that Roger Waters was threatening him, added to his fear that at any moment he might be in trouble, not merely for smuggling, but for committing treason, was compounded not only by the apparent attempt on his life, but also by the posturing of the damned mountebank who had given that silly old woman the chance to twit him.

He banged both fists on the table before dropping his head into his hands and covering his face with them. He thought that, if he had to listen to one more evasive answer, his tottering reason might collapse altogether leaving him fit only for a madhouse.

Ritchie said nothing. He simply stood perfectly still. He had been right: William was on the point of nervous collapse. With luck he might lose his self-control completely and then who knew what might happen next? He was not proud of himself for pushing William to this extremity by his prevarication, but he had no other option if he were to save the poor fool from the consequences of his folly.

William at last lifted his head. Tears were running

down his face. Ritchie's remained impassive, non-judgemental and totally sane, a reproach to him.

'You can have no notion,' William said at last, his voice blurred, 'of what I am going through. To cap everything, there was an attack on my life this afternoon. I was shot at from ambush. I am like to be in the dock at the Old Bailey, being tried for treason if things go wrong, and you stand there fooling with me and I don't know what the devil to say to you. You don't know, you cannot know, of my terrible situation. I only know that I have no idea what to do next, nor do I know of anyone who might be able to help me…'

'Tell me,' urged Ritchie. 'Tell me why anyone should wish to shoot you, what your terrible situation is and why you are like to be tried at the Old Bailey.'

'Tell you?' asked William. 'Why should I? How can *you* help me?'

Ritchie was mentally improvising as rapidly as he had ever done in his difficult time with the guerrillas in Spain. It was essential that William confide in him before he revealed even a part of the truth of his presence at Compton Place to him.

'Why not?' Ritchie said as though he were talking to some green junior officer who was displaying cowardice in the face of the enemy. He leaned forward, both his hands grasping the table edge, and turned his eyes hard on William's. He had seen mesmerists at work with their patients and knew that a fixed gaze and a repetitive phrase used again and again with absolute conviction could compel their patient to reveal their secret fears and wishes—could even make them behave in a particular fashion.

'Why not, eh, William? Why not? Tell me that. Why not? Why not?'

This trick had been successful for Ritchie before and it

was successful now. With men who were not so far gone a swinging watch was often needed as well as the voice. It was not necessary here.

His face working, William choked briefly, but his eyes remained fixed on Ritchie's, so compelling were they, and once his choking was over, out it all came. How his attempt to make money by gambling had ended in him losing what little money he had, and how the debts which had followed his frenzied efforts to recoup his losses had caused him to fall into the toils of the Waters, father and son.

'I didn't know that they were selling guineas to the enemy. I would never have joined with them if I had known that, never. Bringing in drink and tobacco is one thing, helping Boney to fight his wars is quite another. It's treason, you can swing for treason, and Compton Place would go to the Crown, and we've lived here since the Conquest, and between my father's folly and mine we are like to lose it.'

He began to do something which Ritchie had seen the distraught do before; sway and rock in his chair, moaning something incomprehensible the while.

Ritchie, trying to keep his voice as calm as possible, asked William a question of which he had already worked out the answer, but it was essential that William should confess everything to him, 'But why are they threatening you so severely, Compton? Why?'

'Because when I told them I wanted to withdraw from their syndicate they laughed and said that I was too involved for them to let me go. I was stupid enough to attempt to threaten them by saying that, if they didn't agree to what I asked, I would inform the Home Office or the Lord Lieutenant of the county of their activities. They then threatened me with death if I attempted to do any such thing. Since I know that they have already murdered others for attempting to cheat them, or threatening to withdraw, I knew that they meant what they said.

'They also told me that I was to report to the beach at the next landing and help with the loading and unloading or it would be the worse for me.'

He began to sway about and wring his hands. 'Now I don't know what to do.'

'Why not inform the authorities and ask them to protect you?'

'Because some of them are in the pay of the Waters— or so they told me—and I don't know who they are. I could be signing my death warrant if I haven't signed it already. Oh, God, is there no one who can help me?'

'Why not try me?' Ritchie said gently. 'Why not ask me for help?'

He was beginning to see a way out for the unhappy wretch before him. If William told him all that he knew, and co-operated with him, Sadler and the authorities, then he would almost certainly escape the full power of the law being turned on him. With luck he might escape being punished by the authorities or being shot by the Waters if he tried to defy them on his own.

'You?' exclaimed William. 'Why should I ask *you* to help me?'

'Well, since you have already confessed to enough to allow me to go to the nearest Justice of the Peace and ask him to swear a warrant for your arrest, it would be sensible of you to assume that I am not immediately off to him for some very good reason. You could also assume that my presence in your home might be related to this wretched business in which you have become enmeshed.'

'Might it?' queried William, looking baffled. 'All I

know of you is that you are running around under a false name—which is not exactly encouraging.'

'Not entirely false,' Ritchie told him. 'Although I was christened Richard, I have been known as Ritchie since I was a babe in arms, and Edward *is* my second name. It's only the last bit which has conveniently disappeared,' he ended in as engaging and confiding a tone as he could summon up.

His coolness began to infect William, who had exchanged shivering and shaking for staring at his half-brother's tutor who suddenly seemed to have acquired the ability to dominate him in no uncertain fashion.

'Let me,' said Ritchie, 'as I told you at the beginning of this interview, take matters slowly. I am here to discover the details of this cursed venture into treason which the Waters have been running for the past few years. When I say I am here, I mean that I am here officially…'

'*Major* Richard Chancellor, of course,' William was moaning again.

'Of course. I see that you are beginning to understand me. I am Major Chancellor of the Fourteenth Light Dragoons, invalided home as Lady Leominster correctly reported, and sent here by Lord Sidmouth to discover who were the organisers of the trade in guineas, how they carried it out, where the contraband was landed and the coins sent on.

'You told me that you had been tricked over the business with the guineas. I am inclined to believe you as you are weak, but not wicked. In consequence I can offer you the chance to redeem, as well as save yourself, by helping me to trap those who can only be described as traitors.'

'How long have you known that the Waters and I were engaged in running contraband?' asked William. 'Were you told beforehand that we were?'

'No, I was not—and that will help to save you, but only if you do as I ask, to the letter. I discovered the details of the Waters's treasonable dealing after I came here. I was traitor hunting, not fossil hunting.'

He did not add, and the Dark Avenger did not walk in vain, for the less that William knew at the moment, the better.

'How do I know that you are telling me the truth?'

'You don't. I can tell you that I love your half-sister and therefore would not wish to be instrumental in sending you to the gallows. Your common sense should inform you that my false identity was a means of getting me into the district without anyone guessing what I was up to. I have only told you because I think that, between us, we can scotch, if not kill, the snakes who are betraying me and my soldiers to the enemy for filthy lucre.'

The bit about the snakes was a quotation from Will Shakespeare of Stratford, Ritchie's hero, but William was too unlettered to recognise it. Ritchie could only conclude that the second Mrs Compton had been a clever woman, Pandora and Jack were so different from William.

'A further question,' he added. 'How much does Sir John know of all this?'

'Very little, I think,' replied William.

'You think, but you don't know.'

Ritchie was beginning to wonder whether someone in the district had informed the Home Office and might even have suggested that a spy at Compton Place would be well positioned to discover exactly what was going on. Might it be that Sir John was happy to turn a blind eye to the smuggling of drink, tobacco and luxury goods, but drew the line at the sale of gold?

Had Sidmouth not mentioned the sale of the guineas to him because he needed to have someone on the spot who had gone there with no preconceived notions of what he might find?

'My grandfather and I rarely speak to one another,' William said slowly. 'He disapproves of me, as he disapproved of my father. He would certainly never confide in me even if he had suspected what was going on.'

That made sense, Ritchie thought. He fixed William with a cold eye and using his most severe voice, said, 'I will now tell you exactly what I wish you to do. Listen to me most carefully, for we shall not speak of this again. Disobey me in any way and I shall have no hesitation in throwing you to the wolves of the law. On the other hand, if you co-operate with me to the utmost, I shall do everything in my power to ensure that you escape punishment—even if you do not deserve any such favour.

'You will first tell me all that you know of this wretched business and then I will tell you exactly what I wish you to do. If you don't do as I ask—well, you know what the outcome will be. Do you understand me?'

William muttered, 'Yes,' and nodded a reluctant head before obeying the dominant man before him.

When he had finished his recital Ritchie began to speak rapidly and surely to him after the fashion which he had always used with his juniors in the field, his voice carrying a conviction and his eyes a power which held the wastrel before him spellbound, so much so that when he had finished William muttered, 'I suppose that as a further act of good faith I ought to tell you that there are a large number of kegs containing brandy in the crypt at Little Compton church—the one which no longer has an incumbent. They came in with the last consignment but I have not yet had time to move them on, since next week's consignment is more important.'

'Excellent,' said Ritchie. 'The Excisemen can shift that

secretly, so that no one but them and us know that it has gone—and you will get the credit for that... Now I will leave you. If you can think of anything further which you wish to tell me, then I shall be pleased to hear it.'

William nodded again and watched Ritchie—his unlikely would-be saviour—walk to the door where he turned to say, 'By the by, you had better be even nastier than ever to me over the next week so that no one may suspect that we are fellow conspirators. Reassure the Waters that you have changed your mind, have no intention of breaking away, and will be happy to join them on the beach. They will think that their attempts to intimidate you have succeeded and will therefore not be so wary as they ought to be.'

His hearer moaned to himself at the thought of trying to convince the pair of sharks who had been manipulating him for the past year that he was telling them the truth—his only consolation being that he might now have the chance to manipulate them!

When Ritchie returned to the schoolroom he found Pandora there again, waiting for him. She looked up at him, and exclaimed, 'Oh, dear, was William so very tiresome? You look quite done-up.'

Her ability to read him was almost frightening, Ritchie thought. He was, indeed, feeling tired, tired to the bone. By rights he should still have been convalescing in London, taking things easy. Instead he was trapped in the middle of a giant conspiracy, trying to scotch it, pretending that he was something which he was not, and now his task had been made much more difficult because he was attempting to save the worthless half-brother of the woman he loved.

'Not more than usual,' he told her, smiling a little, 'you know William.'

'Sometimes I think that I don't,' was Pandora's answer to that. 'He seems to have such a collection of bees buzzing in his empty head that I never know which one of them is going to attack me next!' Not for the first time, and quite separately, Pandora was echoing something which Ritchie had already thought.

This lively piece of unnatural natural history amused Jack, who said dismissively, 'Oh, William's a nodcock, Pan—let it go at that.'

'A nodcock who has a certain power over us all, more's the pity,' she told him severely.

'Only if Grandfather dies,' retorted Jack, 'and who knows what kind of will he has made—until he dies, that is.'

'William is the heir, after all.'

'But heirs don't always inherit everything, do they, Mr Ritchie?'

'It depends on whether the estate is entailed in the male line,' Ritchie told him.

'There's no entail, that I do know,' said Pandora, suddenly made grave by the thought of her grandfather's death. 'But one must suppose that, since William will inherit the title, what is left of the estate will go to him.'

'True,' Ritchie said. 'On the other hand…' and he was thinking of the Luck of the Comptons which, rightly or wrongly, the old man had given to him '…he may make some dispositions which, while giving William something, would not give him all.'

'Oh, you know so much,' Pandora said, recovering her normal jollity, 'that it is a great pity that you are only a tutor. Except that you are a very good tutor.'

'The best,' Jack told her. 'He makes everything so interesting. Today we were doing King Alfred and the cakes. Do you know that story, Pan? Mr Ritchie acted all the parts. He was very good as the peasant woman who scolded the king because he let them burn. He ought to be on the stage.'

To Pandora's surprise Ritchie's face darkened a little when Jack said that, and he quickly turned the conversation towards other matters—which was strange, seeing that Jack had been complimenting him. It was only afterwards when she was making her way down the backstairs so that William should not guess where she had been spending her time that Pandora thought of something else.

If Ritchie possessed the talents of an actor, could it be that he had been pretending to be unable to ride? The morning after he had tamed Nero she had overheard George talking to Bragg, saying that only a master equestrian could have tamed the stallion so easily. Bragg had suggested that in a tight corner a man might do things which were otherwise beyond his compass. George had denied this vehemently, whereupon Bragg had shrugged his shoulders and walked away, refusing to argue with him further.

But suppose that Ritchie *were* a master rider, what would that mean? Because, if he were, the worrying thing would be that this was not the only deception he was practising since he possessed spectacles which also perpetuated a pretence—that he was a short-sighted schoolmaster. The real mystery, if her suspicions proved to be true, was why he should need to deceive them all from Sir John downwards.

Pandora shook her head to clear it. She must be wrong. George must be wrong and the bees from William's head were buzzing in hers if she really believed that Ritchie was something quite other than what he appeared to be—

a good, quiet scholar who had brought life and joy into Jack's life and love into hers.

She found Aunt Em in the drawing room at her eternal canvas work. Pandora often thought that her own life would be so much easier if that were all she needed to think about. Aunt Em, though, was obviously aware of all that was going on for she took one look at Pandora and half-echoed what she had said to Ritchie. 'Is all well with you, my dear? You look rather paler than usual.'

'Oh, nothing's wrong, Aunt. I have just been up to the schoolroom and I have reason to believe that William has been bullying Mr Ritchie again. He really is the outside of enough. We shall lose him if William is not careful and that would be very bad for Jack.'

Aunt Em put her work down. 'There I must agree with you, my dear. A most worthy young man. We are lucky to have him. Why, even the servants like him—particularly since he saved William's life. I hate to say it, but your half-brother is really a most ungrateful young man if he has begun to tease Mr Ritchie again!'

Aunt Em was even more angry that evening when they all sat down to dinner—it was one of the nights on which Ritchie and Jack were invited—and William immediately began to hector poor Mr Ritchie about his appearance again. So much so that, on seeing Mr Ritchie's meek head bowing over his plate as this torrent of words cascaded over him, she exclaimed, 'William, I must ask you to refrain from upbraiding poor Mr Ritchie in public. If you feel compelled to do so, at least perform that function in decent privacy, except that since Mr Ritchie's conduct has been exceptional since he arrived here, I cannot believe that you have anything to reproach him with!'

William, goaded by this attack when all that he was

doing was obey Ritchie's orders, bellowed at her, 'It's not his conduct of which I complain, Aunt, it's his clothing.'

'That is the second time you have attacked him on this point,' she retorted severely, 'and any decent person's answer would be that if you wish him to be more *à point* you must raise his salary. And that is enough of that or I shall order my dinner to be served in my room!'

William did not know who to glare at the hardest, Ritchie for landing him in this plight, or Aunt Em for defying him so roundly.

'You know that I can't afford to pay him any more,' he mumbled at last.

'In that case, be quiet,' was her fierce response.

Ritchie was perhaps the most uncomfortable person at the table. William was scarlet in the face, Aunt Em was bridling, Jack was bristling, Pandora was looking daggers and he was feeling an acute shame that his attempts to save William were causing such embarrassment.

Fortunately, that was all. The rest of the meal passed in deadly silence. At the end of it William rose, and said, 'I would like a private word with you in the library, Pandora, if you would be so good.'

His manner was so conciliatory that the whole table, and Pandora in particular, stared at him on disbelief.

'Certainly, William,' she said faintly. 'I will accompany you.'

'Excellent,' he said with a little bow which left Pandora staring at him even harder and Jack guffawing.

'You will take tea with me in the drawing room,' Aunt Em ordered Ritchie. 'Where I will try to reassure you that some members of the Compton family do possess a modicum of good breeding. Jack will accompany us. He needs to learn the little niceties of life.'

'Very true,' agreed Ritchie, relieved that for a short

period at least he might not need to deceive and trick all those around him.

Alas, once she had cornered him in the drawing room, Aunt Em began to cross-question him about his family. He answered her by describing them accurately, but by giving them all different names. His twin, Russell, became Francis. His father was translated from peer to the irascible incumbent of a small parish in Oxfordshire which was actually quite near to one of the Chancellor family's mansions. His mother, who was known for her interest in various charities, became the wife who walked round the parish dispensing tea, sympathy and various articles of cast-off clothing.

If he not been unhappy at having to practise such deceptions on the kind old lady, he would have been amused at his own inventiveness. Fortunately it was not long before Pandora rejoined them.

'William,' she told them, 'says, of all things, that he needs an early night. I cannot remember when he last retired before the small hours! What's more, was I the only person at table to notice that he drank very little at dinner and when old Galpin offered him his port at the end of the meal he refused it? Do you think he's ill?' she appealed to her aunt.

'He seemed very much his usual self at dinner,' said Aunt Em severely, 'but yes, I did note that he drank very little. Most unusual and most odd.'

Ritchie knew why William had been so abstinent. It was one of the commands which he had given him. 'A man in drink,' he had told him severely, 'frequently says more than he should. Until after next Friday week you must forgo it as much as possible so that you may not forget yourself.'

'But that would look most strange,' began William, 'seeing that I am usually a heavy drinker.'

'Not at all—explain that you have a flux and the doctor has advised you to avoid all strong liquor until you are well again. That should do the trick.'

One way or another he would try to reform his future brother-in-law. It might be a hopeless task, but the wretched creature had become part of his duty. He owed it to the old man upstairs, to Pandora, Jack and gallant little Aunt Em to at least make an effort to persuade the heir to Compton Place to behave rather better than he had been doing since he came of age.

Later, after Jack had retired to bed with a copy of *Robinson Crusoe* which Ritchie had found in the half-ruined library, he was sitting at the schoolroom table, a map of Sussex before him, when Pandora burst in and plumped herself down in the room's only armchair.

'No one knows that I am here,' she explained, 'so do not have the regal fantods over my presence. William has retired, as has Aunt Em, and I suppose that Jack has, too. We may enjoy ourselves in peace. In any case, I came up the backstairs. I have never used them so often in all my life. I really do need to talk to you—you are the only person of sense that I know.'

She ran down at last. Ritchie surveyed her with fond amusement. He would not have her otherwise than the downright creature that she was. Her honesty and her goodness oozed from every pore, which made his deception of her even more of a reproach to him.

'Now, Miss Compton,' he said gravely, 'tell me what it is that brings you here so urgently.'

'William,' she said urgently. 'It's William. He's madder than ever. In one breath he's so hatefully rude to you that I am ashamed to be related to him. As, for example, at dinner this evening. In the next breath he's suggesting to me that I should make you more at home here! That it would be a good thing for me to converse with a man of sense such as you appear to be. I ask you. Much more of this and I shall begin to think that he's lighter in the attic than Grandfather.'

Not so, thought Ritchie wearily. He's just an impatient fool who has suddenly realised that I am something of a catch and, that being so, it might not be a bad thing for you to catch me before I am attracted to anyone else. Why he couldn't have waited to make this suggestion until the smuggling business is safely over, I can't imagine.

Jack's right. The man's a nodcock and my—and his— life might depend on him not behaving like one when we reach *point non plus*.

Of course, he said nothing of this to Pandora, merely tried to comfort her by pointing out that, by all accounts, capricious had been William's middle name ever since he had been born.

'I know,' she said, her face sad. 'I sometimes think that if he really had to suffer in some way, or face the grim facts of what our heritage at Compton Place has descended to, he might change. Do not tell me that I am supposing the impossible, but if he does not mend his ways soon then our family will have no other course left but to leave the house and lands where we have lived for nearly six hundred years. Whatever would the Dark Avenger have to say to that!''

Ritchie could not, in honesty, reassure her. He could only hope that the events which he had set in motion would prevent part of the ruin which might yet descend on the Comptons by saving William from the gallows and their estates from being sequestrated by the Crown.

In the meantime he said gently, 'My dearest girl, we can none of us foretell the future and like your namesake, Pandora, we can only hope. It would be unhelpful to offer you the old adage, "What can't be cured must be endured", but there is a great, if unpalatable, truth in it. Now try to forget William for a little and live your own life.'

Impulsively Pandora leaned forward and kissed him. 'You are so wise, Ritchie. Why can't William be more like you?'

There was no answer he could make to that, other than to hold her gently away from him and say—it broke his heart to do so—'That kiss was against the rules, my dear girl. We must behave ourselves and if you were to do it again, then I could not answer for the consequences.'

Her answer to that was to kiss him again, her eyes shining with love and mirth combined.

'Oh, damn the consequences, Ritchie, my heart's darling. I am so tired of being good. I think that I would prefer to be wicked for a change.'

'Siren, to tempt me so!' he exclaimed hoarsely. 'Even Odysseus, whom the first sirens tempted so long ago, could not have resisted you—and nor can I!' And she was in his arms and he was kissing her. The passion which they were feeling was even stronger and more fulfilling than anything which either of them might previously have imagined, or hoped for.

To Pandora it was as though a great gale were sweeping her away. She was at the heart of the storm, in her lover's arms and time and chance meant nothing to her, only the magic of the moment. She had not dreamed that the power of their coming together would be so strong. She wished both to conquer and to surrender. To conquer by compelling him to love her in the fullest sense of the word and to surrender by offering herself to him completely, and damn all the rules of conduct which had kept her virgin and chaste for so long.

Thought had gone, words had gone, the body was all, had not Ritchie who, after all, was the more experienced of the two, and who had lived his life by strict rules of conduct which most men of his generation ignored, remembered suddenly who and what he was.

If they had been a pair of the lads and lasses who roamed the countryside, satisfying themselves in the woods, or the unconsidered birds who sang in the trees, or Nero, the stallion, about to mount his mare, then he would not have drawn back, groaning, his whole body one vast ache which could only be soothed by the nymph in his arms.

'No,' he gasped. 'We must stop. Your honour and mine demand it. I must not ruin you—not least because I must not destroy my own honour by taking advantage of my love who is as yet untried and virgin. To do so would make me no better than William and Roger Waters and would leave you my victim.'

'Oh, you should be a clergyman after all,' wailed Pandora. 'Your sermons make you worthy of a bishopric. If I tell you that all I want is you, and you alone, why should you draw back at the very last fence of all and leave us both gasping for what we may not have—but so nearly achieved?'

'Because when we stand at the altar I would wish you to be my virgin bride. No pretence must stain our vows. I know that to behave ourselves is hard but if we do we may look the world in the eye.'

'Does that mean that you are asking me to marry you?'

'No more and no less, and now my darling Amazon, let us sit down and recover ourselves before we each retire to our separate beds knowing that before long we may be able to share one—honourably.'

'And I may tell William and Aunt Em and Jack, of course, that we are to be married?'

'Not yet, my darling. I would wish to propose to you in proper form by asking for Sir John's permission first and, for some most particular private reasons, I do not wish to do that yet.'

Ritchie had not meant to ask her to marry him so precipitately, but in the throes of thwarted passion the words had been wrenched from him and he could not take them back—however unwise he had been in uttering them when wisdom told him that he ought to wait until his mission was over.

He kissed her gently on the forehead. 'So we must be good, for I do not think the time to speak to Sir John will be long in coming.'

'In that case,' declaimed Pandora grandly, 'wickedness must wait a little, although I suppose once we are married what was wicked when we were single will become sanctified. Don't you find that odd?'

What Ritchie did find was that, once again, Pandora had shown that she had a mind as sharp as a knife. His only answer was an evasive one. 'We must obey society's rules,' he told her, 'because they are designed to prevent us from falling back into savagery, and that would never do.'

'Another little sermon,' mocked Pandora, but her eyes were loving. 'And now I must sneak down the backstairs again. I cannot tell you how much I long for the day when we are publicly put to bed and the backstairs are banished forever.'

He gave her another chaste kiss for that and they parted. Pandora reached her room without being seen and Ritchie retired to his hard bed. Each of them dreamed of the other and the day when they might be together as man and wife.

Chapter Twelve

To most of the inhabitants of Compton Place a week had never seemed so long. Outwardly life went on as it always did: beneath the surface, things were very different.

On Sunday the Rector delivered himself of a lengthy sermon about the necessity to lay up treasure in heaven and not on earth, apparently unaware that in the crypt of one of the nearby churches a good deal of earthly treasure had been stored by those who were nodding their heads in silent agreement with him. Only Ritchie laughed inwardly at the hidden and unintended joke. On the other hand, he thought afterwards, it was quite possible that the Rector knew quite well what was going on to the extent that he was buying all his brandy from the Gentlemen.

What men said—even clergymen—and what they did were two quite different things, as Ritchie had often observed.

On Monday Jem Sadler arrived in the stable yard again and exchanged courtesies with Bragg. Bragg, of course, had been told by Ritchie of the plans he had laid down for William and himself to follow on the Friday which would see the latest consignment of contraband arrive and the guineas brought from the City by Roger Waters be made ready for sending to France. Sadler had not been informed by Ritchie of Bragg's true identity and was careful in what he said before him since he was not sure whether Bragg had now been enrolled on the side of the smugglers.

'What brings you here?' asked George, emerging from Nero's former stall carrying an empty bucket. 'Anything in particular? Trouble last night, was there?'

'Not that I know of,' said Sadler cheerfully. 'Young Compton here, is he?'

'Depends which young Compton, you mean,' muttered George. 'Mr William is over at the Waters's and Master Jack is playing cricket with his tutor and half of the stable lads.'

'Cricket, eh,' smiled Sadler. 'Mind if I take a look?'

'Up to you,' mumbled George.

'Well, seeing Mr William's not here, my journey won't be wasted if I have the chance to watch a bit of fun,' and to Bragg's secret amusement, for he was certain that it was really Ritchie to whom Sadler wished to speak, he strolled off in the direction of the lower lawn, leaving a disgruntled George to care for his horse.

Fortunately for Sadler he arrived at a pause in the game when the drinks tray had arrived from the kitchen and was able to speak to Ritchie without needing to invent an excuse for doing so.

'I see you believe in play as well as work, Mr Ritchie,' he said, loud enough for those standing around him to hear what he was saying.

'Depends on the kind of play,' was Ritchie's cheerful response. 'Jack,' he called, 'run to the kitchen and ask Cook to send Mr Sadler a mug of ale by your good self.'

This useful ploy enabled him to get rid of Jack long enough to have a private conversation with Sadler.

'The Yeomanry have taken your advice seriously and will be out in force on Friday night,' Sadler told him. 'Seems that the Lord Lieutenant had a despatch from the Home Office telling him that one of their men was in the area and that any information he might send them must be taken seriously. I've told no one of your name and where you're stationed in case those in the pay of the Gentlemen should try to do for you.'

'Thank you for that, Sadler, and for being a go-between with the Yeomanry for me. I have also discovered that a large consignment of brandy is at present stored in the crypt of Little Compton church awaiting collection—I suggest that something is done about that immediately.'

'Thank you, sir. My masters will be pleased to confiscate it immediately. One further thing I do have to ask you is this: Is Mr William Compton involved in this wretched business?'

'Now that I do not yet know, but hope to do so by Friday.'

Sadler, not sure how truthful his man was being, said, 'It seems that the authorities both here and in the City were sure that the Waters were behind this latest outbreak of smuggling on the South Coast, but until now have had no real evidence which they could use against them. It might be a different matter on Friday.'

'One can only hope so. Now, Sadler, here's Jack with your ale. Shall we drink a toast, the three of us—Jack and I aren't drinking liquor, but let's hope that lemonade will do. Death to all traitors and down with Boney, eh?'

'Splendid,' said Jack eagerly. 'Next time may I have some ale instead of this weak stuff? The other fellows I've met lately all seem to be allowed it.'

'Not yet,' Ritchie told him, winking at Sadler. 'It would spoil your wind, you see. Now let's start the game again. Your turn to bowl, Jack. Try and work the twister in without your victim seeing what you're doing.'

'Back to play, or work,' grinned Sadler. 'Tell Mr Compton I was sorry to miss him, but I was only here to report that all's quiet. Good day to you both—I'll go when I've seen the young master's twister.'

So he did. Ritchie, amused at the man's evident pleasure at being part of a conspiracy which involved such high-ranking personages as the Lord Lieutenant, played cricket a little more savagely than usual, treating his victims to a display of such hard-hitting excellence that Jack told him he ought to be a member of the Marylebone Club.

Which Ritchie was—but he couldn't inform Jack of that!

Nor could he tell him that the matter of trapping the traitors was now in train and that the Gentlemen would find the Yeomanry ready to ambush them on Friday. Ritchie hoped that their captain would have the sense to remain in hiding until the landing of the consignment began, thus putting the guilt of those engaged in smuggling contraband and selling guineas beyond a doubt.

In the meantime there was a game to play and later he would need to prop William up again lest he prove unable to perform his duty on Friday night.

'There seems to be no doubt,' Roger Waters told his father that night after he had received an urgent letter from London, 'that the Home Office has a spy here. It's useful to know that, but the devil of it is that my informant hasn't the slightest notion who he might be. All he can discover is that only Sidmouth knows who he is, and one thing about Sidmouth is that he don't talk.'

'So you've no clue at all as to who he might be,' said his father, lighting his pipe.

Roger shook his head. 'He could be anybody—gentle or simple. My bet is that he's one of those former Bow Street Runners, thrown out for shady practices, whom the Home Office often uses to spy out the land. Except that I would have thought that a London fellow would stand out a mile among Sussex rustics.'

'Someone we might not suspect, then?'

'Exactly.'

For one brief moment Roger thought of Mr Edward Ritchie of the surprising horsemanship, but the man was so much the mild scholar otherwise that such a suspicion seemed absurd.

He was not to think that on the afternoon before the Friday consignment was due to take place when he met Lady Leominster out on one of her afternoon excursions. He had been returning from Compton Place where he had been savaging William Compton in an attempt to bring the silly ass up to scratch. When he first saw Lady Leominster his first reaction was one of impatience that he must submit to the verbal witlessness of the old trout.

He was not to think that for long.

'So happy to see you,' she carolled at him. 'I thought that I might miss enjoying your company—even if for only a few moments—I'm off to town tomorrow. I can't say that I've found much to entertain me on this visit to Sussex—except, of course, having come across Ritchie Chancellor playing the greasy usher at Compton Place, goodness knows why.'

'Ritchie Chancellor?' echoed Roger.

'Yes, Ritchie Chancellor, you must surely have heard of *him*, Major Richard Chancellor, Hadleigh's younger brother. Perhaps *you* can inform me why he's engaged on such an odd masquerade. He can't be wanting the money—that uncle of his left him in a very warm position indeed, and besides that rumour has it that he was a bit of a high-flyer in the Peninsula—or so I am led to believe. A cavalryman, of course.'

'Of course,' Roger echoed again, apparently witlessly, but actually seething with rage and a sudden understanding of what the so-called 'Mr Ritchie' was probably up to if he needed to conceal his true identity while at Compton Place.

'Oh, dear,' cried the lady suddenly. 'I shouldn't have told you all that, should I? He might not want it known. Do you think he's after the Compton gel? Perhaps not, but there again those quiet young men often go after the lively lasses. Oh, well, if you can't tell me what he's up to, then that's that. I'll probably winkle it out of his brother when I get back to town.'

She was so busy talking that she failed to notice how quiet Mr Roger Waters had suddenly gone. She struck her driver one of her favourite blows and was carried away in an aura in which fatuity and self-satisfaction were grotesquely combined.

Roger Waters, left behind on his horse, staring after her, was asking himself a series of urgent questions.

Item: was Mr Edward Ritchie, the humble tutor, Sidmouth's spy?

Item: if so, how much did he know?

Item: had he discovered that the Waters were behind the present wave of smuggling on the Sussex coast?

Item: if he were Sidmouth's spy, however much, or

little, he might know, what steps should he and his father take?

Item: he would, himself, recommend the most drastic treatment.

Item: had that old idiot Sir John Compton sent for him?

Item: did William Compton know that Ritchie was Sidmouth's spy?

Item: if so, he should be dealt with, too. Sir John was too senile to trouble with.

Item: ...

At this point Roger gave up and decided that perhaps the best thing of all would be to do nothing—for the time being—other than to take the utmost care when the next consignment arrived.

His father, when Roger had returned home, was not so sanguine.

'Let's kill the snake,' he ordered bluntly. 'Draw its fangs. I'll order Joss to kill him. He goes out every afternoon with that lad. An accident can be arranged.'

'But suppose Ritchie isn't Sidmouth's spy—is just amusing himself?'

'So?' said Henry Waters. 'What of that? Better be safe than sorry—and ridding the world of yet another useless aristocrat is to do something of a favour for it! Best to take no chances.'

While Roger Waters was running contraband for the money it brought them, his father, who had been a Radical in his youth, was selling guineas to Napoleon to support him and the possibility that, if he won, there might be a new order in Britain; where merit would be all and a man would not be looked down on because of his low birth, or because he was a merchant or a tradesman.

Roger nodded—and agreed to Ritchie's death. As usual, his father probably had the right of it.

Ritchie, unaware that Henry Waters had pronounced his death sentence, was enjoying himself on yet another jaunt in the afternoon of the fateful Friday. He had endured one more conference with William, who was beginning to think him a harder taskmaster than Roger Waters—even if he were trying to save him and not bleed him dry.

That over, Ritchie had proposed to Jack and Pandora— with Bragg attending—a trip along the coast in an attempt to discover further traces of fossils. In reality it was so that he might re-familiarise himself with the terrain so that when night fell he would know exactly where he was.

'I do hope that you're minding your back, sir,' Bragg said in the stable yard while they were readying themselves for the trip. 'Wouldn't do to take too many risks now, either tonight, or even today. I've got a funny feeling about things.'

Ritchie stared at him. He had awoken that morning from a nightmare which occasionally plagued him: a nightmare in which he was once again in the hands of the French soldiers when they had been interrogating him so harshly. He had woken up, sweating heavily, with a feeling of something wrong. Something which he might have forgotten—although he couldn't think what.

'That's strange,' he said slowly. 'I've had an odd feeling today, as well.'

'Aye, then that makes two of us,' said Bragg, looking happy for once—although why, Ritchie couldn't imagine.

'I'll bear that in mind,' he came out with at last.

'Aye, you do that…sir.' The 'sir' came out as an afterthought.

Whether Bragg's odd feeling persisted or not, Ritchie

did not know. What he did know was that his refused to
go away.

It rode on his shoulders all afternoon. He had the feeling that he was being watched. He asked Bragg to reconnoitre for him, but Bragg could not find anything suspicious. Ritchie came to the conclusion that he was
suffering something akin to pre-battle worry, what with
having to coerce William Compton as well as, in Bragg's
words, 'minding his own back'.

He tried to behave as normally as possible, but, as
usual, he could not deceive Pandora.

They were seated on the grass enjoying the impromptu
picnic which Cook had prepared for them. Bragg, a de-
voted angler, had joined in their quest with a will after he
had seen something which resembled the skeleton of a
fish in the stones of Compton church.

'What's wrong, Ritchie?' Pandora asked in a low voice.
'I may be mistaken, but I fear that something is troubling
you.'

He tried to smile back at her, but he was aware that his
smile was stiff. He decided to be as truthful as he dare.

'Yes, I am a little troubled. I have the sensation of
which the country people sometimes speak: that someone
is walking over my grave. You are a clever girl, Pandora,
to detect that I am disturbed—or dare I think that the eye
of love is a penetrating organ?'

Her smile for him was now shy. She had always been
forthright, if not to say loud in her dealings with the
world, but Ritchie always made her feel a lady. Not that
he ever suggested that she was too bold. Far from it, he
liked, nay, loved her for her straightforward approach to
life. He had grown tired of namby-pamby and affected
young women.

Not that Pandora was in the least like Caroline Lamb

in her daring, either. She had a basic fund of common sense, and it was this which attracted him the most. Even her shyness was straightforward. She neither exaggerated it nor spent her time excusing herself when she was occasionally overcome.

She would make a splendid wife for a soldier if he decided to stay in the army when this wretchedly long war was over—or even if, after they were married, she accompanied him to battle, like Harry Smith's Spanish wife. If he returned to civilian life then he could visualise her helping him to run his estate and she would bring up their children to be sensible creatures, neither pampered nor spoiled…

'Ritchie? What is it, Ritchie?' In his musings he had forgotten that she was there, that she was troubled about him, and here he was wool-gathering over their future before they were even married! Love was making him nearly as big a nodcock as William!

Pandora was looking at him so anxiously that he could not resist leaning over and giving her a loving kiss and damn what Jack and Bragg thought. Fortunately they were both so engrossed in discussing angling—Jack had expressed a wish to be taught, and Bragg was promising to take him on his next excursion, Mr Ritchie permitting— that they had no eyes for the other two.

The sensation of being watched was so strong that Ritchie excused himself and wandered on his own through some scrub which surrounded a large stand of trees. He was so distracted between his powerful feelings for Pandora and his own unaccountable attack of the whim whams, that he forgot his usual caution while he was reconnoitring.

He had scarcely reached the trees when he heard an odd noise coming from the thick of them: caution immediately flew back. He threw himself forward on to the ground, the instincts of a lifetime's soldiering immediately taking over to save him.

No sooner had he done so than a shot rang out, disturbing the quiet of the afternoon. He was later to discover that his deliberate fall had saved him from injury or even death. In the distance he heard a shouted oath from Bragg and the sound of two pairs of running feet.

One pair, his attacker's, was running away from him and the other, Bragg's, was running towards him. Self-preservation kept him lying on the ground until Bragg arrived, panting, with Jack and Pandora in his wake, even though he had ordered them to stay where they were for safety's sake.

At the sight of his major—and his friend, despite their difference in rank—lying prostrate and still on the hard earth, Bragg immediately forgot their mission and Ritchie's masquerade.

'You nearly did for yourself this time, sir,' he exclaimed, bending over Ritchie to discover whether he was dead, wounded or neither, 'and you can't say that I didn't warn you. Will you never stop taking chances?'

'And do you never stop croaking, Bragg?' retorted Ritchie, sitting up, and also forgetful, using his own voice of natural command. 'I'm not dead. I think you'll find the tree behind me where I was standing when I heard a noise and threw myself forward.'

'You'll run out of luck one of these days,' Bragg ground out, '…sir.'

Both Ritchie and Bragg became suddenly aware that Pandora and Jack were staring at them and that they were on the verge of giving away Ritchie's true identity.

To try to mend matters Bragg said hurriedly, 'I'll have a look at the tree.'

"It was probably some idiot being careless while out shooting,' Ritchie offered, trying to make light of the situation, although well aware that he had almost certainly been the target of the unknown marksman and not a bird or rabbit.

'I've found the ball,' Bragg announced. 'Do you want me to prise it out?' Ritchie shook his head. Pandora, her face white, had remained unusually silent during this exchange.

Jack said eagerly, 'What made you throw yourself down, sir?'

'I tripped,' lied Ritchie, 'which was most fortunate.'

For some reason, while this answer satisfied Jack it did not satisfy Pandora. It was gradually being borne in on her that quiet, apparently inoffensive Mr Ritchie, whom she had come to love, was once again the centre of yet another odd incident.

This narrow escape from a misdirected shot, added to his sudden and unexpected equestrian prowess, his peculiar plain-glass spectacles, and his rather surprising prowess at cricket, were beginning to make her ask more and more questions about him. Besides that, Bragg's familiar remarks to someone who was supposed to be a stranger were also puzzling her. By the way that they spoke to one another they sounded like old acquaintances, not chance-met servants in a big house.

Ritchie, dusting himself down, was ruefully certain that his clever love might be growing suspicious of what he was really doing at Compton Place. His only hope was, that if all went well at Howell's End that night, the need for him to dissemble would disappear and he could approach her in his true self.

In the meantime he and Bragg must try to look innocent

and hope that nothing untoward happened in the next few hours.

'Went wrong!' howled Henry Waters at his henchman. 'What do you mean, went wrong? Didn't you get a proper sight of him before you let fly?'

Joss growled back, 'Beg pardon, sir, but he stayed alongside the young woman, the boy and that new groom at Compton Place, the whole damned afternoon. I daren't do anything then for fear, that by some accident, I might hit one of them instead. As it was, when he left them to walk about on his own it gave me a splendid opportunity to have a go at him, but by some ill chance he must have stumbled just as I loosed a shot at him. After that there was no alternative but to run or be caught.'

'Or something!' Henry Waters howled again. 'I told you that the bloody man was an experienced soldier and that you would need to be cunning to do for him and then you make a botch of it.'

'I could have another go.'

'Too late. He's probably twigged that the shot wasn't an accident. Oh, well, we shall have to make the best of it, but he's almost certainly the reason why William Compton has suddenly acquired some guts, damn him. With luck we can do for the pair of them tonight.'

If the cunning bastard doesn't do for you first, thought the wretched Joss, but he didn't say so.

The cunning bastard in question was enjoying an early supper with Aunt Em, Pandora, Jack and William Compton. William was so nervous at the prospect of an evening spent in trying to outwit those who had been controlling him so ruthlessly for the past year that he could barely eat.

Kind Aunt Em asked him, her face anxious, 'Are you well, William? You don't look well and, if you will forgive me for making a personal remark, I have never before seen you pick at your food as though your appetite had deserted you.'

'I am quite well, thank you, Aunt,' ground out William, throwing down his fork. 'I am a little tired, that's all.'

Jack, with the thoughtless truthfulness of youth, said cheerfully. 'Tired, William? What could have tired you? I wonder. After all, *you* weren't quartering the countryside like Pandora, Mr Ritchie and me this afternoon.'

Ritchie said, as quickly as possible, to prevent the wretched William from venting his fear of coming events by verbally attacking his half-brother, 'Now, Master Compton, how many times do I have to tell you not to make personal remarks about other people's behaviour? After all, your brother has many responsibilities which he cannot share with others and of which you have no knowledge. A short apology to him would be in order.'

Jack said, mutiny written on his face, 'Well, Aunt Em made a personal remark and no one reprimanded her. As for William and responsibilities, all the world knows…'

'Master Compton,' said Ritchie in his coldest, most severe, voice, hitherto only used on misbehaving junior officers and men, 'all the world shall now know that I am sending you to your room at once to contemplate what punishment I shall inflict on you tomorrow. Civility to your seniors is a lesson you must learn before you can call yourself a gentleman. Bow to us all and apologise for your insolence before you retire and I might commute part of your sentence.'

'Oh, very well!'

Jack rose and did as he was bid. William, who had earlier opened his mouth to rail at him, before being forestalled by Ritchie, said, 'Very right and proper, Mr Ritchie. It is time that Jack learned manners and etiquette—something which that wretched man Sutton failed to teach him.'

Pandora and Aunt Em both stared at him. He had never shown the slightest interest in Jack's behaviour before. Indeed, Jack could have gone to the devil for all he had cared.

Pandora said faintly once Jack was safely out of the room, 'I think that Jack's behaviour has greatly improved since Mr Ritchie arrived to tutor him and I am pleased to learn, brother, that you are ready to support him.'

Her approval for William was shown by her use of the word brother—something which she had seldom called him before. Aunt Em was thinking that if William had had the good fortune to be instructed by a tutor like Mr Ritchie he might have grown up to be a more responsible man.

William offered Pandora a watery smile.

'You have the right of it, sister. My tutor was a careless man—like my father—and I joined a bad set when I went to Oxford.'

Really, thought Pandora, we ought to run up a flag to celebrate the fact that William is showing signs of moral improvement. We can only hope that it lasts.

Ritchie was thinking much the same thing. What was beginning to trouble him almost as much as keeping William up to scratch was that the weather was changing rapidly. On their way home the light had taken on a peculiarly opaque quality and rumbles of thunder could be heard in the distance. George had remarked when they had returned their horses that it was lucky that they had decided on a ride that afternoon since he thought that a storm was on the way and that tomorrow might not be so suitable.

'Summer storms in these parts,' he had said, 'are unpleasant things—worse in their way than those in winter. The sea will be rough tonight.'

Had George been trying to tell him something? It was not the first time that his comments had been cryptic—designed either to warn or to inform him. He almost certainly knew, even if he were not a smuggler himself, that a landing at Howell's End was to take place that night and that a warning that inclement weather was on the way might be useful to anyone who might be present.

Later, while Ritchie was dressing himself in the coarse labourer's clothing which he had worn as the Dark Avenger, the first flashes of lightning filled his room. The thunder which followed was distant and, although the wind had risen, it had not yet begun to rain.

He had arranged to meet William in the paddock behind the stables after ten o'clock had struck and darkness had fallen. But first he needed to brief Bragg who was to keep watch over them from a distance, although that might be difficult if the thunderstorm arrived and proved to be severe.

His mirror showed him someone quite unlike either quiet Mr Ritchie or the soldier who was Richard Chancellor. He looked like every local Gentleman who had defied the Excisemen for the last hundred years.

Bragg had found him some boots like those which both smugglers and Excisemen wore which would enable him to melt into the crowd which would assemble on the beach. William would be wearing the clothes of an aristocratic sportsman out shooting.

Before he left, Ritchie rubbed the cold ashes from the

fire grate on to his face and hands and dishevelled his hair
beneath a woollen cap with a pom-pom on the top which
some of the locals wore in bad weather—waterproof
sou'westers being beyond their means. Thus disguised, he
hoped to escape detection by Roger Waters or his henchman who had tried to shoot him.

So it was down the backstairs for him again and out
into the open where the thunder had moved nearer and
nearer as darkness fell. Lightning flashes were beginning
to shoot across and down the night sky. He felt rather
than saw or heard Bragg following him at a distance.

William Compton, as instructed, was standing at the far
end of the paddock by the gate which led into the park.
A groom, not Brodribb, was holding two horses and it
was plain by his offhand manner to Ritchie that his disguise was working since he was not recognised.

'I had begun to think that you weren't coming,' William said after they had mounted and were on their way,
leaving the groom behind under the delusion that his master was on his way to help with landing the incoming
cargo. It won't hurt him to soil his hands for once, was
his dismissive judgement on that.

'I had to wait until the backstairs were clear,' Ritchie
told him. 'I didn't want anyone to see me and possibly
recognise me in this clothing. No one must know that I
am with you.'

'Well, looking as you do, no one could possibly guess
who you are.'

After that William fell silent for a time, carefully picking his way across the rough ground which descended to
the sea. There was a break in the cliffs at Howell's End
which made it easy for the smugglers to carry contraband
up to the by-way along which William and Ritchie began
to ride through an ever-increasing downpour. The rain

which had been threatening for some hours had finally arrived.

'I'd give anything not to be doing this,' William confessed when they reached a place where the by-way ran along the edge of a wood. The rough path from the by-way led down to the beach just before the wood was reached. It was here that they were to tether their horses.

'Me neither,' confessed Ritchie, dismounting and making sure that the pistol beneath his rough coat was in position.

'Eh, what's that?' exclaimed William. 'I thought that you soldiers relished this kind of thing.'

'Oh, we're only men after all, not gods, and battle is best when it's not in the immediate future and after it's over—if one survives, that is. Immediately before is always the worst of all. On the other hand, when you're in the thick of it you haven't time to worry. Survival is all.'

Whether this cheered William up or not, Ritchie had no time to find out. They had begun to scramble through the scrub and on to the sandy beach which shelved down to the sea. A large number of men were already assembled there. A cutter was standing out at sea but there was no sign of an approaching boat. The dark night and the curtains of rain made it difficult to see anything clearly, even when lightning briefly lit the sky.

Two carts stood waiting, loaded with wooden boxes which presumably contained the guineas about to be sent to France which would be replaced by incoming contraband. Brodribb had suggested that silks and luxury goods would be coming in and not liquor which was probably why Howell's End was the venue.

One group of the Gentlemen stood by the carts, another stood further to their right and nearer to the incoming tide. Through the driving rain Ritchie made out Roger Waters and another man neither of whom was wearing the usual smugglers' garb. They were using their night-glasses to look out to sea. He prodded an unwilling William in their direction. William was shivering in his good clothes, which were proving most unsuitable for the dreadful weather. Ritchie was thankful for his own coarse disguise. There was, as yet no sight or sound of an approaching band of Yeomanry or of Excisemen.

'Remember to tell Waters that I'm Brodribb's brother, taking his place because he has a distemper,' Ritchie reminded William, for that was the story which he had concocted to explain Brodribb's absence and his own presence. 'He might be suspicious of a stranger suddenly appearing after you had tried to renege.'

One of the waiting men near Roger Waters was flashing his light, signalling to the distant cutter.

William said, raising his voice over the noises of the inclement night, 'Here I am, Waters, as I promised you.'

'But late as usual, eh, Compton? I was just about ready to believe that you would never appear at all. Who's that with you? Where's Brodribb?'

'Took sick this morning so I've brought along his brother. He's another useful fellow.'

'Well, he'd better be,' Roger said, dismissing Ritchie who had given him a bow so servile that it hid his face. 'There's a few missing tonight—there are those who don't like this weather; a pox on them, eh, André?'

The man by his side said something in French which William failed to understand but which Ritchie did—it was a slight on the courage of Englishmen, at which Roger laughed. Ritchie also understood that with luck they were going to net themselves a spy who was about to be returned to his homeland.

The man with the light called out, 'The cutter's signalling that it's about to send the boat, Mr Waters.'

'Right.' Roger cupped his mouth with his hands and bellowed to the men around the carts. 'Come on, lads, get the boxes on to the sand instanter ready to leave, and you,' to the other group, 'start unloading the boat immediately it comes in. We can't afford to waste time in this weather. Compton and Brodribb, you can help to unload the carts.'

Privately Ritchie had to admire the man's competence, however much he disliked what he was doing. He was conducting the whole operation in the most professional fashion. There was nothing amateur about what was going on, no suggestion that smuggling was only a jolly pastime. On the contrary it was a serious business which was making fortunes for those who, like the Waters, were running it from the top.

Still there was no sign of the Yeomanry. Ritchie did not lose heart, although William muttered in his ear while they walked to the carts, 'I wouldn't mind heaving those bloody boxes around if I thought that the authorities were going to arrive and save me from being Waters's prey—but if they don't you can have the sack without a reference, Ritchie whoever you are. Not that that will trouble you, but I like the thought of doing it!'

'Patience,' whispered Ritchie. 'The Yeomanry will want to catch them in the act and that's not quite yet.'

'Well, I wish they'd blasted well hurry. I'm wet through already and the rain is getting worse.'

'Not long now,' Ritchie told him while they were lugging one of the boxes down towards the sea. 'The boat is well on its way, and when it arrives I think our rescuers might.'

William, unused to heavy manual labour, was, for a moment, too exhausted to reply. He wiped a brow which, despite the rain, was also running in sweat. 'I think that I've ruined my back for ever,' he moaned.

Even as he did so the incoming boat reached the sand not far from where they were standing. The leading oarsman leapt out and yelled something at the men waiting to unload it. Exactly what, neither Ritchie, nor William, was ever to learn for, as if an unseen signal had been given, there was the roar of galloping hooves coming from round and through the wood which William and Ritchie had skirted on the way to the beach.

The Yeomanry, Sadler, and some of his fellow Excisemen had been waiting there, unseen, since shortly after Roger and his men had arrived. The dark night and the noise of the rain and thunder had enabled them to remain hidden and unheard.

The leader of the charging Yeomanry, his sabre upraised, shouted, 'Stop, in the name of King George, I bid you cease…'

He might as well have saved his breath for the end of his sentence was lost in the noise of the storm. It was now raging directly overhead and the rolling of thunder had become virtually non-stop. A battle royal began in the pouring rain, with some of the smugglers running from the men on horseback towards the by-way in order to escape, and the others trying to pull the riders down and beat them with whatever weapons they could find.

Ritchie began to drag a fearful William away from the battle and up the far side of the beach towards the by-way and safety. He had no wish for them to be cut down by mistake for one of the Gentlemen, but it was a risk he had had to take.

Almost immediately they were accosted by Roger Waters who had left his post at the sea's edge to run after them. The Frenchman who had been beside him had been knocked down in the Yeomanry's first charge and, dazed, had been arrested by a pair of Excisemen who were hauling him up the beach towards the by-way where a couple of wagons had been posted to carry the prisoners away.

'I suppose it's you I have to thank for this,' Roger roared at William. 'Informed on me, did you? And how the devil did you do that without my people learning of it?'

William began to stutter and, foolishly, turned to look at Ritchie for help. Roger followed his eyes and suddenly, his expression changing, said, 'It wasn't you, though, was it? I do believe that this fellow isn't Brodribb's brother, but Sidmouth's bloody spy. Well, Mr Ritchie Chancellor, that get-up no longer fools me and, by God, one of you will pay for what you have done…now…since I've nothing further to lose.'

In the middle of the next roll of thunder which was accompanied by a series of lightning flashes which temporarily lit up the whole scene, he raised his right hand in which he had been holding a pistol.

Ritchie, who had, as usual, been on the *qui vive*, ready for anything, and whose own pistol had proved difficult to draw from under his heavy clothing, reacted immediately to Roger's threat by beginning to fall backwards the moment that Roger began to level his pistol at them. He took William with him by gripping him round the waist as he fell. They reached the ground together, William trapped beneath Ritchie, as Roger's shot rang out.

'Oh, by God, I've been hit,' shrieked William.

'No, you haven't,' said Ritchie, wryly. 'I have.' He rolled away from William and watched Roger Waters run down the beach and into the shallows where the half-unloaded boat was making ready to leave before it became a victim of the law. He had to scramble aboard in the most undignified fashion. Ritchie's last sight of him was of his legs, waving in the air.

'What? What's that?' William was exclaiming, and sitting up in his turn. 'Injured! Where? How? When? What shall we do?' he gabbled.

Someone had to talk sense, even if it were the genuinely injured who did, and not the fortunate man who had escaped, Ritchie decided. 'It's nothing, just a nick on the shoulder,' he said as gently as he could. 'By great good luck I'm not even dead, nor like to die. I shall lose some blood, but not too much, I hope, since the ball didn't pierce my shoulder, but flew on after it had gashed me.'

For once in his selfish life William Compton thought of someone else. 'Let me have a look. Is there anything I can do?'

'You can help me to my feet, take off your cravat and wind it round my shoulder. Further treatment will have to wait until we reach home again.'

Through the murk Sadler panted up to them. 'I saw that,' he gasped. 'I was too far away to help. I saw you fall. Was either of you hurt?'

'We didn't fall, well, not exactly,' said William who was bandaging Ritchie's shoulder. He had now calmed down enough to understand what Ritchie had done. 'Mr Ritchie pulled me down when he saw that Waters was going to shoot. His shoulder has been nicked. It's bleeding, but not too badly, I hope.'

'Good,' said Sadler, but spoiled his praise a little by adding, 'Why did you let Waters get away?'

'Well,' Ritchie said, wry again. 'We weren't exactly in a position to stop him. On the whole it's a good thing he's gone. He's saved the country the cost of a trial, you've nabbed his father and the French spy who was on the way home, so all in all I'd call it a successful night's work. Besides, what are the odds on him finding a decent life in France? Not very good, I'd say.'

Sadler was looking out to sea over Ritchie's shoulder. He raised his night-glass. 'I agree with you—if he reaches France, that is.'

He could see the French cutter beginning to move away at speed. It had sighted an English cutter, its blue and white striped flag aloft, moving towards it, ready for battle. The outgoing rowing boat, caught between the pair of them in heavy seas, was now falling behind in its effort to reach safety.

Sadler snapped his night-glass shut. Behind them the unequal struggle, later to be known as the battle of Howell's End, had ended. Those dejected Gentlemen who had not managed to escape and who were still able to walk, were being led to the wagons, to be transported to Lewes Gaol. Excisemen followed them, dragging the bodies of the wounded up the slight slope before flinging them, higgledy-piggledy, among their uninjured fellows.

'It's over,' he said, 'and successfully. I have to thank you both. And now, Mr Ritchie, your task accomplished, I wonder if you would have the goodness to tell me exactly who you are. The Captain of Yeomanry will wish to speak to you now, and the Lord Lieutenant tomorrow. I should like to know how to introduce you. After that I will arrange for you to be driven home.'

'Oh, Mr Compton and I have horses waiting for us near the by-way.'

'Nothing to that,' Sadler retorted. He thought that his man was looking weary unto death and was swaying a little. 'Your injury needs attention and Mr Compton also scarcely looks fit to ride a horse.'

'Oh, very well, Sadler, we'll do it your way. And as for who I am, since Mr Compton found out who I was by accident and has subsequently been bravely assisting me in my duties, I must confess that I am Major Richard Chancellor of the Fourteenth Light Cavalry. I was sent home on furlough from Spain to recover from my wounds and because of my experiences there I was asked by the Home Office to come here in secret to try to discover who was organising the trade in guineas.'

Sadler smiled ruefully. 'Our difficulty lay not in knowing who the organisers were, but in catching them at their treasonable trade. You, sir, enabled us to do that. The law is already on its way to arrest Mr Henry Waters.'

'Excellent,' muttered William. After this night's work, and his assistance of Ritchie and the excise officers, he knew that he need have no fear of what Waters might say about him.

'Isn't that your groom, Bragg, coming towards us, Compton?' asked Sadler. 'I don't think that I saw him on the beach. Was he helping with the cargo?'

'Not Mr Compton's groom,' Ritchie said, all need for secrecy now being over, 'but my sergeant, who has been keeping watch on us from a distance. Isn't that so, Bragg?'

'Aye, sir,' said Bragg, who had a night-glass in one hand and a sniper's rifle, bought from the widow of a rifleman in the Peninsula, in the other. 'Not that I could do too much to help you when that bastard Waters tried to shoot you. The light was so bad that if I'd tried to get in a shot I feared that I might hit you, or Mr Compton. I might have known that my help wasn't needed. If I may say so, sir, another one of your neat tricks worked like a charm.'

'Yes, you may well say so,' grinned Ritchie. 'A gashed shoulder is better than a ball in the head or chest.'

While they had been speaking the thunderstorm had

retreated into the distance and the lightning had lessened. The moon had ridden from behind the clouds. Out at sea the French cutter had sailed further away from the English one which was trying to manoeuvre itself into a position to open fire on an enemy which was almost beyond the range of its guns.

The smugglers' rowing boat was still struggling to reach the French cutter and was now at an equal distance between the two rival ships. Curious, despite his weariness, Ritchie took his night-glass from Bragg to look out to sea just as the English cutter opened fire.

For a moment or two the night, having lost the sound of thunder, was now briefly alive with the noise of cannon fire from both ships, out of range though they were. When it ended, Ritchie searched the sea for a sight of the rowing boat.

It had disappeared. It had certainly not had time to reach its master ship, and whether the cannon fire, or the heavy seas, had done for it, was never to be known. Roger Waters had exchanged death on the scaffold for death in the sea which had been the author of his, and his father's, fortune. Like him, that fortune was to be lost forever.

'Time to go home, sir,' said Bragg urgently, 'after you've spoken to the Captain of Yeomanry. He's waiting for us on the by-way. The doctors would be furious if they knew what you had been getting up to. You must know that you have done more than you ought tonight.'

'No, I don't know that, Bragg,' Ritchie retorted, but everything about him showed that he was lying. His shoulder was bleeding more profusely than he had at first thought, and Bragg, swearing, made him lie down so that he could check William's handiwork.

'Time for us all to go home,' said Sadler tactfully. 'We'll take you there in the chaise that we brought with us, after you've reported to the Captain. It's beyond the wood we used for cover. One of my men can knock up the doctor for Mr Ritchie on the way back.'

It was over.

Ritchie's mission had ended.

What had not ended was the unexpected consequence of his mission: his love for Pandora. What would she have to say to the man who had been deceiving her so successfully for the last two months?

Henry Waters was pacing in the study of his recently acquired country home. Again and again he pulled out his hunter to look at the time. Roger should have been home by now, this latest transaction successfully accomplished.

He was in the middle of yet another anxious examination of his watch when he heard the sound of hooves outside, of a door being slammed, and of his name being shouted.

Could this be Roger? He walked into the entrance hall to find Bunce, one of his most trusted men, standing there. He was drenched to the skin and his eyes were wild.

'Quick, master,' he urged. 'You must leave at once, there's no time to lose. They'll be here to arrest you at any moment. Everything went wrong tonight, what with the damned storm and the Yeomanry coming, and being betrayed by Compton and Sidmouth's spy, Ritchie, and all our fellows being arrested.'

'And Mr Roger, where's he? Was he arrested?'

'Lord, master, I scarce know how to tell you. He took to the Frenchies rowboat when it was plain all was lost and they tried to return to their ship…but…'

'But what, man? Speak up.'

'It went down with all hands. Perhaps it was the cannon from the English cutter or maybe it was the heavy sea did for it, but gone it is. All drown-dead, and Mr Roger with them.'

'You're sure, Bunce? Quite sure?'

'Aye, master. I escaped into the wood and watched from there.'

Henry Waters stood for a moment in thought, his head bent. At last he looked at the shivering man. 'I suppose that you were not the only one to get away?'

'Perhaps not. It was dark. Hard to see much except when the lightning flashed.'

'Then you must leave at once. You must not be found here. You've been a faithful fellow. Go to Richters in the City and tell them that I have sent you and that they must find you work. Go at once. Take the horse.'

'And you, master? Will you be leaving?'

'Yes, Bunce. I shall be leaving. Be sure of that.'

Henry Waters watched the heavy door close behind his faithful servant before he returned to his study. He sat for a moment, resting his head in his hands. He was quite sure of what he had to do next—especially now that Roger was dead. He had no intention of standing in the dock at the Old Bailey, of being publicly mocked while he was dragged through the streets of the city which had made him rich, and of being publicly executed for treason.

He rose, walked over to a cupboard which he unlocked and fetched from it a case containing two pistols. Quite calmly, as though he had done this many times before, he put one of the pistols to his temple…and pulled the trigger.

Chapter Thirteen

The noise of Ritchie and William's return in the chaise, with Sadler, Bragg and the two riderless horses clattering in the rear, awoke Pandora from an uneasy sleep. She walked to the window on the landing and watched the little procession, led by the chaise, enter the stable yard. What in the world could be going on? And who could possibly be visiting Compton Place in the early hours?

Pandora pulled on her dressing gown and slippers and walked down the backstairs, through the kitchen and the door which led to the stables. Never mind that she was informally dressed, she had the right to know what was being done in secret, since no one had forewarned her of this. By now the rain had stopped, the clouds had dispersed and the moon was casting its light everywhere so she began to walk towards the stables.

She never reached them. Bragg and Sadler, supporting Ritchie between them, came walking towards her through the archway. William and George were following them. Ritchie, who was scarcely recognisable in his Gentleman's disguise, had a bloodstained bandage around his shoulder. Beneath the smeared dirt his face was white and he was walking unsteadily, almost as though he were drunk.

She was not far wrong in thinking this. Sadler and Bragg—William hovering nearby—ignoring Ritchie's protests, had persuaded him to drink a large quantity of brandy from a flask which Sadler always carried with him. By then he was so far gone from exhaustion and loss of blood from his flesh wound that he gave in to them after a mere token resistance. He was also painfully aware that his body had not yet fully recovered from his experiences in the Peninsula. On the whole oblivion had seemed a better bet than consciousness at that point.

'Ritchie! What in the world have you been doing?'

Pandora's agonised voice had him opening his eyes to stare at her. What could he say to her? He was in no condition to explain anything—in no condition to say, or do, anything sensible at all.

'My duty…' he began, before oblivion finally claimed him and he began to fall forward.

'Damnation!' cursed Bragg. 'I knew he'd overdone things. Him and his bloody duty. It's always been the same with him.' He turned to Sadler. 'Help me to get him to his room and into bed. Miss Compton here will show us the way. George, go and see if the doctor is coming.'

Pandora watched them lift Ritchie up. He stirred when they did so, raised his head a little, opened his eyes, and gave her his sweetest smile before lapsing into unconsciousness again.

His duty? What did he mean by that? What sort of duty took him out in the night, dressed like a smuggler—and with William, and Bragg? And why did Bragg speak to him as he did? Half-respectfully and half-disrespectfully? And how had he come to be wounded? And what was William doing with him? And Sadler?

After that Pandora ran out of questions although she was sure that there were more she would wish to ask. Up the main staircase she led them, first to the schoolroom and then to Ritchie's bedroom where they laid him gently on his bed.

Pandora asked, her voice sharp, 'What in the world have you and Mr Ritchie been up to, Bragg?'

Bragg looked up from where he was unfastening the bandage around Ritchie's shoulder. Sadler was pulling off his heavy boots before fetching water from the jug on the washstand by Ritchie's bed and, using his kerchief, began to wipe his face.

'Now that I can't tell you, miss. Not without asking for *his* permission,' and he jerked a thumb at the semi-conscious man on the bed.

Pandora felt like stamping her foot, but in the present distressing circumstances decided not to. She said to Sadler, sharply, not at all in her usual briskly cheerful manner, 'And I suppose that *you* won't give me an answer, either.'

Sadler, more respectful than Bragg, said gently, 'I can only repeat what Sergeant Bragg has just said.'

He knew immediately that he had been careless in revealing Bragg's rank. Bragg threw him a reproachful glare, and said, not respectful at all, 'It would be helpful, miss, if you left us at once so that we can undress him for the doctor.'

Pandora was about to inform him that she had no intention of being told what to do in her own home when the door opened and Jack came in, wearing a nightgown and one slipper. The other was in his hand.

'I say, Pan, what's going on? There's the devil of a noise downstairs, William's routed half the servants out of bed, the doctor is coming—and what's wrong with poor Mr Ritchie, and why is he wearing such odd togs?'

'Don't ask me,' said the exasperated Pandora. 'Only Sergeant Bragg and Mr Sadler know, and they won't tell me.'

'Why ever not? I say, he's not going to die, is he? That would be too bad.'

'Not yet, young shaver, or so I hope,' muttered Ritchie, trying to sit up, having regained consciousness again, only to be pushed down by an officious Bragg.

'And did you say *Sergeant* Bragg, Pan? What is he sergeant of?' exclaimed Jack, whose conversation seemed to be limited to the asking of questions which no one wanted to answer.

'How should I know? All I do know is that he is giving the orders round here, and since he wants us to leave so that Ritchie may be undressed I suppose we had better go. Except…' and she walked over to take Ritchie's hand, and to ask him '…is that what you want, Ritchie?'

After Pandora came out with this, all her hard-won composure broke down and forgetting etiquette, Sadler, Bragg and Jack, she fell on her knees beside Ritchie's bed and began to wail, 'Oh, whatever have they done to you, Ritchie, my darling? Who did it? And what did you mean by speaking of your duty?'

Through the haze of brandy and exhaustion which consumed him, Ritchie was able only to lift her hand to his lips and kiss it, also forgetful of their wide-eyed audience.

'I can't explain now, my love,' he murmured. 'I'm so tired, tomorrow perhaps, when…' His voice broke, his eyes closed and Pandora began to sob, until he opened his eyes again and summoned up the strength to say, 'Do as Bragg wishes, my darling.'

Pandora kissed his hand in return, then rose. 'Come, Jack,' she told him, trying to keep her voice steady. 'We must leave at once so that Sergeant Bragg and Mr Sadler can ready Mr Ritchie for the doctor.'

'Does kissing his hand and calling him darling mean that you are going to marry him?' said Jack, finding yet another question to belabour her with. 'If so, may I be your page at the wedding? I suppose that William will have to give you away, seeing that Father is dead and Sir John is past it.'

Jack's reward was a weak laugh from the man lying on the bed. Bragg seized the young man by the arm and marched him to the door, Pandora following.

'You heard him,' he said, 'explanations tomorrow. He's lost a lot of blood doing his damned duty, but be sure that we'll look after him, eh, Sadler?'

Sadler nodded his head. When the door closed behind the brother and sister, he asked, 'So they don't know who he is—or who you are and why he is here?'

'None of them,' Bragg told him. 'Only that ass, William Compton, who found out by accident. Now let's have the Major ready for the quack when he comes.'

Pandora thought that she would never go to sleep. She heard the doctor arrive and had to tell herself sternly that she must do as Ritchie wished and not go to his room to discover what his diagnosis was. Immediately after she had left him she had had to be extremely severe with Jack who was still full of questions and was demanding that they find William in order to discover what had been going on that night.

She was sure that it was something to do with smuggling, but why that should involve Ritchie was a mystery yet to be solved. In the end exhaustion claimed her and she slept much later than usual and was only awoken by

Jack knocking noisily on her door and shouting, 'I say, Pan, let me in.'

'Oh, very well.' She lay back in bed and watched him enter, full of himself. Were all boys like Jack? she asked herself, noisy, curious and full of life just when a poor girl wanted a rest.

Today he was worse than ever. His eyes were shining and he could scarcely speak for excitement. 'Oh, Pan, you'll never guess. It's like a story book, only better because it's about real people. I woke up early and went down to the stables and they, and apparently the whole countryside, were full of what happened last night.

'There was a battle, a real battle, down at Howell's End last night between the Smugglers, the Yeomanry and the Excisemen. There was a bit of a naval battle, too, and you'll never guess who was in the middle of it all.'

Now Pandora was really interested. She sat up, her eyes wide, 'Not Ritchie. Why should he be in the middle of it? Is that how he was injured?'

'Oh, yes, and William, too.'

Information cascaded out of Jack. He was so excited that he was barely understandable. 'Mr Ritchie was injured saving himself and William when Roger Waters tried to shoot them when he found out that they had informed the Yeomanry that he was smuggling guineas to France. Roger tried to escape in the Frenchies' boat when the Yeomanry arrived but it was sunk before they reached the cutter. And guess who found out about him and the smuggling? Why, it was none other than Mr Ritchie! He pretended to be the Dark Avenger in order to discover what the smugglers were doing!

'He's probably saved William's bacon, too, they were saying, because he made William help him. And Bragg is Sergeant Bragg, and guess what—'

He ran out of breath temporarily and Pandora said, her heart sinking, 'Never tell me that Ritchie's a soldier, too?'

'Oh, yes. He was sent here by the Home Office to find out who's been shipping the guineas to France and to try to catch them at it. He's a Major in the Cavalry—'

'In the Cavalry! You mean that he was a real horseman all the time—so *that*'s why he could ride Nero, it wasn't a miracle, just something all in the day's work for him. Oh, how could he deceive us so!' And, to Jack's astonishment, Pandora began to cry.

'Goodness, Pan, what bee's in your bonnet now? He was jolly brave saving William and pretending to be the Dark Avenger. Brodribb was really cross when he found that out, I can tell you. You must remember that the Avenger had a right go at him!'

'So he isn't a poor tutor, and Ritchie isn't his real name, either, I suppose.'

'No, but I didn't find out what it is. Bragg came in while Rob was telling us all this, he's Sadler's cousin, and Bragg made him shut up. He used the most dreadful language, Pan—just like a real sergeant, I suppose.'

Pandora was too annoyed at finding that Ritchie wasn't a hero at all, just a soldier, who took everything in his stride, as the saying went, to care whether Bragg was a real sergeant. It was more important that Ritchie wasn't a real tutor, even if he had been a good influence on Jack.

The worst of it was that he'd only come to Compton Place to spy on them all. Was it even possible that he'd been toying with her, pretending to be in love with her just to pass the time when he wasn't concentrating on his real task?

As for saving William! Well, so he ought! That must have been part of his damned duty which Ritchie had been talking about when Bragg and Sadler had brought him back to Compton Place last night. On second thoughts, though, he had been trying to save William all the time that William was being monstrously rude to him. For some reason this made Pandora crosser with poor Ritchie than ever.

'I say, Pan, you're not really angry with Mr Ritchie, are you? Rob says that he deserves a medal.'

'Young Rob's a silly boy. What does he know about anything?'

'He knows about soldiers and being brave. Mr Ritchie's even better than that. He was a splendid tutor, too. He's taught me more in the short time he's been here than Mr Sutton did in two years. He's clever as well as brave. Bragg told me that he never talks about himself.'

'Oh, a real paragon is Mr Ritchie, I'm sure.'

Jack took her cutting remark seriously. 'Oh, yes, and he didn't run after the maids either, only you. You *are* going to marry him, aren't you? We could do with him in the family. Sir John likes him and he could keep William in order.'

Pandora gave a great moan. He *had* asked her to marry him, hadn't he? Or rather the poor tutor, Mr Ritchie, had. Major Whoever-he-was was quite a different matter. She had thought him honest and true; she had told him so more than once—and all the time his life at Compton Place had been a lie.

He was no better than any other man; they were all liars and cheats. She hated them, so she did: Mr Ritchie most of all. She never wanted to see him again. No, that wasn't true, she wanted to know what the doctor had said of his injury. Oh, what a benighted fool she was: she hated him, but she couldn't bear to think of him suffering.

Jack was staring at her agonised face. 'I say, Pan, are

you A-one at Lloyds? You aren't going to faint, are you?
You never do missish things like that.'

'I'm certainly not going to faint, Jack, but Mr Ritchie—
is *he* A-one at Lloyds this morning?'

'Bragg says he is. Pan! Pan! Where are you going?'

Pandora had no time to waste in talking to Jack. She
jumped out of bed, pulled on her dressing gown and ran
in the direction of Ritchie's room. She had to find out
how he was, and then, if he was fit enough, she would
tell him exactly what she thought of him and his masquerade.

Honest! He didn't know the meaning of the word.

Jack stared after her. Women and girls, you never had
the slightest notion what they would do next. Rob, the
groom, had told him that it was even harder to understand
them when they grew older—so it was no wonder that
Pan had suddenly turned light-headed. Before Mr Ritchie
had arrived at Compton Place she had been as common-
sensical as any boy, but now...

He shook his head and wandered off to the stables to
check whether they had any more exciting news to pass
on.

Pandora was out of breath when she reached the schoolroom. She stopped a moment before she knocked on Ritchie's door.

Silence.

She called, 'Mr Ritchie, may I come in?'

Still silence.

Well, damn this for a tale, she would go in and find
out what he was up to now.

Well, he wasn't up to anything in his bedroom. It was
empty, the bed had been made, and there was no sight or
sound of him. Pandora collapsed on it and put her head

in her hands. Dear God, had Bragg been lying to Jack? Had he died in the night and they had already taken his body away without telling her? No, never say so!

She thought that she was going to be sick, but what use would that be? None at all. She must try to recover her common sense and her composure. She would walk quietly downstairs and try to find out what had happened.

On the first landing she met William.

'So there you are at last, Pandora,' he said, all merry and bright for once. 'Don't you want any breakfast this morning?'

Breakfast! How could he talk of breakfast when she didn't know whether Ritchie was alive or dead?

'No, William. Where's Mr Ritchie? He isn't in his room.'

'Of course not. The morning's nearly over. Nuncheon will be served shortly.'

Pandora closed her eyes. Could her wretched half-brother think of nothing but food? She stamped her foot at him. 'William, *where* is Mr Ritchie?'

'In the library. He'll be leaving to visit the Lord Lieutenant after nuncheon, before travelling on to London to report to Sidmouth about last night's excitements.'

He had barely finished speaking before Pandora was off again, and running as fleetly as any racehorse entered in the Derby. So, he wasn't dead after all, was he?—just busy doing his duty. Well, he owed her the duty of telling her the truth, didn't he, after telling her all those lies about himself and so she would inform him in no uncertain terms.

She burst into the library to find Ritchie writing at William's desk. He was still wearing his shabby tutor's clothing. His face was grey, there were shadows under his eyes, and the left sleeve of his jacket hung loose to allow for his bandaged shoulder. Yet he still looked exactly like the quiet and kind man she had fallen in love with. How dare he!

'Good morning, Major Whoever-you-are. Were you, your *duty* done, returning to London without saying a word of farewell to me?'

Ritchie closed his eyes in a pain which was not physical. Something which he had spent the last weeks fearing would happen, had happened. Pandora had learned of his mission before he had had an opportunity to tell her of it himself.

'So you know already. I had hoped to explain to you why I came to Compton Place myself. Unfortunately I was too far gone to be able to do so last night—I might have guessed that the story was too good for it not to be about the county in no time. Of course I was going to say farewell before I left, my darling girl. Why ever not? And how did you find out?'

'Jack told me. What you have done is the talk of the stables, and yes, I suppose, of half the county of Sussex, too. It seems that I was the last person to know that you came here under a false name, pretending to be who and what you are not. I, in my innocence, thought you were the only honest and truthful man whom I had ever met, but all the time you were deceiving us—and me. How am I to know whether I can believe in anything you have ever said to me?'

Ritchie came round the desk to comfort her. He could see that his gallant girl was perilously near to breaking down. This was what he had always feared, that she would recoil from someone whom she thought had tricked her. No, not thought: he *had* tricked her, had he not?

'Believe me when I tell you that I truly love you and that I was not lying when I asked you to marry me. I wanted to tell you the truth myself, but by some ill chance it was not to be. I wanted to reassure you that, although I came here solely to do the duty laid on me by Lord Sidmouth himself—that was to identify those responsible for smuggling sovereigns to France—I didn't bargain on meeting you when I came to Compton Place. Nor did I bargain on falling in love with you when I did.

'But, Pandora, I'm so glad that I've found you. Please also believe me when I tell you how much it troubled me that I was deceiving you. There were many times when I nearly compromised my honour—and possibly your safety—by telling you the truth. As for my name, at least the Ritchie and Edward parts are true.

'May I introduce you to Major Richard Edward Chancellor of the Fourteenth Light Dragoons, always and ever at your service. I am currently on furlough. I am known to my family and friends as Ritchie, and also to you, I hope.'

He bowed to her before straightening up and looking into her glorious green eyes which were brilliant with unshed tears.

'Say that I am forgiven, my darling heart, so that I may travel to London a man happy in your love.'

All Pandora's anger flew away. She had only to hear him speak to her in the kind voice which was so much a part of Mr Edward Ritchie that she could forgive Major Richard Chancellor anything.

'Of course, you are forgiven—but I am sure that you can understand how I felt when Jack came running in with his news.'

He put an arm around her and said in the voice he used to tease her, 'Like I did just now when you came bursting in on me with your news, I suppose. You and Jack are more alike than you think.'

'So long as we are not like William,' said Pandora fervently. 'Though I can only hope that what has happened recently may have sobered him a little. Are you going to kiss me, Ritchie? I think a few kisses might make me feel happy, even though I am going to lose you to London again this afternoon.'

'But I shall come back for you soon, I promise you. As for the kisses, since I have finished writing my despatch for Sidmouth, you may have as many as you like if it will banish that forlorn look you came in with. The only proviso is that we must not be late for nuncheon, I promised William I would not be.'

They were not late for nuncheon, but their rosy and fulfilled faces told a tale which both William and Aunt Em had seen before in others. The more forthright Jack, who had been allowed to join them since Ritchie was about to leave, said, between mouthfuls, 'I see that you have made it up with Mr Ritchie, Pan, so I suppose that the wedding is on again. William spoke to me this morning about going to Harrow this autumn, so I hope that you will arrange it before then so that I can be your page.'

Aunt Em opened her mouth to reprimand him, but caught Ritchie's amused eye and forbore. Apart from that, the only other incident in the meal was when Galpin came in and said that Mr Sadler had arrived and wished to speak to Mr Compton and Major Chancellor. He had important news for them; most particularly for the Major who, he understood, would be leaving for London shortly.

'Tell him to come in,' said William. 'We have almost finished. He can share a glass of wine with us.'

This was so different from William's normal manner with Sadler that both Pandora and Ritchie hoped that his recent experiences had taught him a few lessons.

'Sorry to disturb you at your meal,' said Sadler, accepting a glass of wine, although refusing anything more, 'but I thought that you ought to know that the constables went to arrest Henry Waters early this morning—only to find that he had forestalled them by committing suicide. They searched the house and discovered documents incriminating several of those in the City of London who were doing business with him.

'At least he's saved us the expense of trying him. I suppose his son's death at sea was the last straw. Some of the bodies from the boat were washed ashore this morning, but not his. I thought that the authorities ought to know of this as soon as possible, Major.'

'Best tell Sir John when you see him before you leave,' William said to Ritchie later. Which was what Ritchie did, as well as confirming what William had already told him of the previous night's events and how they had come about.

The old man was in good form, apparently quite aware of all that was going on. Ritchie thought it extremely likely that the two large footmen who always hovered behind Sir John kept him well-informed about everything which was going on in Compton Place. When Ritchie took the Luck of the Comptons from his pocket and told him that it had already done its work in saving William, and that it ought to return to the family, Sir John shook his head.

'No,' he said, his old voice firm for once. 'Keep it, I beg of you. I know, as surely as I know that you will come back to marry Pandora and that when your Army service is over you will look after Jack and William, that at some time in the far distant future it will return to Compton Place to save it again. So put it back in your pocket. Oh, and by the by, remember me to Sidmouth when you report to him.'

Ritchie duly did as he was bid and went downstairs to start his journey to London, but not before he had kissed Pandora goodbye and promised that he would be back to claim her as soon as possible.

Ritchie had been gone a week which seemed more like a year to Pandora—she missed him so much. Sometimes she feared that he would never come back and that he had forgotten her the moment the carriage taking him away had been driven through the main gates of Compton Place.

She had visited Sir John shortly after Ritchie had left and found him at his vaguest, except that just as she was leaving, he said, winking at her, 'I must congratulate you, my dear. I hear that you are going to marry that soldier fellow after all. Why did everyone pretend that he wasn't one?'

Then, one afternoon, she was going over the estate books with William, whose change of heart was beginning to look more and more permanent now that he had escaped the gallows, when old Galpin came in, his face one smile.

'The Major has come back, Miss Pandora, and Sergeant Bragg. He's on his way. I thought that I'd warn you.'

'Warn me! I don't need warning.' Pandora jumped to her feet and ran into the entrance hall just as Ritchie came in; but the man who was facing her did not look like her dear, shy Mr Ritchie at all. He was superbly dressed, magnificently *à point* from his fashionably dressed hair to his shining boots. He held himself like the soldier he was. He looked, in fact, exactly like all the men who had frightened her in the past… She scarcely knew what to say to him.

And then he smiled at her—and he was her own dear Ritchie again.

He had a piece of paper in his hand which he waved at her before he took her into his arms, saying, 'Guess what this is, my darling girl? Nothing less than a special licence. We can be married in the week so that you may come with me, back to the Army, to live and, if necessary, march with me like Harry Smith's dear wife does. What do you say to that?'

The glorious green eyes which looked up at him were shining with mischief. 'That like Ruth said to Naomi in the Bible, ''Whither thou goest, I will go,''' she told him, 'and as soon as possible—on two conditions.'

'And what might they be? You know that you can ask anything of me.'

'That Jack must be my page, whoever else attends me, and that you throw away your plain-glass spectacles!'

'Anything, my love, anything, to get you into my bed as soon as possible. And if, once we are married, you care for me as you have cared for William, Jack and everyone at Compton Place, then I shall be a lucky man.'

'Not so lucky as I am, and now let us tell the others our news.'

Hand in hand, the Dark Avenger and his soon-to-be wife walked into the drawing room and their new lives together.

* * * * *

Modern Romance™
...seduction and
passion guaranteed

Tender Romance™
...love affairs that
last a lifetime

Sensual Romance™
...sassy, sexy and
seductive

Blaze™
...sultry days and
steamy nights

Medical Romance™
...medical drama on
the pulse

Historical Romance™
...rich, vivid and
passionate

29 new titles every month.

*With all kinds of Romance for
every kind of mood...*

MILLS & BOON®

Makes any time special™

MAT4

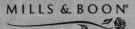

MILLS & BOON®

Historical Romance™

WEDDING NIGHT REVENGE by Mary Brendan

Beautiful, witty heiress Rachel Meredith is a happy
spinster, until her father gambles away the family
home. The new owner is handsome bachelor
Connor Flinte – a man she has already jilted!
Rachel knows she must marry, and Connor wants
revenge. He'll return the deeds – if she'll give him
the wedding night he never had…

Regency

THE INCOMPARABLE COUNTESS by Mary Nichols

One long, hot summer Frances and Marcus had
meant everything to each other – then he had
betrayed her by marrying someone else. Years
later, Marcus comes to reclaim his childhood
sweetheart but is confounded to find the ice-cold
Countess of Corringham in place of the fiery
seventeen-year-old he had known. Can he
persuade Frances to succumb to her youthful
dreams and desires once more?

Regency

On sale 7th December 2001

*Available at most branches of WH Smith,
Tesco, Martins, Borders, Eason, Sainsbury's
and most good paperback bookshops.* 1101/04

FREE!

2 Books

and a surprise gift!

We would like to take this opportunity to thank you for reading this Mills & Boon® book by offering you the chance to take TWO more specially selected titles from the Historical Romance™ series absolutely FREE! We're also making this offer to introduce you to the benefits of the Reader Service™ —

- ★ FREE home delivery
- ★ FREE gifts and competitions
- ★ FREE monthly Newsletter
- ★ Books available before they're in the shops
- ★ Exclusive Reader Service discounts

Accepting these FREE books and gift places you under no obligation to buy; you may cancel at any time, even after receiving your free shipment. Simply complete your details below and return the entire page to the address below. *You don't even need a stamp!*

YES! Please send me 2 free Historical Romance books and a surprise gift. I understand that unless you hear from me, I will receive 4 superb new titles every month for just £2.99 each, postage and packing free. I am under no obligation to purchase any books and may cancel my subscription at any time. The free books and gift will be mine to keep in any case.

H1ZEB

Ms/Mrs/Miss/Mr ....Initials..

BLOCK CAPITALS PLEASE

Surname...

Address...

....

....Postcode ....

Send this whole page to:
UK: The Reader Service, FREEPOST CN81, Croydon, CR9 3WZ
EIRE: The Reader Service, PO Box 4546, Kilcock, County Kildare (stamp required)